GOOD TOGETHER

A CARRIGANS OF THE CIRCLE C NOVEL

CJ CARMICHAEL

TULE
PUBLISHING

GOOD TOGETHER

The Tule Publishing Group, LLC

ISBN 978-1-940296-23-4

Dear Reader,

What should you expect when you pick up *Good Together*? A love story, of course, one that makes you believe in the amazing goodness of the human heart. But there is also an end-of-love-story, one that reminds us that not all beautiful things last forever.

You should expect to revisit the Circle C ranch in Marietta, Montana. You'll visit all four Carrigan sisters, as well as their austere father Hawksley. You'll find out more about the troubles between Hawksley and his deceased wife Beverly. And you'll get to spend some time with Sage Carrigan (from *Promise Me, Cowboy*) as well as her smoking hot boyfriend, Dawson O'Dell, and his precocious daughter, Savannah.

You'll also be introduced to the Tennessee Walking Horses at Bishop Stables, and I want to thank Rick at Rick Wies Stables for giving me and my guy a tour of his operations in Big Arm, Polson. These are indeed beautiful horses, and I hope I've managed to convey why Mattie Bishop loves them so.

Two more stories will be coming this autumn for Dani and Callan Carrigan. You won't believe the surprises in store. Make sure you sign up for both my newsletter, and Montana Born's so you don't miss them!

Thanks for being someone who loves books and reading!

CJ Carmichael

CONTENTS

CHAPTER ONE

Mid-October

Mattie Carrigan's subconscious figured out the problem first. She was dreaming that she and her husband Wes were in the airport. "You screwed up the reservation," he was yelling. "We're booked on two separate flights."

She opened her eyes, heart racing, relieved to be in bed at their ranch in the Flathead Valley of Montana and not—as had been the case in her dream—trying desperately to get to Denver where one of their twin daughters had started college two months ago. They'd picked different schools, Portia and Wren, one moving south to Denver, the other west to Seattle, which drove Mattie crazy. It was difficult enough having her children leave the nest. Couldn't they at least have chosen the same college?

The night was still, dark, and silent. Curtains fluttered in the breeze from the open window to her left. Wes was in the bed to her right, his naked back a wall blocking the digital time display on their alarm clock.

What time had he rolled in from his latest rodeo? This one, the livestock exposition and rodeo in Billings, was about a seven-hour drive from home. So if he'd left at five, like he'd said he would, he should have been back before she'd gone to bed around one a.m.

Maybe he'd delayed his departure to have dinner with friends. Or had trouble with the rig. In either case, he must have been dead-tired when he got here. Yet, judging from the Head and Shoulders scent of him, he'd taken the time to shower before crawling under their covers.

She wanted to move closer and snuggle up against his warm, tanned skin. But something—a nasty stew of resentment, fear and hurt—stopped her. He might have called to let her know he'd been delayed.

Again.

Pushing aside her covers, Mattie slipped to the bathroom down the hall. A weak nightlight—installed eighteen years ago when the twins were babies—kept her from stubbing her toes on Wes's boots. Damn, why hadn't he taken them off in the mudroom?

She'd seen his bull-riding scores posted on the Internet and they'd been low, so he wouldn't have brought home any prize money. He hadn't for the past six months. A sign that at thirty-nine, he was getting too old to be a rodeo cowboy.

The rosemary and bergamot infusion sticks on the back of the toilet tank couldn't mask the odor of horse manure and cowboy sweat that permeated the pile of Wes's clothes on the tiled floor. As she peed, she stared at his faded Wrangler jeans and old blue and white checked shirt.

Not that long ago—definitely less than a year—Wes would have woken her up when he got home, no matter how late. They'd make love and then he'd tell her how things had gone. The bulls he'd drawn and the scores he'd made. He'd fill her in on the latest gossip—who'd been injured and who was riding high. And the romances. Someone sleeping with someone else's wife... it happened all the time.

Mattie stared at her reflection as she washed her hands. The low light was flattering, masking the new age-freckles that had popped out this summer. Now that she was almost forty, she had to be more careful with her sunscreen, she supposed, though she'd never been one for fussing about her appearance.

Her sisters would say she relied too much on the looks she'd inherited from their mother. And she knew it was true, and that she'd been lucky. Good bones and teeth, thick hair and pretty eyes. She'd taken these assets for granted, never guessing that one day they wouldn't be enough for her husband.

Because that had to be the reason they were drifting apart, right?

He no longer found her attractive. Maybe he'd found someone new...?

Mattie put a hand to her chest, feeling the pain as she entertained this new suspicion... that her husband had fallen for somebody new.

But then common sense prevailed. This was Wes, her husband of nineteen years. They were a team. Had been a team forever. Raising their girls. Running the ranch. They did everything together. And he valued that as much as she did.

She'd never doubted Wes in all the nineteen years of their marriage, even though they'd spent a lot of that time apart. And she wouldn't doubt him now.

They were just moving into a new stage of life, that was the problem. Every couple went through this when their children moved away from home. For sure she and Wes were handling the change differently. She was clinging in every way possible—text messaging the girls many times a day, sending care packages from home—whereas Wes rarely mentioned them. Wren said he hadn't called her once since she'd left.

Mattie hung back in the doorway, watching Wes sleep, feeling oddly distant, like she was observing a stranger. They'd met at a rodeo, when she was only eighteen. Ended up married and pregnant before either one of them was twenty. Not a recipe for marital success.

And yet, they'd defied the odds.

Just a year ago she would have called them happy. Wes was her partner, the father of her children, her best friend. They told each other everything.

But not anymore.

"Mat? What's going on?" Wes lifted his head from his pillow. His dark hair all but covered his eyes.

"I had a bad dream."

"Worried about the kids?" His head flopped back. "Don't. They're fine."

He always said that. She was the one who worried. But this time, it wasn't about Wren and Portia. "We need to talk."

Wes groaned. "In the morning. Get back to bed. It's damned freezing in here. Did you leave the window open again?"

She loved fresh air when she slept, but Wes preferred to be toasty warm. That meant open windows in the summer, but come October when the cold winds blew off the Mission Mountains, they had to be closed.

She pushed aside the curtains, then cranked the lever until the window was flush with the wall. Quietly she crept back under the covers, loving the coolness of the sheets on her side of the bed. On her back, she stared at the ceiling, waiting to see if Wes would turn and pull her into his arms.

He didn't.

Before dawn, Mattie was up, dressed for work in old jeans and a flannel shirt. She stood by the bedroom window as she fastened her buttons. In the faint light she could see mist hanging low to the ground and clinging to the Mission mountains. It would be cold outside. She slipped an extra pair of socks on her feet.

Wes was still sleeping and she closed the door after herself so he wouldn't be disturbed.

He generally slept late after a rodeo. She never did. Nothing happened in her day until the horses had been fed. Wes insisted this was ridiculous because they had hired men to do the morning chores. Well, these days it was only Jake. But Mattie had been raised on a ranch and the rules on the Circle C had been inviolate. No one eats before the animals.

Mattie brought up the twins the same way. From a

young age, no matter the weather, she'd bundled them up and taken them to the stables with her. They'd adored trailing the feed cart as she doled out rations, petting the barn cats, and jumping in the wood chips that were used for bedding. But when they hit their teen years, suddenly Wren became a night-hawk and couldn't drag herself out of bed any earlier than fifteen minutes before the school bus arrived, while Portia's new hair and makeup routine required at least an hour of prep time, rendering her unavailable for anything as prosaic as ranch chores.

Mattie missed all of this—the early childhood years and the stormy teenaged years—with an intensity that made her chest ache. Something vital had been scooped out of her body the day she and Wes drove the twins to the Missoula airport. Was she always going to feel this hollow?

After filling a to-go mug with coffee that had been programed the night before to brew fresh at six a.m., Mattie almost tripped on the sleeve of a jacket that had been tossed toward a stool—and only partially hit its target. The light navy windbreaker was Wes's. She bent over to pick it up, wrinkling her nose at the scent of tobacco smoke—he must have worn it into a bar. Intending to hang it on one of the pegs in the mudroom, she paused when she noticed a key had fallen from one of the pockets.

She picked it up, frowning because their house keys were silver-colored, not brass. Besides, Wes kept all his keys on a ring. So what was this for?

She placed it on the butcher block island and went to put her boots on.

Mattie's spirits lifted the moment she stepped outside. The crisp air was like a health tonic, and everywhere she looked there was beauty. From the long-needled, elegant ponderosa pine trees that had been planted by Wes's mother to buffer the house from the road, to the reflective, aquamarine waters of Flathead Lake to the north. A film of ice coated the brick path that led from the back of the house through a break in the lilac hedge to the graveled farm yard, and her boots skidded a few times as she walked. Another sign that the first snow would be coming soon—probably before Halloween.

Wes's truck was parked in his usual spot, the trailer door left open after he'd unloaded Whiskey Chaser. With the rising sun behind her, she saw the fields glistening brightly and it took a few moments for Mattie to locate the golden quarter horse gelding grazing with the rest of the herd at the far end of the north pasture.

Chaser was a relatively young horse, and this was only the second year Wes had ridden him for bulldogging. Mattie wondered if he was the reason Wes had performed so poorly lately. But last season, Chaser's first, he'd done pretty well.

Mattie slid open the main door to the barn and unzipped her insulated vest at the welcoming warmth. It was designed and built over thirty years ago, and she was impressed anew every time she stepped inside. Her father, Hawksley Carrigan, a practical cattle rancher who owned more than ten times the land of the Bishops, would never have approved of the expensive wood interior, the brick floors, the airy open-topped stalls with their wrought iron gates.

Wasteful. Extravagant. She could hear the adjectives in her father's voice, but that didn't prevent her from appreciating the attractive setting.

Jake Webster was already in the feed room, to the right of the main door, doling rations into the cart which everyone in the family referred to as the "gravy train." It was built on wheels, so it was a simple matter to push it down the broad main corridor and measure out the feed and supplement according to the charts outside each stall door.

"Morning Jake." Mattie picked up a scoop and started filling the back side of the cart.

Jake had been hired by Wes's father and was in his late fifties. His hair was thick and straight—and pure gray. He shaved every day, but in the evening, so he had a perpetual grazing of stubble over his long, lean face. When he'd been younger and his hair was dark, this look had been rather attractive. Now, however, the stubble merely accented his age.

He was still lean, though, and healthy, getting as much done in a working day as he ever had.

"I see Wes made it home last night. Where was he this time?" The note of disapproval in Jake's voice was customary any time he referred to Wes's "other" life, as a rodeo cowboy. Jake considered Wes's bulldogging and bull-riding to be a ridiculous and dangerous hobby, whereas running a horse breeding and training operation was a real man's career.

Mattie sometimes felt the same way. Over the years there'd certainly been many times when she'd wished Wes spent more time at home.

But whenever she went to watch him at one of the rodeos, she could understand why he was hooked. He was so talented, and he knew how to play to the crowd. His rides always earned him roars of approval, no matter the score. Over the years, he'd made a lot of friends, too. His rodeo family meant almost as much to him as his real-life one did.

"Billings," she kept her answer brief, knowing where the conversation was heading and not looking forward to it.

"Don't suppose he bought us any yearlings while he was out there?"

The Northern International Livestock Exposition, where Wes had gone for the rodeo, also held auctions for some of the best horses and yearlings that money could buy. Here was another sore point with Jake. In the old days—when Garth Bishop was in charge—they'd kept more than a hundred horses. Now they were down to twenty-two.

She shrugged. "Not sure. We haven't had a chance to talk yet." But she'd be surprised if he had. "Look at it this way—no new horses means less work for both of us."

Jake snorted. "Hardly worth you guys paying me a fulltime salary if this place doesn't require fulltime work."

She rolled her eyes. "Yeah, you've got to stop spending so much time on your iPhone, Jake."

He gave her an affronted look. Then they both laughed. She and Wes had had to practically threaten to fire him before he'd finally agreed to accept the thing and keep it charged and in his pocket while he was working.

"This way, you run into trouble, and you can call for help, quick," Wes had told him.

"More like, you can reach me anytime to give me more work to do," Jake had grumbled. But the man wasn't lazy. It was the infringement on his privacy and his innate dislike of change—especially any change involving technology—that had made him reluctant to accept the phone.

A lot of the older ranchers in Montana were suspicious of change, Mattie's father included. Rich newcomers from places like California and Washington were buying up the relatively cheap Montana land for hobby ranches. Money to spare, and a lack of appreciation for the way things were done around here, led to a lot of animosity toward the interlopers... and the fancy contraptions they brought with them.

But over time, Jake had started to appreciate certain features that came with the phone. Like the weather app. And sports updates. Portia had even taught him how to download apps for video games.

"Ah well," Jake sighed. "Maybe this winter I should sell my horse and buy me a nice little trailer. Head south to the desert and soak up some rays."

About this time of year, Jake always made the same threat. Mattie didn't take him seriously. She couldn't imagine Jake being happy if he wasn't busy working with horses. And if he hadn't left Montana ten years ago, after his wife Chris died, she didn't figure he ever would.

About an hour later, all the horses had been fed, their water checked, and most of the stalls were mucked out. Mattie checked her watch. "Think I'll head inside. Wes should be up by now."

Jake made no reply to that. But he stopped working and straightened, meeting her gaze with an expression that was partly a frown. And partly concern. To Mattie it felt as if a sheet of ice had been slipped down her back.

Jake's look told her that he'd noticed the new distance between her and her husband.

Which meant it wasn't in her head.
Their problems were real.

CHAPTER TWO

The smell of burned toast and eggs greeted Mattie as she replaced her boots with a pair of gray canvas slip-ons. After washing up at the stainless steel sink in the mudroom, she headed for the kitchen. Wes was at the island, his head bent over his iPad as he finished up his breakfast with a cup of coffee.

"Hey. How are things out there?"

Since he hadn't stood to give her a hug, she wrapped her arms around his neck and laid her cheek on the top of his head. Her husband was a small-framed man, but solid muscle. "Want to come out with me when you're finished with that coffee? We've got a couple horses that could use some work this morning."

His answer was a sigh. "I'm pretty sore after the weekend." His gaze dropped back to the iPad, that had gone dark. "Not that I have anything to show for my aches and bruises."

"Bad draws?" She had years of practice at saying the right, sympathetic thing. The score in the rodeo ring was only fifty percent under the cowboy's control. The bulls were assigned by random draws—and not all of them were star performers. But bad draws couldn't explain his sad bulldogging times.

"I guess."

She rinsed out the cup she'd taken with her to the barn, then refilled it. Still lots left in the pot. Both girls had become coffee drinkers after they turned sixteen and were allowed to drink the beverage at home. Mattie no longer needed to make a full pot every morning. But it was one of those habits that was tough to break.

Like cooking too much food and checking the girls' rooms for dirty clothes when it was time to do laundry. And waiting for them to come through the back door after the school bus drove by...

She leaned her back against the counter, sipping the hot coffee and eyeing her husband. He was looking at the iPad again, as if her presence was nothing but an interruption. That was when she noticed the key was no longer on the counter.

"I found a key on the floor by your jacket this morning."

Wes nodded, head still lowered. "Yeah. Thanks."

"So... what's it for?"

Wes hesitated a moment before answering. He seemed annoyed that she felt it necessary to ask the question and he answered with exaggerated patience. "I crashed with the Wilkinson's this weekend. Peter gave me a key to their guest cabin and I forgot to return it. I'll put it in the mail later today."

A wild impulse rose in her—a desire to take his silly iPad and toss it into the garbage. What was he reading on there that was so damn fascinating? After four days apart, was it so unreasonable of her to expect to have a proper conversation with her husband?

Mattie willed herself to be calm. She'd try again, bring up another subject.

"Jake wondered if you'd bought any yearlings?"

"Why would I do that?"

She raised her eyebrows. There was no point in telling him they only had twenty-two horses in their stables right now. Wes was gone a lot, but he still made all the business decisions around here—and paid the bills. He was aware that last year they'd barely broken even. And without new clients or horses, they'd be lucky to do as well this year.

"What's going on, Wes?" she asked softly.

He grabbed onto his mug with both of his tough, sun-darkened hands and gazed down into it, his posture sagging with a sort of sadness Mattie had never seen in him before.

"Why won't you look at me?"

He did raise his head then, but only briefly. Getting up from the stool, he went to the far window. The house had been designed open concept with a seamless transition between kitchen and family area. A river-rock fireplace with a heavy walnut mantel grounded the south end of the room. Large paneled windows to the west and north looked out to the pastures and Flathead Lake in the distance.

Mattie set down her mug next to her husband's and went to stand beside him. She'd lived with this view for nineteen years, but never took it for granted. From here you could see almost all of their land. And it was beautiful.

Wes shifted, putting an extra foot between them. "Mattie—I've been thinking it's time to sell."

"What?" This was something they'd *never* discussed. She wouldn't even have considered it an option. "But—this land is..." She couldn't find the words to go on. She'd been raised to consider land the most important and valuable thing in the world. Her father's ties to the Circle C were blood and marrow deep. And, being married to Wes, she'd come to feel the same way about Bishop Stables too.

"I'm getting too old to rodeo, but I'm not interested in breeding and training Tennessee Walkers. That was Mom and Dad's thing. Not mine."

She wasn't surprised that he was making this admission. She'd suspected as much for years. "But—what about the girls?" This land was their heritage, their birthright. But then an ugly suspicion rose up in her. Unlike her father who had made no secret of his disappointment in fathering four daughters, Wes had never seemed to care that they had no sons. After the twins were born he'd agreed with her that their family was complete.

"Would you be saying this if we had a son?"

"Of course... Hell, Mattie, that's not what this is about."

She was relieved to hear that. But only for a second. She was beginning to see that he'd been thinking about this a long time, and by the firm set of his jaw, he'd already made up his mind.

Without any discussion with *her*.

This was not how their marriage worked. At least, up until now it wasn't.

"But, how will we earn our living? We have four years of college to pay for."

"Only because you pushed the girls to go. I still don't know why. Neither of us went—and we did just fine."

The further education of their daughters had been a no-brainer to her. With Wren, it hadn't been an issue. She'd been excited to go, had already picked out a program at the University of Colorado. Portia, however, had required some persuading.

Mattie had been shocked when Wes sided with Portia, and they had argued privately for over a week. "Let her learn a trade, instead," Wes had said. "She could be a hairdresser or work in one of those nails places. I see them everywhere I go."

Finally he'd backed down and gone silent on the subject, leaving her to persuade her lovely, less academic daughter that secondary education these days was a must.

But all of this had taken place a year ago. She wasn't going to let him pull her back into that argument now.

"Even if the girls could fund college on their own—what about us? How will we support ourselves, not to mention save for our retirement? It's not like we have a big nest egg set aside." Making payments to registered plans had never seemed important. After all, they weren't yet forty.

"The proceeds from the ranch will be enough to take care of the girls." Wes hesitated. "And you."

Mattie stared at him. Finally he was looking at her, too, and his eyes didn't look like Wes's anymore. They were cold and distant as a stranger's.

Understanding hit her like a bullet. She gasped, felt a physical pain explode in her gut. *This must be what it's like to die. You're living your life—and suddenly you aren't.*

When he didn't say anything, she was forced to put words to the awful thing.

"You want to sell the ranch. A-and you want to leave me."

He moved restlessly from the window, to the sofa, where he straightened a cushion before shifting to the fireplace. Resting one hand on the walnut mantel, he turned back to look at her. "Yeah."

Mattie clasped her arms around her torso, feeling a wintery chill, and also, a sense that this simply couldn't be happening.

It was only last Christmas that she and Wes had sat in this very room talking about their future, once the twins were off to college. One more year of rodeoing, he'd promised her, and then he'd have more time to dedicate to the ranch and more time for her. Maybe they'd take a few trips—see a bit of the world outside the continental US.

Was he going through some sort of midlife crisis?

"Is this about Dex's accident last spring?"

In May a cowboy had been killed in the rodeo ring in Texas. Dex Cooper had been a bull-rider, competing in the same event as Wes. Mattie had found out about the death online, when she was checking for her husband's scores. A video of the accident had even been posted on YouTube, but she hadn't watched. It appalled her that people filmed these things—and then, rather than deleting them, actually put them on the Internet for other people to view.

Who were these other people who got such thrills out of tragedy?

Reading about the incident had been horrible enough. It was her worst nightmare, of course, that Wes would be mauled by a bull and be terribly injured—or worse.

The fact that it had happened to some other woman's husband, this time, didn't make it easier to bear.

But what troubled her even more was that Wes hadn't called to tell her what had happened. She'd assumed he hadn't wanted to frighten her. But in the past, he'd shared everything with her. The good. And the tough.

When he came home, she could tell the accident had

affected him deeply. How could it not? But even then he refused to talk about it, leaving the room if she so much as mentioned Dex Cooper.

That was when Wes's rodeo scores had started dropping.

It was so obvious now, Mattie couldn't believe she hadn't made the connection earlier.

"Dex's death is part of it," Wes agreed. "You know I was planning to quit next year anyway. But that kind of cinched matters for me. And I started wondering what it was all for, anyway. All those years in the rodeo ring. Sure I won some belt buckles and made some money. But for what?"

Finally he was being honest. But why had he waited until it was too late?

"You rodeoed because you loved it. And the money you earned helped us raise our daughters."

Unconvinced, Wes glanced over the pictures on the mantel. His parents and hers. Their daughters. Their wedding photo. God, they'd been young.

"I understand why you're quitting the rodeo. It's time." Few men continued to compete into their thirties, and even less once they hit forty. "But why sell the ranch? Seems to me that it's the perfect time to be expanding—not getting out."

Wes rubbed his face and sighed. "You don't get it. I'm done, Mat. I'm just...done."

How dared he say that? "What about the rest of us? I'm not done. I love this ranch and I've worked harder at it than anyone. And what about Portia and Wren? If we sell, where are they going to go for Christmas and the summer break? This is their *home*."

"You don't get it, Mat. You think the girls are going to keep coming back here all the time—well they won't. They'll get a job in the city and they'll meet a guy and we'll be lucky if they visit one week out of the year."

Maybe. Eventually. But there were a lot of years to go before that day. "Aren't you rushing things a little?"

"The twins are eighteen. How much time did you spend going back to the Circle C once you were that age?"

Heat flared over her. "That's not a fair comparison.

Those were different days. And Hawksley wasn't the kind of father that you are." Her father had been disapproving and distant—always. He'd never given any sign that he cared whether his daughters came to visit or not. The only ties Mattie felt to the Circle C were to her sisters. The four of them, despite the gaps in their ages, were very close.

"Parents have to step back when their kids are grown. That's just how it is."

He'd never talked like this before. "Our roles change," she agreed, talking slowly, trying to figure out who this man was. She'd always felt that their parenting styles blended perfectly. But looking back now she could see that Wes had connected better with the girls when they were younger. Their adolescent stage had confused him. And maybe he'd pulled back more than she realized. "But they still need us."

"Portia and Wren haven't needed me since I taught them to drive."

"Why are you being so literal? You know being part of a family is more than doing jobs for one another. Family provides our emotional bedrock. None of us ever grow out of the need to be loved."

"And I'll never stop loving them," Wes said, his voice subdued once more.

The implication of his words hit her with another ferocious stab of pain.

He'd never stop loving their daughters.

But he had stopped loving *her*.

A Week Later

Nat Diamond left his doctor's office in Polson with a feeling of relief at an unpleasant task finally behind him. Ever since his mother's death, twenty years ago, the result of a misdiagnosis, followed by a drug which had stopped her heart cold, he'd had a profound, if somewhat illogical, distrust for the medical profession. He'd been dreading that appointment for weeks. Now, the day opened up to him full of possibilities.

He'd start with lunch. The Mexican place on the shore of the Flathead was his favorite. He'd order steak fajitas and a glass of Corona. Then treat himself with a long ride on the new colt when he got home.

The colt had turned out to be a nice surprise. Spirited, but anxious to please too. Handsome and gaited, strong and graceful. He couldn't wait to show him off to his neighbor Mattie. When she'd sold the horse to him three years ago, she'd said he had promise. But she'd be thrilled to see just how much.

At the restaurant, Nat asked for a booth at the back and sat so he could look out at the lake. The patio had been closed off for the season and at the moment nary a boat could be seen over the expanse of the silvery blue waters, speckled with whitecaps. The Flathead was the biggest freshwater lake this side of the Mississippi and it didn't take much wind to get all that water churned up.

Despite the cooler temperatures—and the knowledge that snow would soon be coming—Nat was relieved summer was over. He didn't care for the influx of cottagers and vacationers who jammed up the roads with their cars, and the lake with their motor boats every July and August. September was the best, but October was good too.

He'd enjoy this month while it lasted.

The gal who seated customers walked by, disrupting his view as she led an older man to the table next to his. Nat gave a double-take. It was Jake Webster, foreman at the Bishop's place.

"Hey there, Jake. Want to join me?"

Jake nodded, then took the bench seat with his back to the lake. "Good to see you, Nat. I've been meaning to call. You must be planning to move your cattle in soon."

"Next week. You in?"

"Absolutely."

One long day of work would see the job done. In the past, when they'd had more cattle on the Double D, pushing the cows down closer to home for the winter had required a two-day trail ride. Nat had loved those days riding with his mother and father, eating dinner around the campfire and sleeping under the stars.

Recent years, though, he'd been downsizing the operation. He'd leased a large portion of his land to a neighbor to the south. Reduced the herd. It was easier this way. And he sure didn't need the money.

Jake ordered enchiladas and a beer and with their drinks came a basket of tortilla chips and a small bowl of watery salsa. Trying to scoop some up, without dripping on the table, was a challenge Nat almost never met.

"I thought we'd bring the cows in next Monday. With the twins in college, I suppose Mat will want to come. And Wes, if he's home. Should I call her, or will you pass on the invite?" Nat worded this carefully, because he was treading potential dangerous waters here. Mattie loved any excuse to be out on the range riding all day. Her husband, despite his horse-breeding operation, and love of the rodeo, did not.

Nat wasn't sure if it was the work—or himself—that Wes objected to. They'd been friends once upon a time. How could they not be, when they'd grown up on adjacent ranches? But once Wes married Mattie, that had changed.

Wes was away from home a lot. And he made it clear that he didn't want Nat stepping in to fill his shoes while he was gone. Good old Jake—decades older than Mattie—was there to handle any problems that came up.

Only Jake couldn't handle everything.

And it was Wes's own fault that he wasn't home more. If Nat were Mattie's husband, he sure wouldn't be taking off to a new rodeo every second week.

Tensions between them eased a little when Nat married Julia. But his marriage hadn't lasted five years before Julia moved back to Seattle. He should have known better than to pluck a woman out of the city and try to transplant her on a ranch.

He'd resumed his bachelor lifestyle without much difficulty. And Wes had gone back to glowering at him if he spoke so much as one sentence to his wife.

Their food came then, and Nat was half finished his plate before he realized Jake hadn't answered his question. He looked up to see Jake pushing food around on his plate.

Nat set down his fork. "What's up?"

"Well. It's Mattie. I'm kind of worried about her."

"Why?"

Jake sighed. He wasn't one to gossip, especially not about the Bishops, about whom he felt incredibly loyal. But sometimes a man had to make a call and speak up, if the situation warranted it.

And this time, apparently it did.

"She hasn't stepped outside of the house for a week."

That wasn't like Mattie. "Is she sick?"

"Don't think so. She says not. But she won't let me in to check on her." Jake swallowed. "Thing is, Wes drove off seven days ago, without his trailer or his horse."

Jake raised his eyes from his plate, and in his tired gaze Nat could see his concern. The reason for it was obvious. If Wes hadn't taken his horse, then he wasn't off to another rodeo. So where had he gone?

CHAPTER THREE

There was not a single tea leaf left in Mattie's kitchen. She'd gone through so many pots in the last week that she'd depleted not only her favorite English Breakfast, but also all the herbal brands her daughters had accumulated over the years.

She'd also worn out two decks of cards playing solitaire. She found the game soothing, for some reason. Shuffling and dealing the cards, logically sorting them, keeping her mind busy so she couldn't dwell on the unthinkable thing that had happened last Monday morning.

She and Wes had had their "talk" shortly after eight in the morning.

By noon he had left, most of his clothes packed in two suitcases, along with his damned iPad, the check-book, and a box of files he'd removed from the office. She had no idea where he'd gone. She could send him a text message or e-mail if she needed him for something, he'd said on his way out the door.

The implied message was that he was hoping not to hear from her at all.

And he hadn't.

Despite composing numerous messages to him in her head, from *you lousy jerk* to *what did I do wrong?* she had maintained silence. Every time she felt the urge to reach out to him, she thought about his eyes and how empty they had seemed when he looked at her. As if all the laughter and love that they'd shared had bled out of them.

He no longer saw her as Mattie, the love of his life, but as Mattie, the woman who was standing in his way.

And God, but it hurt. Her husband and this ranch were as much a part of her body and soul as the twins were. How could she survive the loss of all of them? What would be left, who would she be?

And what about Portia and Wren? In about five weeks they'd be flying home for Thanksgiving. What would she tell them if their father wasn't here? Or if he lived up to his promise to put the property for sale? She was so afraid of this happening that she hadn't answered the phone all week.

Not even calls from her daughters. She'd texted them instead, silly messages like, "Busy right now. Love you lots!" She'd even missed their regular Sunday Skype call yesterday, sending yet another text message. "Computer on the fritz. Getting it fixed. Skype next week?"

An out-and-out lie.

She was ashamed. But also desperate. One look at her face—she'd hardly stopped crying all week, even when she played cards the tears streamed down her cheeks—and they'd know something awful had happened.

She couldn't trust her voice on the phone, either. She'd tried calling Sage earlier—and been forced to hang up and send a text message. "Sorry, I had to hang up before you answered. I'll try calling later in the week."

Thank God for the impersonal text message. It was saving her butt, big time.

But she couldn't put off the people she loved forever. Eventually she was going to have to face them. How would Portia and Wren cope? It wasn't fair for their first year at college to be spoiled by something so dreadful as this.

Damn Wes—how could he have written off his children

CJ CARMICHAEL

as if they simply didn't matter anymore? At one time he would have done anything to protect them.

And her.

Mattie reached for the tissue box. She'd scavenged them from every room in the house and this last one she'd taken from the drawer of Portia's nightstand. The tissues smelled faintly of Portia's white sandalwood perfume.

Which only made her cry harder.

Just eight weeks ago the four of them had sat down to dinner together, celebrating the girls' last night at home before college. Not that Mattie had felt like celebrating—tears kept popping into her eyes as she prepared all of their favorites. Broccoli soup for Wren, ribs for Wes, lemon pie for Portia. The occasion had to be marked, she was determined about that.

Never had she guessed that it might be the last time the four of them would eat together as a family.

That thought started another spate of tears. Mattie tenderly dabbed her cheeks, avoiding the raw area around her nose. She ought to take a shower and change out of her sweats. Prepare herself a proper meal. Go out and buy a few essentials.

Instead, she crawled under the quilt she'd moved to the living room sofa. It was old, she'd found it in the linen cupboard, something she'd taken with her when she moved from the Circle C to her new home with her husband. Her grandmother Bramble had stitched together the quilt—she'd made one for all of them, except Callan who'd been born after their grandmother's death.

Mattie liked to imagine that some of the squares of fabric on her quilt were from old clothing of her mother's. She'd been twenty-two when her mom was killed in a ranching accident. Already married, with babies of her own. But her mother's death had shattered her. Even then, though, she hadn't fallen apart like this.

Mattie pressed the soft flannel backing against her cheek. She wished her mother was here now, to comfort her. What would she say? Mattie knew her parents had gone through rough patches too. Yet their marriage had survived.

Was it possible hers would too?

Blissful relief shot up in her heart every time she considered this. But the hope never lasted long.

Wes wasn't the kind of man who acted on impulse. He considered long and hard. And when he acted, he rarely turned back.

How long had he been thinking about leaving her? She felt that she should know the exact second he'd first considered it. Had they been together at the time? Maybe she'd said or done something annoying to him...

Stop it! She was driving herself crazy.

She tried to summon the energy to get off the sofa. She spent all her nights here now, unable to face either the room she'd shared with her husband, or the girls' abandoned beds. Not that she slept much. When she became too tired to play solitaire, she turned on the TV and watched old re-runs of Gilmore Girls.

What she needed was fresh air. And work. If her father could see her right now, he'd be disgusted. Which she totally deserved. She had animals out there depending on her... and yet, she couldn't make herself go out and face them—or Jake. Not when she knew Wes was planning to sell. For all Jake's talk about heading South for the winter, he'd be lost without this job.

When the doorbell rang, the sound was so foreign it took her a moment to realize she must have a guest. Jake had been by a few times this week to check on her, but he always knocked.

So who could this be?

She'd just be quiet and wait for them to leave.

The doorbell rang again, and then a knock sounded on the door. Whoever was out there was being damn persistent.

Mattie went to the powder room across from the foyer. She was expecting to look bad, but what she saw shocked even her. Matted hair, blotchy skin, puffed eyes, red nose—and wrinkled sweatshirt. She bet she smelled bad, too.

There was another knock, loud enough that it made her jump. Then a man's voice. "I'm not leaving until I know you're okay, Mattie."

That was Nat Diamond's voice. What was *he* doing here? Jake must have said something—there could be no other explanation. Unless Wes had been talking to him? Maybe sounding him out to see if he wanted to buy the ranch.

A sob caught in her throat, and she put a hand to her mouth. It came away damp. She was crying again, but there were no more tissues, so she pulled off a long piece of toilet paper, then went to the door.

Nat Diamond was a good neighbor. In the old days, when they'd had more horses, he'd been generous about letting their Tennessee Walkers graze on his land in the late summer when their own pastures were picked over. He'd been known to stop and warn Mattie when a storm was moving this way, or to help her unload a truckload of feed when Jake's back was troubling him.

He never put on airs, despite the fact that he owned the largest and most successful ranch in the county. Wes was a good-looking guy, but Nat, he was handsome enough to be a movie star. He didn't smile much, or flirt, but he had charisma all right, and aside from a brief period of time when he'd been married to a very beautiful woman from California, he'd been the most eligible bachelor of the county by a long shot.

And he'd always been sweet to the twins.

But Wes had never liked it when he heard Nat had been around and so Mattie had learned to keep her distance. She didn't think Wes was jealous—he just felt guilty when he heard Nat had been helping them out. He didn't like the idea that he couldn't be counted on to look after his own ranch, and his own family.

But the simple fact was—sometimes he couldn't be.

As for right now, well, telling Nat what was going on just wasn't an option. Mattie was low—but she still had her pride. And no one—*no one*—was going to see her this way.

She went to the door and sank onto the slate-tiled flooring. She could feel a cool draft from outside. The weather stripping needed replacing. Another chore to add to the list. "Nat, this is Mattie. I don't know what Jake told you, but I'm fine."

"Then invite me in."

"I'm not presentable."

"I'll wait."

She groaned. Damn it, why were all the men in Montana so intractable? Wes, her father, Jake—and Nat. "I'd really rather be alone right now."

"According to Jake you've been alone for a week. He's worried. So am I."

She closed her eyes, touched by the concern of her foreman and her next door neighbor. Had Wes given a thought to her after he'd walked out? Had he wondered how she was doing—if she was falling apart? He couldn't have, since she hadn't heard a word from him. This callous unconcern, more than anything, proved that he really didn't love her anymore.

There was a long pause before Nat spoke again. This time, his voice was softer, but she still had no trouble making out the words.

"Mattie, I know Wes is gone, and not to another rodeo. If this is pride talking, then just remember I've been in the exact same place as you."

He was referring to when his wife left him. It had been somewhat of a scandal, because Julia had taken up with some rich dude from New York City—met him on the Internet of all things. It was all anyone could talk about for several weeks, but despite all that, Nat held his head high and calmly went about his business. No, the man who had lived through that was not going to cut her any slack over Wes.

"Then you know I'm not fit for company. If you really want to help, I could use some tea and a few boxes of tissues."

"Tea?"

She could hear him chuckling. Damn him for finding that amusing.

"I hope you haven't been drinking it black. You aren't that far gone, are you?"

"Damn it, Nat. You're annoying."

"I try."

She smiled then, just a little smile, but enough to make

her dry lips hurt.

"Tell you what. I'll make you a deal. I'll go get that tea, but when I return, you'll let me in. We'll knock back an entire pot of tea and get all crazy sad and depressed together. You can even cry on my shoulder if you want."

Oh, Nat. What had ever possessed Julia to leave a man like you? "It's a deal. But be warned. I look like something from *The Walking Dead*."

He chuckled again. "You forget. I've seen you on horseback in the driving rain after a day out on the range."

Good point. She rarely looked her best when she was with Nat Diamond. Which was probably for the best.

"I'll bring something with me to fix that weather stripping," he added. "Though I have to admit, the gap in your door has certainly been useful today."

CHAPTER FOUR

"First things first," Nat said when he returned an hour later. He didn't look at Mattie too closely—didn't want to make her feel uncomfortable. But one quick glance was enough to confirm that she'd been crying all week. She had showered, however, and her chestnut-colored hair fell in gleaming waves to her shoulders. She was wearing clean jeans and a button-up shirt that had been tailored to follow the depression of her waist and the curving out of her hips.

Pretty as a descriptor didn't do justice to Mattie Carrigan. She had the kind of beauty that could withstand driving rain, hard work, exhaustion, and yes, even a week of crying. If anything, the ravages of the tears only made her eyes seem brighter, her mouth more tender—and kissable.

Nat wasn't the kind of man to covet his neighbor's wife. And he sure wasn't the type to take advantage of a damsel in distress. But he couldn't deny what was right before his eyes.

Mattie was a very desirable woman.

He had four grocery bags in one of his hands, a tool box

with his hacksaw and rubber mallet in the other.

"This is for you." He passed along the groceries. He'd bought, not only tea and tissues, but some fresh fruit and veggies and a steak for her dinner. The food had been a smart addition. She looked like she needed a decent meal.

Before she could thank him, he added, "I'm holding you to that pot of tea, so you'd better put some water on to boil."

Then he started to remove the front door from its hinges. "That little draft will feel a hell of a lot colder in a few weeks. I picked up a replacement weather-strip at Ace Hardware."

"Nat—that was nice of you. I can pay you back for all of this—the groceries and the kit. And I can do the install, as well. I've done it before."

He couldn't help but be impressed. Mattie was nothing if not self-reliant. But then, she'd had to be, with her husband on the road so damn much.

"Just make the tea. By the time it's brewed, I'll be finished."

The job actually took a half-hour to complete, but when he was done the door opened and closed smoothly and the draft was gone.

Mattie had put on some music, and when he came around the corner to the kitchen, Mindy Smith was singing her version of Dolly Parton's "Jolene." Mattie was at the sink, her back to him, but he could tell by her hunched shoulders that she was crying again. No wonder. The music was so unbearably sad that he couldn't take it either. The docking station was on the counter, bracketed on one side by the home phone and on the other by a pile of *Western Horseman* magazines. He moved ahead to the next track, only to get another song written in a minor key.

"What is this playlist? Songs to slit your wrist by?"

He was going to make another change when a message popped up on the screen, along with the opening strains from *Modern Family*. This wasn't an iPod. It was Mattie's phone.

And the message, he couldn't help reading it, said, "Are you OK Mom?"

"From one of the girls, I think." He dislodged the phone from the docking station and handed it to Mattie.

She grabbed a fresh tissue and wiped her eyes before she turned around. "That'll be Wren."

Of course she'd have different ring tones set up for each of her daughters.

She glanced at the screen, then replaced the phone, selecting a different playlist this time—rock from the seventies. The Bee Gees started singing *How deep is your love...*.

"Oh, God. I can't win today." She hit the off button. Sighed.

"Aren't you going to reply to Wren's message? She sounds worried."

"I've made up every excuse I can think of. First, I told them my computer was broken so I couldn't talk to them on Skype as usual on Sunday evening. Then I pretended one of the horses had the heaves and that's why I wasn't answering the home line..." She slid onto a stool, sagging her arms onto the island.

He found the remote control for the TV and put on the Weather Channel for background noise. And also because, he liked the Weather Channel.

"Maybe you should be honest with them."

"I can't give them the news that their father left me over the phone." Mattie sank her head down on the counter, into the nest she'd made with her arms.

He put a hand on her back. "Is that what happened?"

She blinked very rapidly. "I think so. It was so fast. One minute I was asking Wes if he'd bought any yearlings in Billings. The next he was saying he wanted to sell the ranch and move on. Without me."

"Sell the ranch?" Nat hadn't expected this complication. "You sure?"

She nodded. "I half expected you to already know. I mean—" She pulled her body upright with some effort, and looked at him curiously. "It occurred to me that Wes might have already approached you to see if you were interested in buying him out?"

It made sense. If you wanted to sell land, the first

people you talked to were your neighbors. Often someone was happy for the chance to grow their operation. Or, at the very least, prevent the sale of adjacent land to someone with massive development plans like... oh, say, a retirement village or an eighteen-hole golf course.

But in this case, "No. Wes hasn't talked to me. Or anyone else." If he had, Nat would have heard about it. This kind of news traveled fast. "How do you feel about selling Bishop Stables?"

The look she gave him was pure misery. "I hate it. I probably love this place more than he does. Well, I guess that's obvious. And while neither one of the girls has shown any interest in working here, or maybe taking over one day, that could change. They're so young right now, and they deserve a chance to get out and see a little of the world. But who knows—in ten or fifteen years, they might realize that this is where they want to be after all."

"Maybe," Nat agreed. But odds were against it. Most of the kids who grew up around here tended to move away when they finished school. There just weren't that many jobs or careers to entice them to stay.

Still, as Mattie said, generally families at least gave their children a chance to take over if they owned a farm, orchard or ranch. Wes didn't seem prepared to do even that.

Then again, maybe he needed the money. To finance his divorce. And his new start in life.

Nat kept those thoughts to himself. Mattie was already coping with enough.

"Oh," she said, getting up from the stool as she remembered the tea. "I put a cozy on the pot. I hope it isn't too cold."

She poured the tea into solid white mugs and as she took her first sip, her eyes flitted around the room. Was she wondering how much longer she'd be living in this house? She looked so forlorn, it almost broke his heart.

What she needed was something to look forward to.

"We're moving the cattle next week. Want to come?"

Usually Mattie jumped at these offers. In all the years she'd been living here, she'd only missed out on a handful of roundups because the girls were sick, or once, when Wes was only home for a few days before heading out to his next rodeo.

Today though she looked wistfully, she shook her head, no.

"I've been neglecting my work here for too long. Poor Jake must be run off his feet."

"I saw him for lunch earlier today. Looks like he's holding up."

"I guess someone around here has to."

The volume on the television increased, and they turned to see an ad for winter tires come on the screen.

"I hate how the commercials are always louder," Mattie said. Tears were forming in her eyes as she said this. Nat didn't think she was worried about the volume of the television. Or the need for winter tires, either.

"It's going to be okay," he told her believing with all his heart that this was true. Whether her marriage to Wes withstood this storm, or not, she'd emerge stronger than ever.

But the look she gave him was full of doubt.

After Nat left, Mattie had to allow that his visit had done her good. Not only was her door better prepared to withstand the winter blizzards coming their way, but she was stronger, too. And she realized that cutting herself off from the rest of the world had to stop.

Today.

She'd start by phoning one of her sisters. Dani, a professor of psychology at the University of Washington, was the closest to her in age and the most obvious first choice. But Mattie could imagine how that call would go. Dani would be cool and collected. She'd pass on whatever the statistics currently were for failed marriages and tell her this was not the end of the world. She'd give her a pep talk and tell her to protect herself and hire a good lawyer. She'd also suggest counseling—of course!—and putting her name up on an Internet dating site.

Dani, for all her supposed insight into the human condition, would have no idea how it felt to be looking at the end of a nineteen-year marriage.

Driven and career-focused, at thirty-four, Dani had never been in a serious relationship. She'd eschewed clinical practice for the joys of research and teaching. Nothing got Dani more excited than a bunch of data and the opportunity to run a statistical analysis.

As for telling the twins the awful news—Dani would probably be full of advice for how to do this, as well. But Dani didn't know how it felt to be a mother. She didn't understand the need to protect.

And she didn't know Portia and Wren.

This was going to crush them. Especially Wren, who was less social than Portia, and didn't have a large group of friends for support.

Mattie paced from the kitchen to the far windows and back again. Several times she reached for the phone, then hesitated.

Callan was the youngest of her sisters, but also the toughest. If Mattie called her, she'd probably find her out on the range somewhere, repairing fences, or making other preparations for winter on the Circle C. Callan would be full of fury toward Wes. She'd talk about revenge and making him pay.

And Mattie wasn't up to that.

Maybe she *should* be storming around having fits of outrage and indignation.

But she was too sad and worn-out for such theatrics.

So no. She wouldn't call Callan yet, either.

Which left Sage. Of course it did. The third of the Carrigan girls, Sage had a quiet way about her. She would listen to Mattie. She would be sympathetic. And best of all, she would not presume to tell her what to do.

Though all of them had grown up in the saddle, Sage was the most talented rider. On horseback she looked like a ballet dancer, all strength and grace. Their father, seeing her gift, had convinced her to become a barrel-racer.

Disappointed in his brood of females, he'd taken momentary pride in Sage's rodeo accomplishments, until an accident had resulted in Sage injuring her knee—and giving up the sport.

That had really ticked Hawksley Carrigan off—but Mattie had never seen her sister more at peace than since she'd made the decision to hang up her spurs and open her own chocolate shop back home in Marietta.

Phone in hand, Mattie returned to the windows and the view. She couldn't stand to think about the possibility that one day—maybe sooner than she thought—this view would no longer to be hers to enjoy.

As she waited for her sister to answer, she turned her back on the windows and tried to picture Sage in her shop. Her sister's red hair would be tied in a ponytail or braid and she'd be wearing one of the shop's signature aprons. All around her would be copper-tinted boxes filled with confections of chocolates, nuts and specialty flavors, the air smelling so rich, you could put on weight by just breathing.

Maybe, at the very least, she could ask Sage to send her a package of those delicious salted caramels...

"Hi, Mattie. Good timing, a customer just left. How are you?"

The question hung out there. Mattie realized, damn it, that she'd started to cry again. From her pocket she dug out a couple of tissues, taking a deep breath at the same time.

She had to say something quick or Sage would worry someone had died or something.

"W-Wes is gone. He wants a d-divorce."

"Oh, Mattie. Hang on." Almost a minute passed before Sage came back on the line. "I've left Rose Linn in charge of the shop. I'm in the kitchen now, with lots of time to talk. When did this happen?"

As she recounted the events of the past week, somehow Mattie's load felt lighter. Nothing had changed, the news was all still so very, very bad. But with Sage to talk to, and listening to her sister's calm, kind voice, Mattie's feet were finally able to feel the stability of solid ground again.

She wasn't just Wes Bishop's wife. She was a Carrigan. She had a father—even if he was a mean bastard—and three sisters. And she had a home that had belonged to her even longer than this one had.

"Wow, Mattie, Wes really hit you with a lot. Leaving and selling the ranch, too. And this was the first time he'd talked to you about any of it?"

"In so many words, yes. But I believe my subconscious picked up on certain signs. Because I had this dream the night before, Sage. I was in an airport and I'd booked the two of us on separate flights." She closed her eyes, remembering how, in her dream, she'd been so upset. Beyond what was called for in the circumstances.

"How intense. I bet Dani will have a lot of fun analyzing that one."

"Eventually. But don't tell her yet, okay? I need to break this news to the twins, first." And suddenly Mattie knew how it should be done, and when. Her feet were not only back on the ground, but her strength was returning. "I'll tell them in person when they come home from college for Thanksgiving."

"That's a good idea," Sage agreed. "It'll give you and Wes a little time to sort things out. I assume he'll want to be there with you when you tell them."

"You'd think so, wouldn't you? But the way he's been acting, I really don't know."

A beep from her phone signaled an incoming call. Mattie glanced at the screen, expecting to see one of the twins' names. But it wasn't.

"Can I call you back later, Sage? Looks like Wes is finally ready to talk."

CHAPTER FIVE

Amazing how many thoughts can race through the mind in just a few seconds. In the time she took to disconnect the call to her sister and accept the one from Wes, Mattie wondered if this was more bad news. Maybe he'd found a buyer for the ranch. Or had he realized he'd made a big mistake and wanted to come home? Did he miss her?

Maybe he was calling just to talk...

"Wes?" She stopped pacing. Stood breathless and anxious, her eyes on their wedding photo displayed on the mantel.

But it wasn't her husband, after all. It was a woman.

"You don't know me, Mattie—"

Oh, how Mattie resented the sound of her name on this stranger's tongue. This stranger who was using Wes's phone to call her and invade her own personal space. "Don't call me that. I'm Mrs. Bishop."

"I'm phoning as a favor," the unknown woman continued, ignoring the correction. "I'm sure it's hard, but you have to let Wes go without a fight. He doesn't love you anymore. You may find that hard to believe, but it's true.

Trust me."

This—couldn't be happening. Mattie sputtered at the effrontery. And then anger exploded. "Trust you? Who the hell *are you?*"

The phone went dead. Mattie glared at the screen which had suddenly gone pale, then hit the "End" button with a shaking finger.

Had it occurred to her that there might be another woman in the picture? Of course.

But, just as she avoided the problem signs in her and Wes's marriage, so too had she shied away from thinking about the possibility he was having an affair.

But clearly he was. Or at least he was on the verge.

The key she'd found that morning. Maybe it hadn't been for the Wilkinson's cottage at all, but a room where he'd been meeting this mystery woman? Her body reacted then, not with tears, but with a sudden, violent need to purge. Mattie ran to the bathroom getting there just in time as her body rejected everything she'd eaten in the last twenty-four hours, the way her mind wanted to reject everything that had happened in that same span of time.

When it was over, she felt weak, trembling... and very cold. She ran a hot bath for herself, and let herself be soothed by the scented water.

She would not let that woman get to her. This was *her* life and *she* was the one who was in control.

Wes could leave her, he could sleep around, he could even fall in love with someone else—she couldn't change any of that. What she could control was the way she reacted.

And the most important thing, she realized, as she was toweling off and selecting clean clothes, was being a strong mother.

"**D**o you think something's wrong with Mom?"

Portia glanced at the message, then turned her phone face down on her desk. She was in her Introduction to Psychology class—and the instructor was her Aunt Dani.

One of the reasons she'd decided to come to the University of Washington was to be close to her aunt. Her mom thought it was good for her to move away from Montana—expand her horizons and all of that. But Portia hadn't admitted that she felt nervous about being on her own.

Ideally she and Wren would have gone to the same school, maybe even been roommates in the same sorority house.

But Wren wouldn't go for that.

Wren had chosen to go to school in Colorado. As for sororities—Wren claimed she had no time for them.

Being a twin should have been so fun, but it seemed to Portia that Wren was always trying to push away from her. If Portia chose shoes in red, then Wren would pick black. When Portia decided to grow out her bangs, Wren had cropped hers.

Why was she so determined to be different? Probably because she was embarrassed. Wren had always been the smart one, and Portia suffered in any comparison between the two.

At least coming to Seattle had proven to be a good decision. First, she'd been thrilled to discover she was actually going to be in a class taught by her aunt. She'd been worried there might be rules against that, but Aunt Dani had assured her that since the assignments and exams were all marked by TAs—teaching assistants—there wasn't any conflict of interest.

Dani had always been Portia's favorite aunt. Dani was so sophisticated, with beautiful clothes and an elegant way about her. She'd always been really sweet to her and Wren, bringing them gifts when she came to visit and listening to them like they were real people, not just mini versions of their mother—which was how Callan treated them sometimes.

Since she'd made the decision to attend UW her aunt had been especially kind. She'd picked her up at the airport, taken her shopping for clothes for rush week, and given her a tour of the campus. She'd explained to her about the various sororities and made recommendations on which ones she thought Portia would like the best.

Since Portia had settled into her sorority house, every Sunday night Dani invited her to dinner, in her beautiful modern condo with a view of the city. It was painted white with gray furniture and gleaming wooden floors. Real oil paintings were on the walls and all the appliances and lighting fixtures were high tech. One wall was floor to ceiling windows and you could look out at the Space Needle. Portia wanted to live in a place like that when she was older. But she still wasn't sure how she'd earn the money to afford it.

She sure couldn't see herself being smart enough to become a professor.

The lecture today was hard to understand, even though she'd done the required reading. She tried focusing harder on her aunt, who was moving confidently around the stage, not huddling behind the lectern and reading from notes the way some of Portia's professors did.

"The simple fact is," her aunt Dani was saying, "we don't always see what we think we're seeing. Our perception is more than what we take in with the five senses. It also includes the ability to detect changes in another person's body position or movement. Does anyone know what we call that?"

A few of the students sitting lower down in the auditorium-style classroom called out some answers. Portia, at least, could recognize when she heard the correct one. It was *proprioception*.

Despite her aunt's advice to sit as close to the front in each class as was possible—the professors will remember you better that way—Portia was in one of the back rows, hidden among the almost seven hundred students. She was more comfortable here. She was pretty sure being remembered by her professors for being dumb wouldn't work in her favor.

Her phone vibrated against the desk, signaling an incoming text message. Probably another from Wren. Unable to stop herself, Portia turned her phone over to read it.

"I haven't talked to her all week. Have you?"

What was the matter with her? Her sister was getting paranoid. Placing the phone in her lap, Portia used both thumbs to make a quick reply.

"She must be busy."

Portia wasn't worried about her mother the way Wren was. She was annoyed. After making such a big fuss about them leaving, and insisting that the three of them Skype every Sunday afternoon, her mom had been the first to bail out. If her laptop wasn't working, then she could have used the computer in Dad's office.

Or bought a new one.

What kind of mother would go a whole week without checking in with her daughters. And no, text messages did *not* count.

Portia's own proprioception kicked in then, and she glanced up to see that the students were filing out of the auditorium. Her aunt was no longer on the stage, she must have dismissed them and left already. She had to stop zoning out like this. From now on when she went to class she would turn her phone completely off, not just put it on stealth mode.

"Hey, Portia. Have you decided what to wear to the party tonight?"

A redhead with olive shaped green eyes, wearing trendy Citizen jeans that Portia coveted, but couldn't afford, stopped by her desk. Kirsten was in her sorority, they'd met during rush week. Kirsten's family lived in Portland, her father owned a car dealership and her mother managed an art gallery. Portia had seen pictures of all of this, including the mansion where Kirsten lived, the beautiful Irish Setter that was the family dog—and the gorgeous brother who was one year older, and also enrolled at UW.

For some reason Kirsten thought it was cool that Portia had grown up on a ranch and that her father was a rodeo cowboy. It wasn't cool to Portia, though, when on the night they were all presented into the Greek system, almost every other girls' parents came except her own.

Her dad had been at a rodeo, of course.

And her Mom hardly ever left the horses. "That's the

price of owning a ranch," she'd say, whenever Portia complained about not getting to go on holidays like other families. Pretty much the only time they left home was to visit their grandfather and Aunt Callan in Marietta, or, occasionally to watch their father at a nearby rodeo.

But Kirsten didn't get any of that, of course. She didn't understand that owning a ranch meant waking up before the sun came out and scooping horse shit out of stalls. Kirsten watched YouTube videos of Portia's father on the bucking bulls and gasped at how brave he must be.

"I should probably catch up on my reading."

"We'll go later, around ten?"

Portia didn't commit. The late nights were beginning to get to her. The drinking, too.

The one thing she and Wren had in common was a distaste for alcohol, ingrained by their mother who almost never indulged herself with so much as a beer or a glass of wine. When she was a teenager her mom had given riding lessons to a girl named Neve Shepherd until Neve suddenly decided boys were way more cool than horses.

Shortly after that Neve ended up dead—the result of using alcohol and drugs at a prom night party.

Her Mom had been strongly affected by that. And she'd managed to pass her attitudes along to her daughters. Mostly because she'd never tried to be preachy or bossy about it.

Whether to drink or not will be your choice girls. I just hope you do what feels right to you—and don't start drinking just to fit in with your friends. And never if you're driving.

Kirsten was nice. Most of the time they ate dinner together and studied, or went to parties, in the evening. But lately, Portia had begun feeling a little hemmed in. Kirsten had a lot of ideas about the kind of people she liked—and the kind she didn't.

And one of the guys Kirsten definitely didn't like was moving toward them right now.

Hastily Portia slipped her laptop in her shoulder bag, then pocketed her phone, as a tall boy with long hair that brushed over his eyes, gave her a private smile. No, more like a grin. She'd noticed him watching her in classes before.

She didn't know his name, only that he didn't belong to any of the fraternities and none of her new friends seemed to like him. Kirsten joked about his cowboy boots, calling him a *pretend cowboy* behind his back.

Kirsten's eyes narrowed as she zeroed in on the guy, moving their way. Then she frowned and turned her back to block him from Portia's view. "Want to grab some lunch?"

Without waiting for Portia's response, she led the way into the hall.

Mattie cooked the steak for dinner, not expecting she'd be able to eat it. She surprised herself by finishing half, along with a baked potato and several spears of broccoli. Bless Nat, he'd known what she needed better than she had.

The TV was on, tuned to six-o'clock news so she wouldn't be able to hear herself chew. Nothing she hated more since the twins had left than the quiet of mealtimes. When she'd had enough, she cleaned the kitchen, putting off the calls she'd promised herself she would make.

Finally, she dried her hands, then picked up her cell. Since she was most worried about Wren, she called her first.

"Mom! Thank God! Why haven't you been answering your phone?"

Mattie smiled as she settled on the sofa like a cat, her body curled into the corner, with her legs tucked under her. Did Wren realize she sounded just like the mother here?

"Sorry, honey. It's been a crazy week." She wanted to skirt the truth. Not lie. "Plus, my throat has been acting up. It's been difficult for me to talk."

"Is it a cold? Are you okay?"

Her daughter's concern was touching. Mattie blinked, not wanting to risk getting emotional, because one thing would most certainly snowball into another.

"I'm a lot better, today. Don't worry. How are classes?"

"Crazy busy, but I love them all. Poli-sci is my absolute favorite. We're reading about Plato—he's amazing, Mom. Just brilliant. I can't believe he lived more than two thousand years ago."

Wren spent fifteen minutes talking about Greek philosophers, most of which Mattie couldn't follow.

"—and we had to write an essay, and I had the highest mark in the class, Mom. The professor singled me out later and said he was really impressed and that I should participate more during class because I obviously had worthwhile things to say."

"That's wonderful, honey." She was proud of her daughter, but then, she'd never had any doubt that Wren would excel at college level classes. "What are the other kids like in the class? Have you met anyone that you like?"

Wren went silent, and Mattie felt badly, knowing her question had taken the fizz out of her mood.

"Not really. But it's okay. I'm super busy keeping on top of the work load."

That was what Mattie had been afraid of. That Wren would throw herself into her studies and end up with zero social life. If only Wren had agreed to go to UW, then at least she could have visited her sister and aunt when she was lonely.

"Can I talk to Dad?" Wren asked, after Mattie had updated her on the well-being of the horses and the cats.

"Sorry, honey, but he isn't home."

"I thought he had a clear schedule for the two weeks after Billings?"

Trust Wren to be up-to-date with her father's calendar. Often she knew better than Mattie where Wes was supposed to be on any given day.

"His plans changed and he had to go. But I'll tell him you called and if he gets a chance he'll get in touch."

They said goodbye after that, exchanging "I love yous" and "I miss yous."

Mattie called Portia next, which was easier, since Portia didn't hit her with as many questions, or ask what was going on with her father. For twenty minutes Portia chatted about sorority parties and a new friend of hers named Kirsten. When Mattie turned the topic to her classes, Portia just sighed.

"They're hard, Mom."

Portia might have kept chatting for another twenty minutes, but a friend came to her room and so she finally said good-bye. Mattie put down her phone, then closed her eyes, thinking about her daughters, wishing they weren't so far away. She was relieved that they both sounded okay. But that didn't prevent her from feeling guilty about being out of touch for so long. Falling apart wasn't an option when you were a mother. She would have to do better.

O ctober was slipping away and with it, the long days that came with spring and summer in Montana. The advent of winter was almost harder to bear than the season itself. Five long months of snow and ice, cold, and dark lay ahead. Maybe Jake's idea about heading south wasn't so dumb.

Mattie had already been awake for an hour when the morning alarm went off. The news came on, but she couldn't focus. Then the weather. A cold front was coming down from Canada. She didn't want to get out of bed. The cheerful prattle from the radio announcer didn't fool her.

She was alone.

No man was sleeping in the bed next to her, waiting to give her a good-morning hug. No children needed her to make lunches or hurry them along to catch the bus. Even the horses outside didn't really need her. Jake could manage on his own, one more time, if he had to.

But. She'd promised herself that this morning she would do it, resume her life, in some form or fashion.

So she hauled her body out of the bed then pulled on her work clothes.

Her first sip of coffee promised her she could do this.

She could face the cold, the work... the emptiness.

Fifteen days since Wes had left. The longest she'd been alone in her life.

Maybe she'd feel different, stronger, more capable, if she hadn't married so young. But she'd moved from her childhood home to this one. Babies coming along so soon, she and Wes had less than a year to enjoy being newlyweds.

Taking her to-go cup with her, Mattie went to the mudroom and piled on the layers, then added her boots, gloves and hat. Outside a lightening of the sky promised that morning would be coming. Eventually. Her gaze snagged on the two sugar maples that the girls had brought home in third grade after a school trip to a nursery.

Maples weren't indigenous to Flathead Valley and Mattie had babied those trees. Putting up chicken wire to protect the trunks and watering them faithfully during the hot, dry summers. Now they rewarded her every autumn with brilliant red leaves that stood out from the gold of the aspen and cottonwoods. They'd been at their peak the last time she'd come out to do chores. This morning, however, less than a dozen leaves remained on the slender gray branches. What made some leaves cling harder than others? Were they in denial that the season was changing, or just hanging in there to enjoy one more day?

She turned from the depressing sight and made her way to the barn.

Jake was in the feed room, wearing his winter parka and a knitted cap instead of his usual Stetson.

"Damn cold," he said, after giving her a quick once-over.

"It is."

They worked silently for the next hour, the repetitious chores a soothing balm on the ache of her heart. Every horse got an extra pat from Mattie that morning. Their nose butts and whispered nickers brought tears to her eyes.

Ever since she'd been a child she'd known that if you treated an animal kindly, they'd give you affection and loyalty in exchange. Never once had this equation failed her. And never once had it meant as much as it did today, especially with the specter of a potential sale looming in her future.

When they were finished in the barn, she and Jake went out to flake hay into the corrals where the majority of the horses were kept. The eastern sky was lighter now, and Mattie leaned against the whitewashed fence to take in the view.

There were ten horses in this pasture, all of them familiar, beautiful animals, who moved with the grace of dancers as they shook out their kinks from the night and welcomed the new day. In the distance a layer of mist clung to Flathead Lake, and the air held a stillness that seemed almost mystical.

In all the years of her marriage, this view never failed to fill her with awe. Even though Bishop land lay before her, almost as far as she could see, she had never been filled with a sense of ownership. The very idea that one person could lay claim to a tree, a field, a lake, seemed full of gall to Mattie.

No, she preferred to think of herself as a steward of the land. Here to enjoy and reap blessings before giving up her space to the next generation.

She'd imagined herself growing old living here—with Wes.

She'd pictured them riding horses still, when their hair was gray and their middles were thickening. She'd seen them hosting family meals on holidays, and sitting alone on the porch after everyone was gone.

If Wes wasn't coming back, if he really was going to sell this land, what would her future look like?

She didn't have a clue.

And that was terrifying.

The fence shifted a little as Jake came up beside her and propped his boot on the first rung.

"We should get that pump repaired before it gets much colder," he said.

She nodded. "You think the horses are dreading the winter as much as we are?" Her gaze was on Wes's horse now. Whiskey Chaser and her favorite mare, Rosie, named for her disposition, were standing parallel to each other, each facing opposite directions, the way horses often do.

"Nah," Jake scoffed. "Horses been living in these hills long before ranchers started building barns and filling food troughs. They're tougher than we are. Built for survival. I think they prefer this weather to the scorching days of summer. And frankly, so do I."

It was a funny admission from a man who had recently threatened to pack up and head south. The upward twist of his lips told her he recognized the irony himself.

"You okay?" he asked.

It was his first reference to what was going on with her and Wes. Mattie nodded, suddenly afraid to speak in case sobs came out instead of words.

"I've been at Bishop Stable for almost forty years," Jake said, his tone slow and thoughtful. "Wes's folks, Garth and Jude, were all about the business. They cared about the horses, but even more they cared about their reputation and doing things right. They weren't what you'd call warm. They treated Wes just fine, the same as they did the horses, actually..."

His voice trailed off and Mattie was left to her own thoughts of the Bishops. She'd been worried about impressing them when she first started dating Wes, but they'd been so hard to read that even today she wasn't sure if they'd liked her or not.

They'd moved into town after she and Wes were married, but Garth had continued to come out to the ranch most days of the week and Jude had kept up the garden and put away her preserves every fall.

Jude had been the first to pass away, ten years ago now, from ovarian cancer. Garth had died five years later. Mattie had been surprised and saddened by how little they were missed by Wes and the twins.

"The Bishops built this ranch and established a first-rate reputation for the horses. But when you moved in, Mattie, you made this place a home. Those girls of yours laughed more in one day than Wes did his entire childhood." Jake sighed. "What I'm trying to say is, whatever happens here on, you should know you did good work here."

"Thanks Jake." Montana ranchers didn't do compliments. Which made his words all the more meaningful to her. But how much did he know? "Has Wes told you about—his plans?"

"Not yet. But I know that boy. Stews over problems in his head, makes up his mind and only then does he talk."

Yes. That was Wes all right. "He's left me, Jake. And he wants to sell the ranch."

Jake's sidelong glance didn't reveal any surprise. "His interest in the horses has been slipping for years. But your marriage—that I didn't see coming. I'm sorry, Mattie."

She leaned over the fence, resting her head. Jake's hand settled on her shoulder, warm and solid.

"Makes me wonder what I've been doing the past twenty years when I thought I was investing in my family."

"That's exactly what you did. And you were successful at it. Some people think that if something isn't permanent, it doesn't count. But everything changes in this world. You'll still have your family Mattie—and good memories besides. Keep them close. You earned them."

For Jake, it was quite the speech. Mattie straightened her back. "You're a wise man, Jake. Makes me wish you were more of a talker."

He chuckled. "Me a talker? Not likely." He pushed away from the fence. "Better get back to work. You got time for a ride this afternoon? Valley Girl could use some work."

Mattie nodded. The fresh air and exercise would be good for her as well as the horse. Of course no one understood that better than Jake.

"Make sure you take your phone with you," Jake cautioned.

It was Mattie's turn to chuckle. "Never thought I'd hear you say those words to *me*, Jake."

"Change, Mattie. Happens to all of us."

After lunch Mattie worked Valley Girl in the arena for half an hour, taking her through her paces, before heading out on one of her favorite, and shorter, trail rides, following Chatterbox Creek up into the low hills, then running along the crest of Ponderosa Hill before returning along the lake-side slope which offered one of the more picturesque views of Bishop Stables.

Mattie took her time showering, drying, and grooming Valley Girl, crooning to the horse as she worked, the radio playing softly in the background, set as usual to Jake's favorite country station.

He'd gone out to buy parts for the pump, but he'd be back in time to handle the evening feeding. She knew he wouldn't mind if she left him to it, and went inside for a shower of her own. But before she made it to the house, Nat Diamond's grey truck appeared on the road and she watched as he slowed and pulled into her lane.

Mattie rubbed her hands clean on her jeans as she walked toward him. She didn't want to analyze why her heart suddenly felt lighter. Nat was a neighbor and a friend. Why shouldn't she be glad to see him? She waited for him to park and open his door. "You have a knack for catching me at my best."

He stepped down from the cab, wearing jeans, boots, and a sheepskin jacket. The man was so damn handsome, all decked out like a model on the cover of *Western Horseman*. It wasn't fair.

"Dirt suits you. Been out for a ride?"

"Yeah." The sun had broken through the clouds around one o'clock and the day had actually turned quite warm. "Enjoying the last of the fall colors."

"Good. I brought you a gift. But maybe you don't need it." He pulled out a shopping bag and handed it to her.

She peered inside and grinned when she saw several boxes of tissues and canisters of tea. "Seems like I've got myself a reputation."

"Some women like flowers. But you've always been unique." He hesitated. "I brought something else. You don't have to keep it. Just thought it might come in handy..."

It was unusual for Nat to look unsure of himself. She watched as he reached down to the floor on the passenger side of the truck and then gasped when he pulled out a small dog carrier. Inside were two border collie puppies.

"Twelve weeks old," Nat announced, as he freed them from the padded carrier. The two puppies looked to be all hair, with dark noses and adorable round eyes. "I ordered one of them a while ago. Asked to bring along one of her litter mates. In case you wanted one. But I can see you're not a dog person."

She was on the ground, scooping up the puppies, petting them and laughing. "Oh, they're so sweet. I wish Wren and Portia could see them."

"Take a video with your phone, then send it to them." Nat kneeled beside her and scooped up one of the dogs. "This is Buffy. She's mine."

Mattie could tell they'd already bonded. "You named your dog after a vampire slayer?"

Nat looked confused. "The breeder named her. I didn't know Buffy was a—what did you say? Vampire slayer?"

"I'll lend you the DVDs sometime. Portia has the entire collection." As she spoke, her eyes were on the other puppy. Almost identical to Buffy, but with a different look around her eyes. "Did the breeder name this one?"

"Tuffy," Nat admitted, his tone somewhat apologetic. "Want to guess what the other two puppies were called?"

"Fluffy?"

He laughed. "Yup. And the last?"

"Hopefully not Huffy."

"Nope. Muffy."

"Buffy, Muffy, Fluffy and Tuffy," Mattie repeated. "Wow."

"You could always change the name. If you want to keep her, that is. Like I said before, no obligation. I just thought having a dog around the place might be a good idea."

Mattie picked up Tuffy and buried her nose in her soft hair. She understood what Nat was thinking. A woman living on her own in the country needed protection. A dog could offer that. But by the time Tuffy was big enough to ward off strangers, would Mattie still be living here?

If not—where?

The truth was, getting a dog right now didn't make any sense. What if she ended up living in town? Or, God forbid, back at her father's place on the Circle C? Having a dog in tow could make things really complicated.

But then Tuffy cocked her head to one side. God, she was cute.

It was too late for logic. She was in love.

"I'll keep her."

CHAPTER SIX

"The puppy was genius. Tell me again about this neighbor who brought her?"

Sage was on the floor by the fireplace, playing tug-of-war with Tuffy with one of the toys Nat had left behind.

Turned out he'd come prepared with everything Mattie needed to become an instant dog owner. There was special puppy food, a dish, a bed, and several toys. And the cutest little collar.

Once he'd helped her carry everything inside, Nat had left, refusing her invitation to stay for dinner, which was just as well because no sooner had Mattie taken the puppy with her to the bathroom and had a shower, than her sister Sage had shown up unexpectedly. It was a four-and-a-half-hour drive from Marietta, and so not an easy trip. Mattie had hugged her sister fiercely.

"You didn't have to do this."

"I just wanted to. But I can't stay long. We have a big party at the store on Halloween so I'll have to leave after lunch tomorrow."

Sage had brought dinner—butter chicken and rice—which was now reheating in the oven. She'd also packed chocolate, of course. A box of her salted caramel chocolates and several of her signature milk-chocolate cowboy hats. Since Sage preferred dark chocolate, Mattie knew these were for her.

Mattie was thankful she'd not only showered, but dried her hair and put on jeans and a nice sweater as well, because Sage looked fabulous.

She'd recently cut her thick, wavy red hair, and was wearing a new shade of lipstick that suited her ivory complexion perfectly.

Or... maybe it wasn't the haircut and lipstick that made Sage look so beautiful. Happiness glowed like a halo around her. Mattie remembered her talking about a cowboy the last time they'd been together, at the Copper Mountain Rodeo in their hometown of Marietta.

Back then Sage had sounded annoyed that this dude from her past had the nerve to come to *her* town. What was his name again?

"Oh, you're so sweet!" Sage kissed the puppy, then released her end of the tug toy. "You win. It's time for me to make a salad to go with that curry."

"It smells delish," Mattie admitted, not sure whether to follow Sage to the kitchen and help chop veggies, or stay here and make sure Tuff didn't have an accident. Fortunately most of the flooring in her house was wood, however so far Tuff was showing a preference for the handmade Pendleton rug that she and Wes had splurged on five years ago.

Wes. She couldn't go five minutes without thinking of him. She wondered how he'd feel about the puppy. They'd had a dog when the twins were little, but when Sparky died at the age of twelve, they'd all been so heartbroken they'd decided to wait a few years before getting another.

Noticing a sudden restlessness in Tuff, Mattie picked her up and took her out to the yard. Sure enough, after wandering and sniffing for a few minutes, Tuff peed beside one of the maples.

"Good, Tuff. Good." Mattie heaped her with praise and gave her one of the doggie treats from her pocket before taking her back inside. The rich, spicy aroma of Sage's cooking had her immediately feeling hungrier than she'd been in weeks.

She blockaded the dining area with chairs, so Tuff couldn't escape, then set out plates and cutlery while Sage served the curry, rice and salad. "It sure is nice to be waited on."

"Good. You deserve it." Sage took the spot—Wes's spot—to Mattie's left. "Now, tell me about the neighbor who dropped off Tuff."

"Not much to tell. We've known Nat Diamond forever. He has a huge ranch, even bigger than the Circle C. Back when we had more horses we used to graze on some of his land."

"Does he have a family?" Sage spooned a mound of fluffy brown rice onto her plate.

"Both his parents have passed away. A few years later, he did marry a woman from Seattle, but that didn't last long. She couldn't hack the ranching lifestyle."

"Not everyone can."

Mattie knew Sage included herself in this category. "So what happened with that cowboy friend of yours who came to Marietta for the rodeo? Callan told me he helped with the fall roundup this year. Did pretty well for a greenhorn, she said."

Down in Paradise Valley winter came early and cattle were moved out of the hills at least three or four weeks sooner than here by the Flathead.

"Callan invited him, not me. But I ended up being glad she did. Dawson and I—well, we've mended fences, you might say."

"Didn't you tell me he'd been married? And that he has a daughter?"

"Savannah is a great kid. As for the wife—that's over. Before we hooked up again, I made sure Dawson had the official divorce papers."

The word hit the air like a bomb blast, reverberating long after both sisters had fallen silent.

Divorce. Divorce. Divorce.

A word that just one month ago, Mattie never would have thought would apply to her.

Her first few tastes of the butter chicken had been delicious. Now she set down her fork, convinced she couldn't handle another mouthful.

Sage looked concerned and apologetic. "I'm sorry. I shouldn't have said that."

"Don't be silly. No sense avoiding the subject, since I know that's why you're here." She reached over to squeeze Sage's hand. "Something I very much appreciate by the way."

"Of course I came. I've been worried sick since your call. Have you heard anything from Wes?"

"Nothing. Not a word in sixteen days." She watched the puppy... tired from all her frolicking, she'd finally fallen asleep on the fuzzy dog bed Nat had given them. "I don't even know where he is."

Sage's eyes widened. Mattie could tell that she hadn't expected the situation to be this dire.

"Rodeo weekend you told me he'd been badly shaken when a buddy was killed last spring."

"Yes. Dex Cooper. He was about five years younger than Wes. And it must have been awful for Wes to see it happen to someone he knew personally. Normally he talked to me about stuff like that, but this time he didn't say a word. It was eating at him, though, I could tell. I thought maybe he'd finally retire. I didn't expect—"

She stopped, not needing to say the rest.

"Why would you expect him to leave you? You guys were so good together."

"I thought so," Mattie said softly.

"You *were*," Sage insisted. "And you will be again. Don't give up too easily. Sixteen days seems like a long time now, but when you compare it to twenty years of marriage, it's just a hiccup."

Mattie really wished her sister was right and this stormy period was something that could pass. But she hadn't told Sage everything. So she filled her in about the key and the phone call from the mystery woman. "The signs point to Wes having an affair..."

She waited for Sage to disagree. But she didn't.

"Maybe he is. Maybe he isn't. But even if Wes has been

unfaithful, that doesn't have to spell the end."

"Are you kidding me?"

Her sister studied her closer, her gaze intense. Then she took a deep breath. "I have a secret to tell you. I've kept it from you, Dani, and Callan for a long time. But I think it may help you see your current situation differently."

"What is it?" She could tell the secret was a big one. And if anyone in their family was capable of keeping quiet about something important, it would be Sage.

"Let's talk in the family room," Sage said. "I've lost my appetite and I see you have too."

Mattie cleared the plates, feeling guilty for ruining a meal that her sister had gone to so much effort to prepare. While she stored the food in the fridge so they could eat it later, Sage set a couple of birch logs in the fireplace, started the fire, then brewed a pot of tea.

Once the work was done, Mattie tucked herself into her favorite corner of the sofa, feeling cozy and safe. Sage curled up at the other end, resting her feet on the large oak coffee table.

"So what's the big secret?"

Sage looked uneasy. "I hope what I'm about to tell you doesn't change how you feel about Mom."

Suddenly apprehensive, Mattie asked, "Why would it?"

"I know how close you two were. You were always her favorite."

"Not true," Mattie said automatically, though she suspected it sort of was. Not that her mother had loved her more than her sisters. But she'd been the only one of Beverly Carrigan's daughters to give birth to grandchildren and after the twins were born, during the weeks Mom came to stay with her on the ranch, they'd had so many opportunities to share stories and experiences, to bond as women, rather than as mother and daughter.

"You're the oldest. Which automatically means you had more years with her than the rest of us."

Their mother had died, tragically, when the twins were only two years old. The accident happened after midnight, on a cold night in March. She'd been in the barn with her husband, trying to help a cow manage a difficult delivery.

The cow had gone wild and rammed her poor mother into the concrete wall of the barn.

Death had been instant. No suffering, the doctor told them later, which was of some comfort, at least.

The damn cow and her calf had been fine. Her father had sold both, wanting them off the ranch. But of course, the sale had come too late. Nothing could change the outcome. Or the awful knowledge that their mother, who had always been terribly nervous around cattle, would only have been helping under duress.

"I was twenty-two when Mom died. So you were—"

"Twelve."

"Gosh. So young."

"Callan was only eight," Sage pointed out. "I wonder why there were so many years between us? Five between you and Dani. Then four more between Dani and me, and another four between me and Callan. Did Mom have trouble getting pregnant?"

"She never said so." Mattie was still mulling over how young Callan and Sage had been when their Mom died. Maybe that was why they didn't seem to harbor the same anger toward Hawksley that she did.

Her bad feelings toward her father had even deeper roots than her Mom's death, dating back to the arguments she'd overheard from behind their parents' closed-and-locked bedroom door.

Hawksley had an awful temper.

And no one had borne the brunt more than his wife.

"Given what a beast dad was, I'm surprised she stayed in the marriage as long as she did. She would have had options." Their mother had been born Beverly Bramble, after all, an ancestor of the original Brambles who founded Marietta. They'd built a fortune on the copper buried into the mountain of the same name. And diversified into banking once the ore was depleted.

The original Bramble Manor was still one of the grandest homes in Marietta. These days Great Aunt Mable lived in the stately Victorian, along with cousin Eliza, who had turned the place into a bed-and-breakfast and was reported to be writing a family history.

"There are always two sides in any marriage, Mat. That's kind of what my secret is about."

For a moment Mattie was reminded of her own marital woes. Did Wes have a list of grievances against her? If so, she wished he'd at least given her a chance to hear them. "Compared to Hawksley, Mom was a saint."

"I know you've always thought that." Sage took her feet off the table and shifted into a more upright position. She gazed at the crackling fire for a moment, absent-mindedly twisting a strand of her hair at the same time.

"Because it's true," Mattie said, feeling suddenly tense and uncertain.

"Is it? I saw something, Mat. About a year before Mom's accident."

The room fell quiet, the only sound the snapping and popping from the fire. Tuff picked that moment to wake up and come looking for them. Mattie pulled the little fluff ball into her lap, where she settled immediately back to sleep.

"I was home from school. Sick with a fever, at first, but then I felt better and decided to sneak into Mom's room to play with her jewelry and makeup."

They'd all done that when they were little girls. Their mother had owned a beautiful vanity table, a family heirloom, with dozens of intriguing drawers and hidey-holes.

"Only the door was locked. And not thinking that someone must be in there—because it was early afternoon and the room was always empty during the day—I took a pin and unlocked it."

Mattie could read her sister's face well enough to guess that she'd interrupted a sexual act. But—"who was Mom with?"

"It wasn't Dad. It was—Mr. Sheenan. And, oh God, Mattie, it was so appalling to me at the time. They were having oral sex."

Mattie supposed she shouldn't be shocked. But she sure as hell was.

The Sheenans owned the ranch next to theirs. Their mother had died much earlier, leaving Bill Sheenan to raise five boys and a daughter on his own.

Ever since she'd start school, Mattie had been cautioned to stay away from those "Sheenan brats" by her father. She'd assumed it was a dispute over water rights that had bred the dislike between the two families.

Now she realized the problems were a lot more... personal.

"Frankly, given what a jerk dad was, I don't blame Mom for having an affair."

"Maybe not. But here's the weirdest part. At the steak dinner after the rodeo last month, Bill Sheenan came up to me and apologized for what I'd seen. All these years later! I couldn't believe he had the nerve."

"He must have been feeling guilty for a very long time."

"I guess. But dad saw him talking to me, and came up and popped him one on the jaw."

Mattie had seen the fight. "So that's what was behind it!" Their father had made them all leave the barbecue after that, without saying a word about what was going on.

"I talked to Dad later and found out he knew about the affair. Had known all along."

"Really? Then why didn't he ask for a divorce?"

"That's what I wondered. And Dad told me that there were worse ways you could hurt someone you'd married than by cheating on them."

"Wow." Mattie would never have expected to hear something so... understanding... from her Dad. She had always pictured him as a man who saw things in black and white. Sons—good. Daughters—useless.

"Incredible, isn't it?"

"And you've kept this secret for how long?"

"More than a decade."

It was a heavy weight for a young girl to have carried. Mattie suspected it had taken a toll. She remembered Sage as a young girl—she'd been real chatty, with a sunny disposition and an easy-going nature.

But Sage had changed as she'd gotten older. Become quiet and thoughtful. And this was why. It had to be.

"I'm so sorry you had to deal with this on your own, Sage. I wish you'd confided in someone. Like maybe me?"

"At first I was too scared to say anything. I was afraid

Mom would leave us. Then, after she died, I didn't want to spoil anyone's memory of her."

"No wonder you make chocolates for a living. You are the sweetest, Sage. You really are." Mattie stroked the puppy's soft fur, and considered Sage's reasons for exposing this big secret today. To her.

"You're trying to say that even if Wes has been unfaithful I shouldn't automatically give up on my marriage."

"At least talk to him."

"I want to. He's the one who's gone into hiding."

"Then find him, Mattie. Don't leave it too late."

CHAPTER SEVEN

As Mattie tried to fall asleep that night, her conversation with her sister kept repeating in her brain. Should she be trying to reach Wes?

She lifted the cell phone, which she kept next to her pillow. No missed calls, emails or text messages. Nothing.

Why this wall of utter silence from Wes?

Was he waiting to hear from her?

That didn't make sense. Wes had been the one to say he wanted to leave. And he'd done it. His silence proved he didn't love her anymore.

Still, Mattie's thumb hovered over Wes's name on her contact list. It was past midnight. Where was he? Would he take her call if she had the nerve to hit that button?

Even if he did—she had no idea what to say. And there was always the possibility that that woman would answer. Mattie didn't know if she could bear the certain knowledge that her husband was having an affair.

And yet her father had done it.

Sage's revelation about their mother's affair was still difficult for Mattie to believe. How long had the affair gone on? And why had Hawksley put up with it? The man Mattie knew as her father did not offer forgiveness or second chances very often.

Maybe he'd understood that it was his own lack of kindness and loving that had chased his wife into the arms of another man?

No one could say the same of her and Wes, though. From the beginning they'd been affectionate in private *and* in public. The twins would sometimes complain when they kissed for too long in places like restaurants or street corners. But Mattie had loved Wes's demonstrativeness.

That, too, had eased off recently, she realized, when she couldn't recall the last time they'd shared a kiss in front of others.

Or made love.

Damn, how long had her marriage been crumbling without her even noticing?

Cooking apples and cinnamon. Fresh brewed coffee. French toast and maple syrup. Mattie rolled over in bed, trying to decide if these delicious smells could possibly have been conjured in a dream. Then she heard the sounds of dishes being unloaded from the dishwasher. Hell, Sage must have gotten up before her. How was that possible?

She reached for her phone and saw with dismay that it was after eight. Outside there was just a hint of daylight peeking through the curtains.

Suddenly she was reminded of how it had felt to be a little girl, on Saturday mornings, sleeping in and being woken by her Mom calling that breakfast was ready so get it while it's hot. She so hadn't appreciated how lucky she'd been in those days. If only she could have her Mom back for one day to tell her thank-you for those hundreds of breakfasts that had been made with love and devoured so carelessly.

Like so many things in life, the wisdom of appreciation came too late.

She grabbed her robe and headed to the kitchen, where

she found Sage dusting powdered sugar over the French toast. Tuff was licking the floor by her feet where something yummy must have spilled.

"Oh my God. You're amazing Sage. You made Mom's breakfast."

Her younger sister had such beautiful skin that she looked fresh and pretty, even first thing in the morning. Her loveliness only increased with her smile. "I haven't had French toast for years. But I woke up craving it. Hope you don't mind that I commandeered the kitchen."

"You're kidding, right? Like I would mind. I thought I was dreaming all those delicious aromas. I was afraid to open my eyes." She gave Tuff a cuddle, then glanced out the window at the morning fog and sighed. "Poor Jake. He had to do the morning chores on his own again."

"Not totally. I probably wasn't as much help as you, but I did try."

"What time did you get up?"

"Early. Tuff has been fed and taken out to pee, as well."

"You're an angel."

"Pretty much." Sage placed two slices of the prepared toast on a plate, smothered it in cooked apples and cinnamon, then passed it to her. "Eat up. You hardly had a bite of dinner."

Was that why she felt so famished now?

Her first taste was heavenly. "Tell me more about this new guy of yours. Dawson O'Dell."

"Want to see some pictures?" Sage set her breakfast plate next to Mattie's then sat beside her and passed over her phone.

Between bites of scrumptious maple-infused French toast, Mattie scrolled through several pictures of a dark-blond cowboy with a laid-back air and the hint of a smile on his lips. He lacked Wes's confident, almost cocky air. Instead—"There's something kind of sweet about him, isn't there?"

"He has the biggest heart," Sage agreed. "You should see him with his daughter. He's such a rock. Kind, but firm and so patient."

The two sisters exchanged a glance. Their father had

possessed only one of those qualities, and they weren't kindness or patience.

"So he's really moved to Marietta to stay? He's quit the rodeo?"

"Yup. That's part of the reason it took him so long to come and find me. Not only did he need to extricate himself from his failed marriage, but he also took courses and earned his degree in criminology. Now he has a full-time position as deputy sheriff and he and Savannah live in a super cute house on Bramble Lane."

"Does his daughter like Marietta?"

"She seems to. Though I'm not sure she believes they're really in town to stay. Her life has been a series of moves from one place to another and she finds the routine of school somewhat tedious. You should have seen her expression when Dawson explained she'd have to keep going until she was at least eighteen."

Mattie couldn't wait to meet this kid. She sounded like a real firecracker. "What about Dawson's ex-wife? Why doesn't she have custody of their daughter?"

"Gina's quite the character. Apparently she falls in and out of romantic relationships with regularity and ends up following these guys all over the country. Mostly she's happy to leave Savannah with Dawson, but he's nervous since legally they have joint custody and he's afraid one day she'll show up in town and want to take Savannah away from him."

The mention of custody had Mattie's stomach turning over. Just about the only good thing about her current predicament was that the twins were old enough that she and Wes would never have to fight about things like custody. "Can he get the agreement changed so he has sole custody?"

"He's talked to his lawyer about it. But getting Gina to sign any sort of legal document is unbelievably hard." Sage sighed. "It worries me sometimes that Dawson married such a dipstick."

"Well, he obviously learned from his mistakes." Mattie affectionately bumped her shoulder against Sage's. "Or am I jumping to conclusions when I assume the two of you will end up as husband and wife?"

Sage couldn't stop a smile from revealing the truth. "He's already asked me. I told him he had to wait a year for my answer."

"A year!"

"I need to make sure that all the changes he's made are going to stick."

"Is he really so different from the cowboy you first fell in love with?"

"That's a good question. At heart—no. Or I wouldn't have fallen in love with him all over again."

Mattie was satisfied with that answer. She was glad that Sage had finally found her place in this world. Too often in the past Sage had seemed a little sad, a little lost. Maybe it was carrying the burden of their mother's secret that had weighed her down. As the oldest sister, she should have been there for Sage. But it was too late to fix that now. All she could do was feel glad that Sage finally seemed happy. She really did have it all. A career that fulfilled her. A man to cherish her.

It was almost as if she and Sage were balanced on a teeter-totter. Once Mattie had been up and Sage down. Now it was the other way around. The image wasn't a satisfactory one. Mattie knew that whatever setbacks she was facing now, ultimately she would get through them and be happy again.

But there were still many hurdles to get over before that could happen. First among them was talking to Wes. If he was serious about leaving her then they had to break the news to the twins. Hopefully together.

The secret of her mother's affair, however, had given Mattie new hope. If her parents had weathered such a big storm in their marriage, maybe she and Wes could too. Other than that key and the phone call from the strange woman, she had no reason to believe he was having an affair. Despite all his travel, she knew he'd never slept around. Gossip traveled fast on the rodeo circuit and she and her family had a lot of friends. If Wes had been a cheat—she would have heard.

For all she knew he was already regretting what he'd

done and was too ashamed to make the first move. Later today, after Sage left to drive back to Marietta, she was going to be the bigger person and call him. She had to at least give him a chance to make things right.

Nat had been expecting to hear from Wes Bishop. Still he felt unprepared when he saw his neighbor's name on his phone display. Nat was in his office, reviewing blueprints with Timothy Dundas, the architect he'd hired to make modifications to the sprawling ranch home he'd inherited from his parents. The two of them had been talking for over an hour and gone through three cups of coffee each. At this point they were pretty much done.

He pointed at his phone. "Sorry, Tim, I need to talk to this guy. The plans look great. Thanks for dropping them off."

"No problem. Let me know when you're ready to start the work."

Nat handed over an envelope containing a progress payment toward the project and then the two men shook hands. From the outside they were as different as two Montana born men could be. Nat was tall and broad-shouldered, dressed in work clothes and boots that had a little caked mud between the soles and the leather, whereas Timothy was thin and sophisticated, with wool trousers and a cashmere sweater and loafers that looked fresh out of the box.

Despite their outer differences, they shared an appreciation for aesthetics and Nat knew he'd hired the right man for the job. He clapped his shoulder and thanked him again, before opening the office door.

Eadie Johnston, Nat's housekeeper of fifteen years, was waiting in the hall to see Timothy out. Eadie looked after the five-thousand square foot house, plus made him dinner four nights a week. Kept her recipes and her opinions to herself—best job security going, she liked to say, usually with a grin, because she knew how invaluable she was around here.

Nat closed the door behind his departed visitor and hit the "Talk" button on his cell phone. "Hey there, Wes."

"Nat. How are you?"

The question was meant as a pleasantry and that was how Nat answered it. "Fine. You?"

"Not bad." Some background noises escalated, then a door slammed shut and there was silence. "Sorry. Just got myself a coffee, now I'm back in my truck."

"How's the weather?" Nat asked, wanting a clue as to the man's location.

"Skiff of snow. Cold. Usual Montana shit."

So he was still in the state, at least. "No snow here. At least not yet."

"Won't be long," Wes predicted. "Anyway, the reason for the call is I was thinking of selling Bishop Stables. Of course you'd be my first choice as a buyer. Any interest in expanding? Barns are all in good shape. And you can't beat the views, as you well know."

"This is kind of sudden." And, then, he couldn't resist adding, "What does Mattie think about it?"

"She doesn't own the land. I do. And you shouldn't be surprised. I never took to the horse breeding operation the way my folks did. I figure I'm best to clear out while I'm young enough to try something new."

He'd bet serious money Wes wasn't just talking about a career here, but a different woman, too. If the man had been standing in front of him, Nat would have been tempted to punch him in the nose.

"You might miss it more than you think. Maybe you should sleep on this idea for a bit."

"Is that your way of saying you aren't interested?"

"I never said that." Last thing he wanted was to have the Bishop's land end up with some unknown third party.

"So...?"

"Let me think on it."

"I'll give you a week. Then I'm putting the place on the market."

"Don't rush me, Wes. No one will give you a fairer price than I will."

"That's why I'm talking to you first. But I can't wait

forever, Nat. Think fast—okay?"

And then the call was over.

Nat placed his phone on the gleaming surface of his walnut desk. He was an orderly man, one who kept his papers in file folders and knick-knacks to a minimum. So he had a lot of clear desk space. Which helped him to think.

He spread his large, work-roughened hands over the smooth walnut, and thought back over the generations of Diamond men who had sat at this desk and made decisions about the future.

What would his father, or grandfather, have done if they'd been in this situation?

He had no doubt about the answer. They would have put in an offer on the spot. And they would have started low.

After all, Wes Bishop wasn't in the best bargaining situation. First of all, he was in a hurry. Disadvantage number one.

Second, his chances of finding a buyer who wanted to continue breeding Tennessee Walkers was close to zero. Horse breeding was a dying business and had been for years. Wes might get lucky and find a family to buy the house. But the barns, the arena and other outbuildings? Those would be mostly worthless.

To everyone but him.

He could convert the barns—use them for cattle. The extra land would mean he could increase the herd. His dad, his grandfather, they wouldn't have hesitated. But Nat wasn't in the same situation as they had been. And not only because he didn't have any children to pass this on to. The last few years he'd been doing the opposite of expanding. Nearly thirty percent of his land was currently leased and his herd was smaller than it had ever been.

So no. Buying this land would not be a logical move.

After a few more minutes reflection, Nat picked up his phone and called a woman whose husband had once worked for him. Bernie Howes had been pregnant with their first baby when her husband started drinking on the job. Nat had considered firing him. That was what his foreman, Seth Richards, had wanted him to do. Instead, he'd counseled the guy, talked him around to attending the local AA meeting. Found him a sponsor.

Now Bernie, who worked for the most successful realtor in Flathead Valley, thought he walked on water.

"Hey there, Nat. What can I do for you?"

"Just wondering if you'd heard any rumors about the Bishop place going on the block?" There was a reason he'd chosen to talk to Bernie and not one of the realtors who worked at the firm. Bernie understood the merits of discretion. He could trust her not to use his call as a basis for starting a rumor.

"Not a word," she answered, an edge of speculation in her voice. "Have you?"

"Maybe. But this is just between you and me."

"Understood."

"If you *should* hear anything, though..."

"I'll give you a call right away."

"Text message would be fastest."

"You got it, Nat."

"Thanks." He ended the call and placed the phone in his pocket this time. He ought to get out to the barn. Plans for the roundup happening in just four days needed to be finalized with Seth. But he couldn't seem to clear his head.

He'd never doubted that the problems between Mattie and her husband were real. But hearing from Wes directly, well, that cemented things.

There'd been a time when he might have considered moving in on what Wes no longer appreciated. But that option wasn't open to him now. The best he could do was protect her interests. And if that meant buying land and outbuildings that he had no use for—so be it.

Sage departed for Marietta shortly after they'd polished off the leftover butter chicken, around two in the afternoon. Mattie hugged her sister tightly before letting her climb behind the driver's seat. "You're dangerous for my waistline, but amazing for my state of mind. Thanks for being here, Sage. It meant a lot."

"That's what family's for. But next time, you come up to Marietta. It would be good for you to get away for a while."

Sage's intentions were good, but she was wrong. Mattie always kept her visits to the Circle C few and far between for one reason. Her father Hawksley. She didn't think it was her imagination that Hawksley was harder on her than he was on the other girls. And that was saying something, since he wasn't exactly easy on any of them.

Of course part of the reason their relationship was so fractious was because she'd always blamed him for being so hard on Mom. Now that she knew there'd been another side to that story, maybe she could be more tolerant of her father's rough ways.

But that was a theory to be tested when she felt stronger.

"I'll be in touch," she promised her sister, side-stepping the subject of a visit.

When Sage started the engine, Mattie picked up Tuff who had followed them outside. She didn't want to risk the little puppy getting run over. Tuff wriggled and squeaked until Sage was out of the lane and driving toward the highway and finally Mattie was able to set her down.

"Do your business," she told Tuff, rewarding the pup with a treat when she did.

Though her mind was on the call she intended to make to Wes, Mattie decided to put it off until later and spend a few hours working with Rosie. She took Tuff out to the barn with her—the dog might as well start getting used to the horses now, since she'd be living her life with them.

Hopefully.

Mattie pushed aside the worrying possibility that the ranch might be sold. For now she'd try to stay positive. Sage's visit had left her with hope and she was clinging to it as long as she could.

After saddling up Rosie, she took her into the arena where she put the mare through her paces. A well trained Tennessee walker had three characteristic gaits, all of them smooth and fast, requiring a special pattern of motion whereby no two hoofs touched the ground at the same time. After a brief warm-up, she soon had Rosie in a spirited flat-footed walk. "That-a-girl, Rosie." She eased back into the saddle and let Rosie do her thing, until they'd completed about twenty circuits.

Next she cued Rosie into a running walk, and fifteen minutes after that, a canter. Rosie was much more responsive than she'd been even yesterday—proving yet again the benefits of consistent training.

Mattie had just dismounted and was leading Rosie to the grooming area for a shower and rub-down when her phone vibrated in her front pocket. Out of habit she glanced at the screen even though she had no intention of answering.

It was Wes.

Damn. He'd caught her unprepared. She'd intended to phone him when she was sitting in the family room with a cup of herbal tea and some soft classical music in the background to keep her calm.

But who knew if she would reach him an hour from now. She'd better take this opportunity while she had it.

She sucked in a deep breath. "Hi Wes."

"How are you Mattie?"

If only she could see his eyes. She couldn't tell from just his voice if he really cared what the answer to his question was.

"I've been better."

He didn't say anything for the longest time. Then, his voice quiet, he said, "I'm sorry about that."

A powerful longing swept over her, a desperate need to feel his arms wrap around her as he said those words. But she was alone in a barn with only a talented horse and a mischievous puppy for company. She supposed it could be worse.

"Where are you?"

"I'm staying with friends."

"Friends" being a euphemism for "another woman?" She had to know the truth. "A woman called me yesterday from your phone. Is that the *friend* you're talking about?"

He swore. "She's just someone I was having coffee with. She must have used my phone when I went to the washroom. But forget about her. I'm still staying at the

Wilkinson's guest cottage."

So he was in Montana, not far from Billings. Peter was one of Wes's oldest friends, also a rodeo cowboy. They'd been traveling buddies for years before a shoulder injury sidelined Peter into a career in his family's lumberyard. While Peter and Wes stayed in close contact over the years, they'd never done much socializing as couples. Probably because she and Marg had little in common. Marg worked as an accountant at the lumberyard and she and Peter had never had children. That meant they enjoyed a lot more freedom, including the ability to travel almost anywhere at a moment's notice. A few times Marg and Peter had suggested the four of them take a jaunt to Las Vegas, but while Wes was tempted, Mattie had to remind him that it was hard enough to find someone to watch over the horses—let alone find a sitter for their daughters as well.

That had been a mistake on her part, Mattie suddenly feared.

If she'd made more of an effort to do things with Wes as a couple maybe they wouldn't be in this situation now.

"That's kind of them. How are they doing?"

"The lumber business is thriving. So much so that Pete offered me a job."

Mattie felt as if he'd planted a fist in her gut. "You've taken a job?"

"It's just casual labor. For now."

Mattie let go of Rosie's reins, then sank to the floor of the arena, her knees pressing into the soft dirt. She brought both of her hands to the phone, cupping it like it was a delicate object that might disintegrate if she wasn't careful.

"Wes, I want you to come home. We need to talk."

He didn't answer.

"I need to understand what happened to us." She held back on the word *please*. She wouldn't beg. She deserved this much. What he was doing—it wasn't right.

"I don't know what I would say, Mat. I just need time away."

"How much time?"

She could picture him shrugging. She knew this man so well. The way his right shoulder always hitched up a little higher than the left.

"I can't answer that."

"Damn it, Wes. What am I supposed to do while you're taking all this *alone* time. Just wait for you to decide if you want to stay married to me?"

"Do what you want. You don't have to answer to me."

"What you're describing sounds a lot like a separation, Wes." She felt as if her insides had shriveled, leaving her body at the same time heavy and hollow.

"Yeah."

"I guess I should get in touch with a lawyer. And we'll have to tell the kids. When they're home for Thanksgiving." She couldn't believe she was saying these things. Calmly making plans to end their marriage. Why didn't he stop her? Didn't he realize what an awful mistake this was?

"Whoa. It's too soon for lawyers and telling the girls. I'll come home for Thanksgiving. Let them enjoy the holiday without any worries."

"And what—we'll pretend like nothing's wrong?"

"It's just a few days."

"And when the girls are back in college, what then?"

Again, he had no answer. "We'll figure it out. When we have to."

His words filled her with anger. "So you don't want to talk. You don't want to make any tough decisions. You just want your freedom. Sorry, Wes, it doesn't work that way. We've been married almost twenty years. We run a business together. Have children. You want this to be simple, but it isn't."

"You think this isn't hard for me too?"

Oh, really. He wanted her sympathy now?

"Well it is. And I don't have any answers yet. I'm just asking for some time. Give me to Christmas. Then, if you want I'll go for counseling. Or we can talk to a lawyer. Whatever you say."

Two months of living in the ante-room to hell, not sure if her husband still loved her—or someone else. She couldn't stand that. But did she have a choice?

"I'll only agree to that on two conditions. One—you continue to act as if we're married. That means, no messing around with other women."

"And the other?"

"You don't make any moves to sell our ranch."

She waited through the silence while he considered her deal. Slowly she got to her feet and brushed the soil from her knees. Rosie was looking at her curiously. Probably wondering what in the hell was going on. Tuff had fallen asleep in the wooden box she'd put her in, curled up on the towel she'd placed in one corner. Gosh she was cute.

Finally Wes spoke. "You're putting me in a tough place. But okay, I'll agree to your terms."

"What about Thanksgiving? If you're not here the girls will know something's wrong."

"Hell, Mat. I'll be there."

CHAPTER EIGHT

Wren was in the library, reading Aristotle's *Metaphysics*. The guy was a flipping genius. Every other minute she had to set aside the book to jot down another memorable quote. Her favorite of the night was this one: *It is the mark of an educated mind to be able to entertain a thought without accepting it.*

A group walked by her cubicle and she was momentarily distracted by the fact that one of them had painted his entire face and upper body green.

Oh, yeah. Halloween.

They were having a party in her residence hall. She'd promised a couple of the girls on her floor that she would go. But she'd really rather keep reading Aristotle.

Her first Halloween away from home...

This was going to be a year with a lot of firsts, but she had to admit she was a little sad about spending her first Halloween away from home. Her Mom had always made a big deal of the holiday, decorating the house, helping her and Portia devise amazing costumes, and—since they lived in the country where going door-to-door for candy wasn't possible—hosting an awesome party for all of their friends.

When they were little, they'd set up a spooky maze in the basement, then play games and finish with a ghost story from her dad. The party had evolved over the years as she and Portia grew older. Once they decorated Halloween cookies, another time they carved pumpkins. Somehow, even in their teens, when Portia had started to drive her crazy with her obsession about clothes, makeup, and boys, Halloween had been a time when they, and their two sets of very different friends, could have fun spending an entire evening together.

Overcome with homesickness, Wren pulled out her phone and texted her Mom. "Happy Halloween! What are you up to?"

The answer came in about five seconds. "Not much. It's weird without you and your sister."

Wren felt her eyes grow moist. "Dad there?"

A longer pause this time. Then a simple answer. "No."

Wren's stomach tightened. Something was wrong here. She'd had a few quick text messages from her dad, but he hadn't called once since she'd started college. And it seemed as if he was never home.

"Everything okay?"

"Yes. Aunt Sage came for a visit. House is full of delicious chocolate. Wish I could share. Love you honey. Put down the books and have a little fun tonight okay?"

That made Wren smile. Good old Mom. "I will," she texted. Then stowed her books and laptop into her bag to live up to the promise.

It was Halloween night and on campus that meant one thing. Time to party. Again.

Portia couldn't even remember the name of the frat house Kirsten had dragged her to. She was dressed up as Ann of Green Gables—only Kirsten had vamped her up—shortening the plaid skirt and lending her a pair of over-the-knee black boots. She'd also redone Portia's makeup, pasting on fake eyelashes and dusting her cheeks with glitter.

Really, the only part of her costume that still looked like the wholesome orphan from Prince Edward Island was her wig with the two red braids.

Despite the getup, Portia managed to have fun for the first couple of hours, dancing and laughing with a never-ending lineup of boys who seemed to want to spend a little time with her. All around her kids were taking Jell-O shots, smoking up, passing around mysterious little pills. Portia went so far as to drink the first three beers that were pressed on her, but after that, she began pouring her drinks down the bathroom sink.

It was almost two now and most everyone was plastered or strung out. The few people still trying to dance could barely stand upright. Couples were making out all over the place. And there was a guy following her around who made it clear he wanted to do *that* with her.

She was so tired of this.

"Excuse me. I have to pee." She pushed the boy—Brian?—on the chest so he would give her some space, then slipped through the crowd, stepping over, around and between hot, sweaty bodies, until she reached the room where they had stashed their coats when they first arrived. She didn't like leaving without telling Kirsten, but her friend was all hot-and-heavy with a guy she'd met tonight. Portia didn't even know his name. Kirsten's hookups never lasted long. Portia had learned not to bother being friendly.

Coats were piled everywhere, on the sofas, chairs, and even the floor. Everywhere but the closet which had no doors and was filled with empty hangers. Finally Portia located her jacket and shrugged it over her shoulders. She'd text Kirsten later and let her know that she'd gone. Right now she could hardly wait to inhale some fresh air.

Outside, though, she felt confused about where she was, and cold. Temperatures weren't as low in Seattle as they were in Montana, but the humidity took some getting used to. She zipped her jacket and looked up and down the street, searching for a familiar landmark. She wasn't great at directions at the best of time. And the middle of the night, tired and still a little tipsy, in a city she still didn't know very well didn't add up to the best situations.

Reaching into her pocket, she wrapped her fingers around her phone. She wanted to call her Mom and Dad. "Come and get me. I want to go home."

And oh, how she longed for it in that moment. The security of her own room. A home-cooked meal. Her father tousling her hair as he leaned over to grab the remote control out of her hands. And her sister at the door of the bathroom, asking how much longer she was going to be. The good stuff and the bad, she missed it all.

With her back against the brick wall of the frat house she sank until her butt was resting on the backs of her boots. She sent a text to Kirsten. No answer, of course. She opened Google maps next and tried to figure out where she was. The maze of streets was a total puzzle to her. Now what?

"You okay?"

It was the guy from her psych class. The one Kirsten always snubbed. He was in a dark jacket, jeans and, of course, those dark brown cowboy boots of his. He'd left a group of two other guys and three girls to approach her.

She glanced from him to her phone. "I think I'm lost."

"Yeah, I'd say that was a good assessment."

She narrowed her eyes, not sure how to take his comment. "I don't know where my sorority house is."

"You're a Pi Phi, right?"

How did he know?

"Come on, it's this way." He pulled her up, and she noted how warm his hands felt. How strong. Then he glanced over at his friends, and motioned for them to go on without him. One of the girls, a cute blond in a cat costume, seemed more reluctant to leave him than the rest, but finally she did. The girl was in her sorority, Portia recalled. Her name was Annie, and she seemed sweet, but very quiet.

"I'm Portia Bishop."

"I know."

"How?"

His smile was crooked, but kind of cute. "Hey, I've been a fan of your dad's since I was six years old. I even met him once. Shook his hand."

CJ CARMICHAEL

Oh no. Not another rodeo fan ."Why is it everyone I meet in this city is cowboy crazy?"

"Don't classify me with those uptown friends of yours. I've been on the back of a few bucking broncs myself."

"Right." In his dreams, maybe. "You from Montana, too?"

He nodded. "Helena."

"I'd tell you where I'm from but I suppose you know that already too?"

"I'm not a stalker, Portia. Just impressed with the way your dad handles himself in the arena. So—where *are* you from?"

"Flathead Valley." They'd been walking as they talked and when they came to the corner she was relieved to see a store she recognized. "Thanks. This looks familiar. I'll be fine from here."

She waited for him to walk off, but he didn't.

"It's two-thirty in the morning. I'd better see you to your door."

She could see by the set of his mouth that there was no point in arguing. "Your mother raised you the old fashioned way, I see."

"Some would say the right way." He waited a few seconds then added, "Aren't you even a little curious what *my* name is?"

What a dolt she was. "Sorry. It's been a long night." She waited, and when he didn't say anything she wrinkled her nose at him. "You were going to tell me your name?"

"Maybe I'll make you wait. Build up the suspense a little."

"Suit yourself." They'd reached the Pi Phi house now. As he hung back at the white pillars, she dug in her pocket for her key. "Thank you—stranger."

She held out her hand and he stepped forward to shake it, very correctly, not taking advantage to hold her even a second longer than was proper. Then he stepped back and waited until she had the door open.

The entire encounter was over in less than fifteen minutes. But the odd thing was, once she was in bed, she couldn't stop thinking about it. Kirsten might not approve.

But she thought the guy from Helena was just about the nicest person she'd met all night.

The day after Halloween, Mattie went into town for groceries. She'd been in a funk last night—missing her daughters and Wes so badly that she almost gave in and had a few of Wes's beers. But drinking wouldn't solve her problems, and her habit of abstinence, begun when she was twenty-one, was too ingrained to break.

It was no longer just about Neve—who had died so young and senselessly—but about *every* young person who had to make the choice of whether to drink or drive. It was about her daughters, and wanting to set the best example for them that she possibly could. And it also, truth be told, had roots in her childhood observations of her father and how his meanness would become worse after he'd brought out the whiskey bottle.

Somehow she'd made it through the night—Tuff had been a comfort, that was for sure. She was just the most adorable puppy, Mattie couldn't wait for the girls to see her. Too bad that in four weeks, by Thanksgiving, Tuff would be a lot bigger. Oh well, Portia and Wren would still be thrilled.

Once she'd purchased her supplies, including more puppy food—Tuff was a good eater—Mattie filled the SUV up with gas, then headed for home. Two miles from her gate though, she had to stop because the road in front of her was full of cattle, crossing from one side to the other. She recognized the Double-D brand, not that she'd had any doubt who the Black Angus belonged to since Nat owned the land on both sides of the road.

Looked like he was bringing his herd in for the winter, and not a day too soon according to the forecast.

Snow was expected tomorrow, along with colder temperatures and high winds. The possibility of the first blizzard of the year was what had induced her to stock up on supplies while she could.

Mattie kept the SUV running while she waited. She felt

no impatience, actually enjoying the delay. She'd loved helping to move the cattle when she'd been a kid. It was the one time when her father could be counted on to be in a good mood—as long as nothing serious went wrong. The entire family would spend the night camping in the high hills. There'd be a campfire and her Mom and Dad would sing together, harmonizing with unexpected beauty.

Today Nat's herd was being controlled by relatively few cowboys. She waved at a few as they crossed in front of her truck. There was Seth Richards, short and chubby, but a seasoned cowhand and Nat's trusted foreman. A couple of border collies whizzed by, as well, happily in their element as they brought the occasional stray back in line.

Finally the numbers thinned until there were only a few stragglers left. And bringing up the rear was Nat, on The Duke—the beautiful colt she'd sold him a while back. When he spotted her, Nat directed The Duke to the driver's side of her truck and she obligingly lowered her window.

Always a striking man, Nat was at his most attractive when he was on a horse. Not many men rode with the same calm, commanding presence. He gave her a smile that would have made any of her sisters' hearts go pitter-patter. But she and Nat were neighbors and she couldn't afford to have that sort of reaction.

"Your timing is good," she called out to him. "A storm is coming."

"I heard. We're lucky. I meant to get them in a few days earlier, but we had some complications."

His smile faded, just a little, and she wondered what the complications had been. But before she could ask he was speaking again.

"We missed you—and the twins, of course."

"Not as much as I missed being part of the fun this year." But she'd been right to decline the invitation. Without her girls, it would have felt wrong somehow, to spend an entire day out in the mountains with a bunch of men—and with Nat in particular.

"How's Tuff?"

"Eating me out of house and home. And I love it." She nodded toward the back where she'd stowed her groceries.

"I'll be all stocked up when the storm hits."

"If you need anything at all, give me a call. I take it Wes is still—"

She nodded, glancing away from the concern in his blue-gray eyes.

"Well—" Nat looked like he was going to say something else, but instead he just patted the roof of her truck. "Take care, Mattie."

One minute later the road was clear. But instead of shifting into Drive, Mattie stayed where she was, watching until Nat and his herd had disappeared beyond the cottonwoods.

For the next month Mattie worked harder than she'd ever done in her life. She worked through the blizzard, which lasted four days, then the next two weeks brought a thaw and milder temperatures. Her body ached at the end of each day—which was the point. It was easier to sleep if you were exhausted and she made sure she was. She was losing weight—a fact Jake kept pointing out as he urged her to slow down.

And he really gave her a scolding when he caught her in the tack room adding a notch to her belt so her jeans wouldn't keep falling down.

"Maybe you should see a doctor."

She put away the leather hole punch, then slipped her belt through the loops of her jeans, pleased to see the fit was snug once more. "I'm fine. I couldn't work this hard if I wasn't."

"That's kinda the point. You're driving yourself to exhaustion. And while we're on the topic—you clean this tack room one more time and I'm going to be afraid to walk in there with my boots on."

"That'll be the day. But don't worry. I won't be in your hair much this week. Portia and Wren are coming home on Wednesday. I've got to start baking my pies for Thanksgiving. Apple for you, lemon for Portia, and pumpkin for Wren."

Jake always joined them for the holidays. When his wife had been alive, they'd come as a couple.

"That's plain nonsense—baking three pies when you've only got three people coming for dinner."

Mattie paused, meeting Jake's gaze directly and holding it a few seconds before saying, "Wes is supposed to be here, too."

"He said he was coming?"

"He did." But she hadn't spoken to him since then... and the silence between them grew more painful each day. She was too proud to beg, so she'd just have to wait and see if he followed through on his word.

She could tell that Jake didn't think he would. She could see the skepticism in his eyes. As well as the pity.

But all he did was shrug.

"Three pies is still too much."

The last few days before Thanksgiving passed in a blur. Mattie dusted and vacuumed the girls' bedrooms, washing the clean linens so they would be fresh and putting a potted mum on each of their nightstands.

She didn't stop at three pies—she made six—freezing the extra apple ones, just to have on hand. She also baked chocolate chip cookies and pumpkin spice muffins, and went to Green Valley Farm near Ronan to pick up the fresh, organic turkey that was her standing order.

Ten years ago, back when Wes's parents, Garth and Jude, were still alive and they had at least three or four men working on the ranch, her table had been at capacity for Thanksgiving and Christmas. Now it seemed, every year she set the table for one or two fewer people.

She didn't like this empty nest phase of life, not one bit.

Tuff was growing, healthy and relentlessly energetic. Mattie had laughed, watching her jump and run with delight through her first snowfall. Every day she did something cute that made Mattie smile. And something naughty that had the opposite effect. Tuff loved tussling with Mattie's leather cowboy boots more than any toy.

She'd almost decided to give up and let the pup have them. She needed a new pair anyway.

But was it worth investing in new boots—if Wes ended up selling the ranch?

Almost every hour she butted up against thoughts like this. She hadn't realized how much her expectations of the future impacted her everyday activities, but they did. In the end she decided there was no way to function except to assume she would stay at Bishop Stables.

And so that's what she did.

But her appetite remained dull and her sleep was plagued with disturbing dreams. The night before she was to pick the girls up at the airport, she could feel Wes in bed beside her. The weight of his body on the mattress, the heat of his skin, the smell of his hair. The relief was incredible. *You're home.* She reached out to touch his face but like magic he vanished and she opened her eyes to face a cold, empty bed.

Knowing it was not a habit to encourage, she couldn't resist pulling Tuff up from her bed and placing her on the quilt near her feet. The puppy snuggled in happily. And she decided she didn't give a hoot what the dog training books said.

The next morning she felt a buzz of happy anticipation. In six hours, she would see her girls. She couldn't wait.

She hummed along to the radio as she did the morning chores. She caught Jake smiling a few times, too.

"What time do they get in?"

"Around noon. I booked their flights so they arrive about thirty minutes apart. Hopefully they're both on time. I checked when I got up and so far everything's on schedule."

The drive to Missoula took a little over an hour. Mattie had showered and styled her hair. She was wearing a bulky sweater with skinny jeans and boots—fashionable ones, not the pair she used for work which Tuff had now all but destroyed. Hopefully the sweater would disguise her loss of weight. But some changes couldn't be disguised. The sharper angle of her cheekbones. The lines around her eyes. The jutting of her clavicle.

CJ CARMICHAEL

Wren's flight arrived first, and she came off the plane looking just like the girl who'd left three months ago. Skinny jeans, Ugg boots and a plaid shirt layered with a sweater, then a vest, and scarf wrapped haphazardly over it all.

"Mom. It's so good to see you."

Mattie hugged her tight, not able to say a word. Tears were flowing, she couldn't seem to stop them. She clung to her daughter, thinking no hug had ever felt so good.

"Dad's not here." Wren's voice was flat. Not a question. She had expected this.

Reluctantly Mattie eased her hold. "No. Not yet."

Wren didn't challenge that. Instead she suggested they get a coffee while they waited for Portia.

"Good idea." As they stood in line at Montana Traders, Mattie kept stealing glances at her daughter's face. She'd been wrong when she'd thought Wren hadn't changed. There had been subtle shifts in her face and her posture, reflecting a young woman who was more confident and independent than she'd been a few months ago. The change could be heard in Wren's voice when she placed their orders for lattes, and in the way she organized the lids and napkins, taking care of Mattie the way Mattie was used to doing for *her*.

"Tell me more about the poli-sci class you love so much." Once Portia arrived, there wouldn't be time for serious topics, and besides, this might prevent Wren from asking awkward questions about Wes.

"It's amazing to me how much Aristotle figured out. That was thousands of years ago! And yet we seem to have a lot of the same problems today as the Greeks did back then."

"That's a profound observation. I can see why you've impressed your prof."

"Oh, Mom. I've really missed you. Talking on Skype just isn't the same."

Mattie's shoulders tightened. Was Wren going to mention her father again? "No. It isn't."

"I wish we had more time to ourselves before Portia comes. It's selfish of me. But she'd going to get off the plane looking like a fashion model and talking about all her friends and sorority parties... and make me feel like such a loser just because I went to college to study."

Relief washed over her... along with a dose of motherly concern. If only her girls could learn to be happy with who they were and stop the comparisons. But how did she help them do that?

"Wren, figuring out who you are is one of the hardest things in life. But once you truly are comfortable with your own identity, you'll find other people's attitudes won't bother you so much."

"Are you saying you don't have a problem with how obsessed Portia is about her looks? I mean—it's vain, right?"

"There's nothing wrong with dressing fashionably per se. The question is, why do you do it? Is it because you enjoy and appreciate nice clothing? Or is it because you feel you need to dress that way to make people like you, or to fit in? Being true to yourself doesn't mean dressing in rags. At least, it doesn't have to be."

"Is that how you think I dress? In rags?"

"Honey, no! You look beautiful. Absolutely beautiful."

And it was a good thing she got those words out when she did, because Portia was running toward them now, and she did look as put together as a fashion model in a skirt, tights and a short red wool coat. Taking a firm grip of one of Wren's hands, Mattie abandoned her coffee and rushed forward to greet her second daughter, this time all three of them forming a nice, tight knot.

"It's so good to see you guys."

To Mattie's relief, she didn't ask about her father.

"I can't wait to get home."

"And see Tuff," Wren added.

"Oh my God, I was so excited to see you guys I almost forgot we have a new puppy! Let's get going!"

The puppy was a huge hit with the girls, but to Mattie's surprise, once they'd settled in a bit and had a late lunch, they both wanted to go out riding.

"Seriously?" The last few years she could hardly get either of them on the back of a horse, unless it was for something major like the Double-D roundup.

"I've missed the horses more than I thought I would," Wren confessed.

"Me, too," Portia added.

Mattie couldn't have chosen a better way to spend the afternoon with her daughters. The only dark spot was Wes's continued absence. The girls didn't mention him though, until later, after they'd had chili and cornbread for dinner and finished a movie about zombies that turned out to be more entertaining than Mattie expected.

"So when is Dad getting here?" Portia asked.

To Mattie the room seemed suddenly far too silent. "I was hoping he would be here by now... but it may not work out."

"Oh well. It's still good to be home in our very own house, with you... and Tuff." Portia patted the puppy sleeping in her lap.

Wren said nothing, but Mattie could feel her gaze, and the worry that lay behind it.

Unfortunately there was nothing she could say to set Wren and Portia's minds at ease. Whether or not Wes showed up for Thanksgiving, she was going to have to tell her daughters what was going on this weekend.

But until that moment, she'd do her best to keep cheerful and enjoy their company.

"Tomorrow I expect you girls to help me with the dinner," Mattie said briskly, getting up from the armchair. "You need to start learning your way around the kitchen, and so, I've pulled out all our usual Thanksgiving recipes." She grabbed the cards from the counter and fanned them in one hand. "Do you want to choose what you're cooking? Or make a random pick?"

"Random will be more fun," Portia said. "I'll go first." With Tuff still sleeping in her lap, she covered her eyes and held out a hand. Mattie moved closer putting the cards within reach. Portia's hand hovered... then she selected one.

"Sweet potato casserole." She studied the card a moment. "This doesn't look like your handwriting."

"It's Grandma Carrigan's." Sadly, to her daughters, the name meant little. They only knew her mother from photographs and stories she'd told of her childhood.

She held out the remaining cards to Wren who closed her eyes, then plucked out another of Grandma Carrigan's recipe card. "Cranberry coleslaw. Whew! I was afraid I would have to do the dressing and turkey."

Mattie put the remaining cards back into her copper recipe box. "I've already made the pies, so with you girls helping out tomorrow, dinner will be a snap.

"Oh, that reminds me," Portia slid off the sofa and went to wash the dog hair off her hands. "Nat Diamond called while you were in the shower. He wanted you to know he's moving hay tomorrow morning and did you need any?"

With only twenty-two horses? "We don't."

"That's what I thought. But then I asked him why he was working on Thanksgiving and he said it was just another day to him. So I invited him to dinner."

Mattie froze for a second. Then smiled. "Good."

But it wasn't. If Wes did happen to show up tomorrow and found Nat at the table—he might not be too happy. Then again, that was his problem. She'd raised her girls to be hospitable and of course Portia was right. It wouldn't do for Nat to be on his own at Thanksgiving. Not when he'd done so much for them over the years. And they'd certainly have enough food to go around.

Not to mention pie...

"Mom, Nat used to be married, didn't he?" Wren was taking her turn with the puppy now, playing tug-of-war on the carpet by the fire. Tuff reveled in the extra attention, had barely napped since the girls arrived. The pup would surely sleep well tonight.

"Yes. Her name was Julia."

"I sort of remember her." Portia was in the cupboard now, looking for the chocolate chip cookies. When she found the container, she took a couple. "You want one

Mom?"

"No, I'm fine."

"She was gorgeous." Portia crossed the room to hand Wren the other cookie, then perched on the arm of the sofa. "She had wavy blonde hair and always wore pretty dresses."

"Of course you would remember *that*," Wren said quickly, then flushed when she noticed Mattie's glance. "Not that there's anything wrong with pretty dresses."

"Well, they're not exactly practical on a ranch," Mattie said.

"So what happened to her?" Wren asked. "Why did they split up?"

"It's hard to say. But I'm sure it didn't help that Julia disliked the ranch and the isolation of Montana. I remember her complaining that we weren't even close to an International airport. She liked to travel."

"Well, why'd she marry Nat then?" Portia asked, indignantly. "How did they even meet?"

"Nat had an aunt in Seattle, she owned an art gallery and Julia worked for her. That's how they met. And they fell in love. But I guess Julia never thought through the part where she was going to have to move to Montana and live on a cattle ranch. Or maybe it seemed romantic to her at the time."

Out of respect for Nat's privacy, Mattie didn't mention the rest. How Julia had started drinking shortly after the wedding, and taken any excuse to leave on a trip to visit friends or relatives. Finally she'd run off to New York City with a man she met on the Internet.

"They didn't have much in common, huh? Not like you and daddy."

Mattie stared down at her hands. "True."

"I'm tired," Wren announced abruptly. "Mom, can Tuff sleep with me, tonight?"

Portia looked disappointed she hadn't thought to ask first. "Can I have her tomorrow?"

"Of course. Why not alternate for as long as you're home. A word of warning though—Tuff gets up early. And you have to take her out for a pee right away. She's still a puppy.

"Oh." Wren didn't look nearly as enthusiastic about *that*. But she still cuddled the puppy close to her chest as she stooped over to give Mattie a kiss. "It's been a really nice day."

"For me, too." Mattie ran a hand over her daughter's silky hair, before she left the room. Yawning, she wondered if Portia was ready to sleep as well. But her other daughter was in the kitchen again, putting on the kettle, looking as bright-eyed as when Mattie had collected her at the airport.

And then Mattie remembered—it was an hour earlier in Seattle.

"Want some Sleepy Time tea, Mom?"

"Sure." No matter how tired she was, she wouldn't turn down an offer to sit and chat with one of her daughters. "So—how are your classes? Are you keeping up with the work load?"

"I'm managing, Mom. Psychology is my favorite—Aunt Dani is a really good teacher. The kids pay attention when she's talking."

"Dani's passionate about what she does. She's a great public speaker, too. Smart, funny, with great timing." When she was younger, Mattie had been in awe of her next-in-line sister. Dani's confidence and wit had made Mattie feel dull and slow in comparison.

But over the years Mattie had grown out of the petty rivalry. She'd never exchange her life for Dani's, so how could she resent the gifts that had made Dani who she was?

"What about your social life, Portia? From our calls it sounds like you've made lots of new friends. Are they all from your sorority?"

"Mostly." Portia's voice was bright, but the very brief pause before her answer was telling.

"You mention Kirsten often. Tell me more about her. Do the two of you have lots in common?" Mattie had always been impressed with Portia's ability to make friends. Not only make them, but keep them. Most of the little girls she'd hung out with in kindergarten remained in her circle all the way through high school. She wondered if this new friend would fall into that "keepers" category.

Another pause while Portia poured boiling water into mugs, then carried the tea to the table by the sofa. "We both enjoy dancing. And Kirsten has amazing taste in clothes. She's also rich, so she can afford anything she wants. Not that I'm envious," she added quickly. "Kirsten's really generous about lending me things."

"Don't you have enough of your own?" Mattie was a little worried to hear the answer. It had seemed to her and Wes that Portia's budget for clothing and other extra spending was fair, if not extravagant.

"I do. It's just—sometimes Kirsten likes to dress me up. Like I'm a doll or something. It's just fun, Mom. All the girls in the house share clothes."

Something about that made Mattie uneasy, though she knew Portia had often traded clothing with her high school friends, too. "So you're glad you decided to join a sorority?"

"Definitely."

"I wonder if Wren should have gone that route, too. She's loving her classes but all she ever seems to do is study."

"I *told* her to. But she never listens to me."

Mattie felt a yawn coming and just couldn't stifle it. "Honey, I'm afraid I can't keep my eyes open any longer. We'll talk more tomorrow, okay?" She gave her a hug, and was surprised when Portia squeezed her tightly in return.

"Dad will be here tomorrow?"

This time it was Mattie who paused before answering. "I hope so."

In her bedroom, with the door closed, Mattie took out her phone, dismayed to see no missed calls or text-messages. With a sigh, she typed out a message to her missing spouse.

"What time are you coming tomorrow? Both girls are here. They miss you. Dinner is at six." She hit send, then waited for a reply.

After ten minutes she gave up and prepared for bed, brushing her teeth and her hair, putting on a pair of cozy flannel pajamas. If Wes wasn't going to live up to his promise to be home for the holiday, what did that say about the other promises he'd made? That he wouldn't sell the farm. Would respect their marriage vows and not get involved with other women?

But she couldn't start obsessing about all that now. She was too exhausted—physically and mentally. She closed the drapes, feeling the cold seeping through the glass panes. Another Arctic front moving in, but no snow fortunately. She was going to miss having Tuff at her feet tonight— though having both her daughters sleeping under the same roof as her tonight was more than enough compensation.

By the time she'd turned out the light and crawled into her bed, there was still no reply from Wes. She put the phone on the pillow by her head then went to sleep.

CHAPTER NINE

To Mattie's surprise, both girls were up early to help with chores the next morning. Tasks that they'd often complained about bitterly were performed cheerfully today. Clearly they'd missed not only her, but also Jake, the horses, the barn cats. Jake's step had an extra spring to it as he supervised the goings-on. Several times Mattie caught him watching one of the girls, a smile playing on the corners of his mouth.

Once when he noticed her watching he gave her a wink. "Didn't realize how much I missed those gals. Sure is nice to have them home for a bit."

"I couldn't agree more." She dug her pitchfork under some wet bedding and hefted it onto the wagon in the center aisle.

The girls had brought Tuff to the barn, and made a safe spot for her in the feed room, using sacks of oats and supplements to cordon off an area, setting up a blanket for Tuff to sleep on and a bowl of water. It didn't take long for the barn cats—Harry and Hermione—to come and check out the newcomer. Harry kept his distance, arching his back, then sticking up his nose and prancing off. But

Hermione seemed entranced by the puppy's antics. She perched on the top of one of the feed sacks and watched as Tuff gnawed on one of the chew toys Wren had brought out from the house.

Once the outside work was done, Mattie and the girls returned to the barn to fetch Tuff—and found the puppy and the cat cuddled together on the blanket, fast asleep.

"Oh my gosh. So cute!" Portia took out her phone to take pictures, and so did Wren. While they tweeted and instagrammed—Mattie didn't really understand what either of these things were—Mattie gently extracted Tuff.

Hermione stretched, gave her a disgruntled look, then fell back asleep.

Tuff wiggled to get free, but Mattie waited until she and the girls were out of the barn before setting the pup down. As they all headed for the house, Mattie reminded Jake that dinner was at six.

"Wouldn't miss it," Jake said.

Then she and the girls went inside to shower and start cooking. First a big breakfast, then it was time to truss the turkey.

All this time, Mattie's phone sat, silent, on the kitchen counter. No messages. No missed calls.

She noticed neither girl asked about their father again. Instead, they focused on preparing their dishes, asking for her advice when the recipe directions weren't clear. If Wes had been home, he'd have been watching football on TV. Since he wasn't, the girls took turns plugging their phones into the docket on the kitchen counter, sharing new songs that they'd fallen in love with during the past few months.

After the turkey was in the oven, there were potatoes to peel, the table to set. Mattie put out just five plates. No questions were asked then, either.

At five o'clock they changed for dinner, Mattie putting on a gray and black shift dress with leggings and sparkling earrings. Portia wore another cute sweater and skirt combo and even Wren, who rarely wore anything but jeans, came out in a dress with a long belted sweater over-top.

Mattie checked the time. They still had more than thirty minutes before the guests would arrive. "Let's Skype

Grandpa and Aunt Callan and wish them a happy Thanksgiving."

"Hey Mattie! Hi Portia and Wren. You all look so gorgeous! Wish you were here!" Callan's face appeared on the screen first. Petite and pretty, the youngest of the Carrigan sisters was often underestimated by strangers. In fact she was the toughest and most fearless of them all.

"We've got a full house," Callan said, carrying the laptop around the kitchen so everyone could say hi.

Sage was there, her face glowing with happiness. Helping her with the turkey was her handsome cowboy Dawson, and his cute daughter Savannah.

Sitting at the table, enjoying a glass of wine, was Dani. She blew them a kiss when Callan passed her the laptop. "I was going to stay in Seattle for the holidays, but a last-minute seat sale changed my mind. How are you guys doing? Where's Wes?"

"We're fine," Mattie responded, ignoring the question about Wes. "Just about to put the turkey on the table. Say hi to Dad for us, okay?"

"Hang on," Dani said. "He just came into the kitchen. You can tell him yourself."

Mattie gave her girls a grim smile. Talking to Hawksley Carrigan in person was hard enough. Over the phone, or on Skype, they'd be lucky to get five words from him.

The screen blurred, and then Mattie's father's face came into focus. He was uncharacteristically clean shaven for the special holiday, which made him look younger than usual.

"Hi Dad! You must be happy to have so much company for Thanksgiving."

He just grunted.

"It's great to have Portia and Wren home from college," Mattie gamely continued, carrying the conversation forward on her own.

Her Dad's blue eyes, grown paler over the years, narrowed as he studied the computer. "Is that a dog?"

Mattie relaxed a little. She'd been afraid he was going to quiz her on her husband's whereabouts. "Her name is Tuff. Nat Diamond gave her to us."

"Nice-looking dog."

The girls both said hi to their grandfather and soon after that the conversation stalled. No one could silence a room quite like her father. Even now that she knew her mother hadn't been perfect, Mattie still couldn't feel any warmth for the man. She wished she could, but he had never fostered closeness with any of his children, least of all with her.

"Well, so much for that." Mattie closed the laptop, then glanced around the tidy kitchen, looking for something that needed doing. The spool of cooking twine was on the counter, but as she reached for it to put it back in the drawer, it spun away from her fingers and fell to the floor.

Tuff, roaming the room, probably searching for the source of the delectable aroma of roasting turkey, pounced.

Mattie tried to catch her, but Tuff was much too fast. Ball of twine in her mouth, she looked up, jubilantly, then took off in a sprint, running under the stools at the counter, around each of the girls, then all the way to couch before she reached the end of the roll and was yanked to a dead stop.

The girls, legs trussed as tightly as the turkey's, looked down and then laughed so hard they were doubled over.

"I wish we'd caught that on video. It would be amazing on YouTube." Wren grabbed a piece of the twine and tried to free herself. But as soon as Tuff felt the tug, she pulled back harder, causing the line around Wren's ankles to tighten again.

Overcome by giggles, the girls fell to the floor. This provided the solution as the twine finally went slack and Mattie was able to unwind it from their legs, the stools, and, ultimately work the ball from the puppy's grasp.

Tuff cocked her head on one side, as if to say, "But I was having so much fun..."

Her quizzical look had the girls laughing again.

And that was when a knock sounded at the front door. Mattie felt as if her heart had jumped to her throat. As the girls fell silent, her eyes went to the clock on the microwave. Quarter to six. Was her company early? Or had Wes finally come home?

But Wes wouldn't knock. Mattie gripped the edge of the counter and took a deep breath. She had to stop expecting her husband to show up at any second. If he was coming, he would have called. Or answered her text message at least.

Portia and Wren both ran to get the door and Tuff, excited by the action, followed. A moment later, Mattie heard Nat's voice and seconds later he was in the kitchen, offering her flowers, already arranged in a glass vase, and a jar of huckleberry jam.

"Happy Thanksgiving." He gave her a polite hug and peck on the check. He'd dressed in a dark green sweater that for some reason made the blue of his eyes even more intense. "I nipped the jam from Eadie's pantry. It's good."

"Eadie's jam always is. Thanks Nat. And the flowers are lovely." As she added water, then placed them on the sideboard in the dining room, Nat gave both girls a bear hug.

"You're both too skinny," he said. "What happened to the freshman fifteen?"

"I don't understand why people gain weight when they go to college," Portia said. "The food is way better at home." She gave Nat another squeeze. Both girls were as comfortable around Nat as they were around Jake. They'd known him forever, had been going on the spring and fall roundups ever since they could sit on a horse.

"You smell like Christmas," Portia said.

He laughed. "I was chopping up an old pine tree this afternoon. I did shower, but that resin sticks like crazy."

"Would you like a beer?" Mattie offered. "I'm sorry, I forgot to buy wine."

"Just water is good."

"Want it fizzy? With a little cranberry?" Wren offered. This was their usual drink for special occasions and a pre-mixed pitcher was ready in the fridge.

As Wren filled the tall crystal glasses, Mattie went to pull the turkey from the oven. Right away Nat was at her elbow. "Let me get that. Looks like a twenty-pound bird."

"Only eighteen," Mattie murmured, but she handed him the oven mitts and let him lift the roaster out to the counter.

Nat inhaled deeply. "Can't beat the aroma of freshly roasted turkey. Looks amazing, too."

"We'll let it sit for about half an hour before we carve." Mattie passed him two big forks, which he used to transfer the roasted bird to a wooden cutting board, so she could make gravy from the drippings.

Jake arrived next, exactly on time, and the girls gave him an equally warm welcome. Jake had bought a gift too, a potted ivy in a pumpkin-shaped ceramic container. Mattie gave him a solid kiss on the check. "Oh my gosh, you even shaved."

He patted his face as if he could hardly believe it, either.

It felt good to have men in the house again. Their solid bodies and deep voices added balance and stability. When it came time to carve the turkey, Mattie proffered the knife to Nat. But he shook his head. "Let Jake have the honors."

Was he being courteous to the older man? Or overly sensitive about not stepping into the role of man of the house? Unsure, Mattie was grateful when Jake stepped up and got the job done, turning the conversation to cattle prices at the same time and smoothing over what might have been an awkward moment.

Wes wasn't so much as alluded to after that. Even when they sat around the table no one commented on the one man who should have been here, but wasn't.

The meal was a success from both a food and a conversation perspective. Nat had a friendly, non-judgmental way of talking to the girls that drew them out and Mattie heard tidbits that until now hadn't been shared.

Like that there was a boy who'd gallantly walked Portia home one night but hadn't told her his name.

And, even more surprising, that Wren had met a boy in her political science class who'd asked her out to coffee and who wasn't "a total loser" in Wren's words.

Once everyone had their fill of turkey and vegetables,

they bundled up and went for a walk to Chatterbox Creek, as was family tradition. With temperatures hovering above zero and a full moon and clear sky, conditions were perfect. The girls took turns throwing small sticks for Tuff, who was already showing signs of becoming a master retriever.

After the walk, Nat pulled a couple decks of cards from his coat pocket and announced it was time the girls learned how to play poker. "What makes you think we don't already know?" Wren asked slyly, taking the deck and shuffling like a pro.

From her bedroom, Mattie brought out the penny jar and they played for over an hour, everyone surprised when it was she who ended up with the largest pile of pennies on the table.

"Mom! How did you do that?" Portia wanted to know. "You acted like you didn't even understand the rules."

"When it comes to playing poker, it's smart to let people underestimate you."

Nat grinned. "Well done, Mattie."

After that everyone was hungry enough to eat two pieces of pie each and Mattie gave Jake a smug wink.

The men wouldn't leave until all the dishes had been washed and the kitchen was spotless. By then it was almost midnight and Mattie thought the big talk she'd been planning to have with the girls would wait until morning. But Nat and Jake were no sooner in their trucks, than Wren shut the door and faced her mother.

"So what's up, Mom? What's the real reason Dad isn't here?"

In her mind Mattie had delivered the news to her daughters hundreds of times in a hundred different ways. Now she found the words wouldn't come. Wren's expression softened and she put her hand on Mattie's shoulder.

Speaking softly, as if *she* were the mother, she led Mattie back to the family room. "Let's sit down here, by the fire. Portia, can you grab Mom a glass of water?"

Mattie took the arm chair and waited until the girls were side by side on the sofa, facing her. They looked so young and sweet, and she hated the apprehension and worry on their faces.

"Are you okay, Mom?" Wren finally blurted out. "You look so skinny. You're not sick are you?"

"No. Not sick. And neither is your father."

She could see the momentary relief wash over them. But it didn't last.

"Then what's going on? I can't remember Dad ever missing a holiday or important family gathering before."

It was true. Wes traveled a lot, but he'd always made a point of being here for birthdays, anniversaries, and holidays.

Mattie realized she couldn't avoid it anymore. She had to say this. "I'm sorry to have to tell you this. But your father—left me. He said he needed some time alone."

"When?" Wren asked, at the same moment that Portia burst out with a "Why?"

Poor Portia looked instantly devastated. But Mattie could tell that Wren had been expecting exactly this news.

"Two weeks after the Copper Mountain Rodeo. Your Dad came home from Billings and that was when he told me that—he wasn't happy." She stared down at her hands, fingers linked, lying placidly in her lap. Then she glanced up. Wren looked stunned. Tears were already streaming down Portia's cheeks.

Mattie felt bulldozed by sadness. She felt like she'd just laid waste to her daughters' happy childhoods. Today would be a dividing line for them. The before... when they were a family. And the after... when they weren't.

"I was worried it was something like this," Wren said quietly. "But actually hearing you say the words... I can't believe it."

Portia's tears turned to sobs then. The poor girl looked broken, her face crumpled, black tears laden with mascara rolling down her cheeks. Mattie wiped them away with her thumb, then sat between her daughters, wrapping her arms around their slender backs, wishing they were small enough to gather into her lap.

"I'm so sorry. I wish I could explain how this happened. But—your dad and I, we haven't really talked. He was supposed to be here tonight. We were going to break the news to you together. I don't know where he is."

No excuse he gave would be acceptable. Unless, of course, he'd been in an accident or something. But Mattie didn't think that had happened. On some level she'd known he wouldn't show up.

Once she'd been able to count on Wes keeping his word. Now she wondered about the other promises he'd made and realized she'd been a fool to think they would bind him in any way.

"Th-this doesn't make sense," Portia took a gulp of air. Steadied her voice. "Why wouldn't he be happy? You two are perfect together. Even my friends are always saying they wished their parents would be more like you guys."

"Even the strongest of marriages can sometimes come undone if they're tested too hard. Do you remember last spring, when one of the cowboys was killed at that rodeo in Texas?"

Wren nodded soberly. "He was a bull-rider, like Dad."

"Yes. Your Dad took that hard. He'd seen plenty of injuries in his career. But not a death. That cowboy was younger than him by quite a few years. I believe it made him re-evaluate a lot of things in his life. Not just his career..."

"But that should have made him appreciate you *more*." Wren had never been as quick to cry—or to laugh—as her sister. But a fat tear had been accumulating in the corner of one eye and Mattie watched as it slid slowly down her young, perfect skin.

"Tragedy affects people differently. I can't explain it, Wren." She gathered her nerve. There was something else she had to prepare them for. If she could have thought of a way to cushion the blow, she would have.

But they simply had to be told.

"There's something else your Dad is considering..."

She could feel the girls holding their breath. They could tell by her tone that this was serious. But what could be as bad as the family breaking up...?

"Selling Bishop Stables."

That took longer to sink in. Portia fell back into the sofa cushions. Wren brushed her hair away from her face and squared her shoulders. "He can't do that, can he? It belongs to you, too, right?"

"Why would he *want* to sell in the first place?" Portia moaned. "He grew up here. He was always talking about heritage when we were growing up and telling stories about when he was a kid. He made it sound like this place was important to him. And that it should be important to *us*."

Yes. That was the unfair part. Both she and Wes had instilled values in their children that had taught them not to be selfish but to respect the land and put the ranch and the horses first, in almost all things. To then turn around and sell out, denying them the birthright they had been implicitly promised, was against everything they'd stood for as parents.

"He may change his mind. I hope he will. But just in case—I didn't want you to be blind-sided."

Little Tuff picked that moment to scamper over. She placed her paws on Mattie's knees, waiting to be picked up. As soon as she was, she cuddled in among them.

It was odd that a cute little puppy should be able to offer comfort in the face of so much awful news. But she did. The three of them curled in around Tuff, arms entwined, and Mattie could feel their strength returning.

"At least we have each other," Wren said.

"You still have your dad." The words were hard to say without breaking into uncontrollable sobs. Mattie had to take a breath between each word. "He left me. Not you."

"It doesn't feel that way," Portia said softly.

No. Mattie supposed it didn't.

Her daughters clung close for the remainder of their five-day visit, turning down opportunities to go to town and visit with their high school friends. Mattie felt bad about that but she couldn't deny their presence was a comfort. On the day they were to leave and fly back to their respective colleges, no one had much of an appetite except Tuff.

The puppy gobbled down her breakfast as usual, then proceeded to start pulling clothes out of the girls' suitcases almost as fast as they were packed. Despite everyone's low mood, they couldn't resist giggling as Tuff snatched one of Portia's socks and led them all on a merry chase around the house.

"She's so fast," Wren marveled.

"And tricky." Portia fell to her knees and looked under the sofa, where Tuff was hiding out with her prize, just out of arm's reach.

Never had Mattie been more thankful to Nat for his gift of the adorable puppy. Tuff was a reminder that in the worst of times, there were still reasons to smile, love, and be grateful.

At the airport, she hugged her girls one final time. "I'm so thankful to have daughters like you. Go back to school and try not to worry. Hopefully by Christmas your dad and I will have some things sorted out."

And hopefully by Christmas, Wes would have been in touch with them, as well. Mattie had noticed lots of surreptitious texting going on in the past few days. She suspected they'd been trying to get in touch with their father.

If he'd responded, she would have heard about it, and since she hadn't, she could only surmise that Wes was ignoring their daughters in the same callous way he was ignoring her.

And she would never forgive him for that.

Portia was relieved to say goodbye to her mom at airport security. They shared final hugs and waves, all of them too tearful to say much. Then she and Wren went through the security drill, meeting on the other side of the conveyor belt to put their boots back on, and grab their jackets and backpacks. Finally she was alone with her sister. They only had fifteen minutes before Wren had to board for Denver, but at least they could drop the brave acts they'd been putting on for their mom.

"That was the worst Thanksgiving *ever*. Can you believe it? What is up with Dad?"

"I knew something was wrong between them. But I didn't think it was this bad," Wren admitted. "Keep going," she instructed as she checked their boarding passes for the gate numbers. "We're at the end of the line."

"Has dad answered any of your texts?"

"No." Wren scowled. "He didn't even call on Thanksgiving Day. How lame is that?"

"Do you think something bad happened? Like, he had an accident or something?"

"The authorities would have called Mom. Besides, I heard her on the phone, checking with police and hospitals one night. No, he just doesn't want to talk to us."

That was the conclusion Portia had reached, too. And it really hurt.

She thought back to the last time she'd seen her father—when they'd all driven to the airport together in September. He'd schlepped the bags as usual, complained that they'd packed too much, but she'd seen a tear in his eye when he hugged her goodbye.

"Maybe he was injured at the last rodeo he was in. Hit his head and suffered some sort of brain injury."

"More likely he fell in love with someone else."

Portia stopped in her tracks. "That's an awful thing to say." But it could be true. Why else would he want to leave Mom, forget to call them, and want to sell the ranch? She got an awful, sick feeling in her stomach.

"This really, really sucks."

"Agreed," Wren said. "And it must be ten times worse for Mom. Last night I seriously considered dropping out of college and staying home. At least for the next semester. I hate the idea that she's all alone."

"She wouldn't want you to do that." But Portia understood the lure. She'd wanted to do the same thing, and only knowing how upset the very idea would make their pro-education mother had stopped her.

"Yeah." Wren sighed. In silence they walked the rest of

the way to their gates, which were side by side. Portia was surprised to see that her flight was already boarding. She turned to Wren and gave her sister a huge hug.

"See you at Christmas, Sis."

Portia nodded, crying too hard to say anything back. On the plane, she had a minute to check her phone before turning it off. She noticed a string of text messages from Kirsten. "Yay! Can't wait to see you!" "Party tonight for all Pi Phi!" And then, in a weird twist. "Met this awesome guy—and he has a friend!"

Portia turned off the phone and stuck it back in her bag. She *really* didn't want to go back to Seattle. She hated her dad right now. But she also really needed to see him. If only she knew where he was.

At the Seattle airport, she met up with some of her sorority sisters who happened to be flying back from home at the same time and they shared a cab. One of them, Annie Larimer, gave her a friendly smile. Portia had noticed her on the same flight and remembered that she lived somewhere in rural Montana, too, some small town southeast of Missoula. Not on a ranch, her family ran an orchard or something. They'd worked together on a sociology assignment one night and Portia had really liked Annie. But she didn't have the energy to start a conversation, so she just smiled back then closed her eyes, resting her head on the leather seat and listened to the other girls make plans for that night's party.

Apparently the few girls who'd stayed behind for the Thanksgiving weekend had been working with some of the guys to plan a big welcome back bash for the evening. The party would be off-site, of course, and there would be plenty to drink.

When the taxi pulled up to the sorority house, Kirsten was waiting for her. Portia had hoped to sneak away to her room, and lock the door. Instead she had to listen to Kirsten go on and on about her trip home.

"My friends and I went on a mega shopping trip. Look what I found!" Kirsten spilled the contents of her suitcase onto her bed. Normally Portia would have been insanely jealous of the beautiful new outfits. But today she had zero interest. The effort of pretending to love each item wore away at her, until soon all she could think of was crawling under the covers in her room.

Instead, she and Kirsten dressed and got made-up for the party. When Kirsten offered to let her wear one of the new tops she'd purchased on Black Friday, Portia uncharacteristically stood firm. "I'm okay in this," she fingered the lacy top she was wearing with a gray cardigan.

"Yeah. That's cute," Kirsten said, without sounding convinced. She leaned forward into the mirror as she applied her eyeliner, then stood back to study the effect. "You like?"

"Uh huh."

Kirsten tipped her head to one side as she studied Portia's reflection. "You seem... different."

Portia knew she should explain, but the words wouldn't come. The loss and pain were too fresh. "I'm just tired."

"Yeah, I know. I hardly slept all weekend. It was just one party after another." She went to her mini fridge and pulled out a couple of Red Bulls. "I think we both could use one of these. You don't want to be tired tonight. A couple of guys from my high school are coming to the party tonight. Jared and I hooked up on Saturday night. He's pretty hot and so is his friend Noah. I showed them your Facebook profile and Noah's excited to meet you."

Portia took a long drink—the caffeine and sugar helped.

A few hours later, when the party was starting, she had a beer, and that helped too. She had another drink and then joined a bunch of friends on the dance floor. She let the music flow through her, lift her up from her black mood and transport her a happier, better place. Another drink, a little more dancing, and when a dark-haired guy with crazy blue eyes came up to her and told her he was Noah, she happily put her arms around his shoulders and started dancing with him.

He had some good moves, a natural sense of rhythm.

When she stumbled, they both laughed, and he went to freshen their drinks.

Portia lost all sense of time. The dimly lit room was

decorated with dozens of strands of twinkling lights and LED candles. Couples started drifting to dark corners, making out while the music continued to pulse and pound.

When Noah touched her chin, she lifted her head and let him kiss her.

It felt nice. Really nice.

They kissed while they were dancing, and then suddenly they had moved off the dance floor into an alcove behind some stairs. She wasn't even sure where she was anymore.

"You're a sweet girl, Portia." Noah was kissing her neck now, his hands gliding down to her jeans, then up and under the lacy tank top. She'd taken the sweater off hours ago, and she could feel the heat of his hands against her own fevered skin.

When his hand cupped her breast, she felt a sweet pleasure not only at the peaks of her nipples, but between her legs, too. She'd made out like this for hours with her high school boyfriend, but it soon became clear that this was not a plateau for Noah, merely a pit stop. She could feel his arousal pushed against her hip bone, as he reached for the button on her jeans.

"Hang on."

He immediately stopped what he was doing and kissed her again. "You okay?"

"I'm—" Suddenly the anesthetic of the alcohol and the music and the attention of a cute boy all wore off. She felt alone, sad... and sort of... yucky. She tried to look into Noah's eyes, but they seemed out of focus to her and she instinctively knew that any attempts to explain wouldn't be successful.

And why should they? She knew nothing about this boy. Not his major, or his interests... or even his last name.

"Sorry. I think I'm going to be sick." She broke away and ran, grabbing her coat and somehow finding her way back home, where she locked the door, then fell on her bed and started to cry.

When she returned home from the airport, Mattie was exhausted. She walked from one empty room to the other, feeling too low to tackle the cleaning and laundry that was waiting for her.

If it hadn't been for Tuff, she would have collapsed onto the sofa and allowed herself to sink into a depressed stupor.

But the puppy needed to go out, and so she snapped on Tuff's leash and dressed herself to brave the cold. A thin layer of snow coated the yard today. A big storm was on its way—fortunately not due until well after the girls would be safely at their destinations. She didn't need to worry about stocking up in preparation. She had leftovers to last a week in her fridge and freezer.

And plenty of pie.

Keeping Tuff on a short leash, Mattie headed to the barns. In the past few days she and the girls had done a lot of riding, so none of the horses had been neglected. The tack and feed rooms were still spiffy from her zealous cleaning frenzy of the previous week. Jake had handled the chores alone this morning. He'd be back in another hour to do the evening feed. She decided to load up the feed cart for him, before heading back inside the house.

She'd no sooner made the decision than she heard the rumble of an approaching vehicle—something big and traveling slowly. Sticking her head out the barn door, she was amazed to see a semi-tractor van with a white cab and silver trailer, taking a wide turn into her yard.

Securing Tuff in the feed room first, Mattie pulled on her wool cap and headed back outdoors. The rig had stopped and a driver was climbing out of the cab. He was tall and chunky, dressed in a plaid jacket and down vest, jeans, and work boots. He had his head bowed against the wind as he walked toward her.

She held her ground until he met up with her. Only then did he straighten so she could see a man in his forties, with a round face and serious eyes.

"Damn, I think the storm is coming early."

Weather talk first. Only in Montana. "Wasn't supposed to get here until tomorrow."

"Don't I know it. Hope the snow holds off." He held out his hand. "Guy Medley. You must be Mattie Bishop."

She shook his hand cautiously. "I am."

"Good. We should probably load them up first, do paperwork second."

With her hands on her hips, she shook her head. If he hadn't known her name, she would have been sure this was a mistake. Her stomach churned. She had a very bad feeling about this. "I'm sorry, but I have no idea what's going on here."

Guy's serious eyes widened a little. "Your husband never told you?"

She gave a negative shake of her head.

Guy's chest expanded on a deep inhale. He compressed his lips, then headed back to the truck and returned with a clipboard, which he held so she could see.

"Your husband sold fourteen horses to be delivered to Western Sky Ranch on Spencer Lake near Whitefish. Money's been paid in full. I was supposed to pick them up tomorrow, but when I heard about the storm, I figured it'd be smart to get them moved today."

Mattie grabbed the clipboard, studied the details. Listed were fourteen of their most valuable horses, including Rosie. "Who owns this Western Sky Ranch?" She squinted at the typed name. "Sean Edwards. Does he have experience with Tennessee Walkers?"

"Doubt it," Guy said drily. "He's a reality TV star—my kids watch his show every week. He heard somewhere that Tennessee Walkers make great trail riders and decided he wanted a bunch of them for his new ranch.

She felt sick in earnest now. She couldn't let these horses leave Bishop Stables. They had so much money and time invested in them. Rosie, in particular, was a treasure. Born, bred and raised to be a show horse—not wasted being ridden by rich greenhorns from Hollywood.

She pushed the clipboard back at him. "I can't let you take my horses."

"Well, Ma'am, I'm afraid you can't stop me since they don't belong to you. Your husband signed the papers. And he's already deposited the money."

"He never told me a word about it." Blood flowed to her cheeks, and in her embarrassment, her gaze dipped to the tips of her boots. How awful to have to make such an admission to a perfect stranger.

Guy paused, kicked at a clump of snow and sent it scattering. "I feel bad about that. I surely do. But you need to take this up with your husband. And let me do my job."

She gazed out at the pasture where most of these horses were grazing at the dry tufts of grass still accessible beneath the skiff of snow. Her heart welled with sadness. She didn't want them to leave. She'd been raised to be a practical rancher, but up until now she and Wes had never sold their horses to anyone without vetting them first.

Now he expected her to let more than half the herd go in one big swoop, just like that?

She needed a moment to think. "How about a cup of coffee, first?"

Guy looked up at the mounting clouds, then at his watch. "I suppose an extra fifteen minutes won't hurt."

"We'll go to the house. I have to get my dog." She ran back to the barn where she found Tuff and Hermione snuggled together again, napping. They looked so cute, she decided to leave them there.

She then led Guy Medley along the path to the back door, where they deposited their boots and coats in the mudroom, and she washed her hands before continuing into the kitchen.

"Go ahead and sit. Want some pie? I've got apple, pumpkin, or lemon."

Guy's eyes brightened at that. "Lemon would be nice."

She put on the coffee, cut him a slice, and invited him to sit at the island.

"I'll just make a quick call while we wait for the coffee." Turning her back to him, she went to stand by the windows as she dialed their lawyer. He answered and she quickly outlined the situation.

"Do I have to do this, Stan?"

"I think so. But can you hold a few minutes?"

"Okay." As she waited, she gazed out at the horses. Each one of them had a distinct personality, was loved and pampered, as well as carefully trained. At Bishop Stables they treated all their horses like five star guests. How could Wes just sell them to some pampered Hollywood star who probably didn't have the first clue about running a ranch?

Even worse, sell them without consulting her first.

The coffee pot beeped, and Mattie went to pour a cup for her guest. "Sorry. I'll just be a few more minutes." She noticed he'd already finished his pie. "Feel free to cut yourself another slice."

She went back to the family room and took up the same position at the window. Guy could still hear her, but looking out at the view gave her at least an illusion of privacy. Finally Stan came back on the line.

"Mattie, sorry, but you don't have any option but to let them take the horses. The business is in Wes's name, only. Mattie, you should have pushed for joint ownership when the two of you were first married."

Frankly that had never occurred to her.

"There's something else."

She could hear the tension in Stan's voice and braced for more bad news.

"Wes has been talking to me about... the current situation between you two."

*Aren't you the lucky one. Cause he sure as hell isn't talking to me...*With effort, Mattie kept her sarcastic thoughts unspoken. Feeling betrayed and heartbroken, she managed a simple, "Oh?"

"You should be talking to your own lawyer, too."

"I thought *you* were my lawyer."

He paused. "Not in this case. It's not personal, Mattie. It's just that my firm has been representing Bishop Stables for a long time. And you need a lawyer to stand up for your rights."

She wanted to sink to the floor and curl up into a little ball.

Even her lawyer was rejecting her.

"So I have to let him take the horses?" If her voice came out sounding like a little girl's, well so what? She couldn't help it.

"Yes."

Of the fourteen horses being sold, ten were turned out in the northwest pasture. All Mattie had to do was shake a pail with some oats on the bottom and their ears perked, even the three at the far end of the field.

She didn't try to hide her tears from Guy Medley as the horses came running. These horses trusted her, and she was betraying them, sending them off to unknown pastures and people she had never even met.

All of the horses listed on the bill of sale had competed in shows and so were used to the trailering routine. One by one she snapped on their lead ropes and led them out of the gate, up the ramp and into their box stalls where Guy made sure they were correctly positioned and secured for transport. Mattie was somewhat relieved to see that the stalls were clean and the hay boxes full. The trailer was built to ensure the horses would travel as comfortably as possible.

The last three horses were in the barn—and the very last one Mattie led up to the trailer was Rosie. "Hey, girl," was all Mattie could say, before her voice choked over with tears.

She stumbled going up the ramp, and she could feel Rosie grow tense, then hesitate. The horse was sensing her distress, and didn't want to go further.

Mattie took a deep breath. She had to get a grip. She didn't want to make this experience any more stressful for Rosie than it had to be.

"It's okay, Rosie." She called on all her inner strength to make her voice calm and firm. "Come on, girl."

Rosie's ears moved forward first, then her body. Obviously reassured by Mattie's newfound composure, she allowed herself to be led into the fourteenth box stall, where Guy snapped her into place, then looped the lead rope so it couldn't get tangled in her feet.

Rosie gave Mattie one last look, and Mattie was certain she could read in the mare's soft brown eyes a message along the lines of, *I'm not too sure about this, but since you seem to think it's okay, I'll go along with it.*

Trouble was, Mattie didn't think it was okay.

It was damn treason.

She stumbled out of the trailer, searched both pockets of her coat for a tissue and when she didn't find one, dried her eyes with her sleeve. How could Wes have sold these horses out from under her like this?

"I'm real sorry Ma'am." Guy passed her a clipboard. "I need your *John Henry*. Then I'll get out of your hair."

Her pen hovering over the signature line, she hesitated. "This Western Sky outfit. What kind of a crew does this TV star have working for him? Did he hire competent people at least?"

"I honestly don't know. But I've been in this business a long time and I can size up a person pretty quick. Once I'm done, I'll send you a message. Give you my gut feel on whether they're in good hands."

"I'd appreciate that. Here, let me give you my number."

They exchanged contact information, then Mattie turned away. She didn't want to watch Guy drive off with her horses. But she wasn't ready to return to the house, either. So she trudged with heavy footsteps to the barn. At the barn door, she heard the engine roar to life, then the trailer creak as Guy shifted into gear.

She steeled herself not to look, instead stepping inside and sliding the door closed.

Closing her eyes, she thought back to the first time she'd visited Bishop Stables and the awe she'd felt when Wes had given her a tour of the main barn. He'd been so proud—and with good reason.

Back then, the stables had been full to capacity. Now, all the stalls were empty. The horses that remained— Whiskey Chaser, Princess Bride, Madame Curie, Copper, and four two-year-olds not yet ready to be ridden—were turned out in the south pasture.

She waited for silence. And when it came, she knew her horses were gone. Most likely she'd never see any of them again. She wanted to weep. But she'd done so much of that in the past month and she was so terribly tired of it all.

Her gaze swept the wide aisle, lingering up high where

blue and red ribbons proudly proclaimed the past successes of Bishop Stables. Every year of her and Wes's marriage, the winnings had been a little less than the year before. The trend hadn't worried her. She'd figured they were treading water, waiting for the day when Wes would retire from the rodeo and devote himself fulltime to their ranch.

Looking back, she realized that it was after his father's death that his commitment to the business had really dropped.

There had been signs. All sorts of them. But she'd missed some and misinterpreted others because she hadn't wanted to face up to the truth. It was she who loved Bishop Stables. Not Wes.

And yet it was Wes's name on the legal papers. Wes who signed checks. And Wes who made the deals...

Dragging her boots along the concrete floor, Mattie entered the feed room, and the half-loaded cart. Tuff lifted her head to look at her, then dropped back to sleep. The cat didn't move a muscle.

Mattie stood in front of the cart, feeling defeated. None of this was needed now.

Oh, lord... she sank to the floor, with her back against the wall. Jake would be showing up soon, expecting to do evening chores like usual. She should try to catch him before he left, save him the trip.

But as she pulled her phone out of her pocket, it began to ring.

She didn't recognize the number. But she answered anyway.

CHAPTER TEN

Wes's voice came over the line, so clearly it was like he was sitting right next to her. Mattie cradled the phone with both her hands, as if to take firm hold of the connection between them.

"Wes? Where have you been?"

"I'm still tied up here."

"Where is 'here' exactly?"

He didn't answer. "I tried to make it for Thanksgiving. Were the girls home?"

"Of course they were. Didn't you get my messages? Not to mention theirs?"

"I—lost my phone. Had to buy another."

That explained the strange number. But how convenient that he'd happened to lose his phone just when they'd all been so desperate to get hold of him.

"You promised you'd be home for the holiday. That we'd talk to the girls together."

"Like I said, I tried." His sigh made it sound like*s he* was the one being unreasonable.

"So what stopped you? Were you in an accident or something?"

"No. It's hard to explain."

"I've got time. Lots of it, in fact, since I don't have much in the way of chores to do anymore."

"Um—what are you talking about?"

"I'm talking about the fact that I now have only eight horses to look after. How could you do it, Wes? I suppose it's too much to hope that you would consult me. But a heads-up would have been something, at least."

He was silent for a bit. "I take it Guy Medley showed up today?" When she didn't answer, he added, "He was supposed to come tomorrow. That's why I'm calling. To let you know."

"To let me know what? That you're breaking up our herd? Selling horses I've raised and trained from birth to be toys for some reality TV show star?"

"Calm down, Mat. You should have expected this. I told you, already. I've got to sell everything. No one wants to take over a Tennessee Walking Horse operation these days. That means selling off whatever I can, and then putting the land on the block."

"You're not wasting any time, are you?" Mattie pulled herself up from the floor, dusted off her jeans. When she'd initially heard Wes's voice on the line, she'd experienced a tiny flicker of hope.

That he was coming home. That he was ready to talk.

She'd even dared to hope that he might rescind the sale, call Guy Medley and tell him to turn his rig around and bring back the horses.

But that flame was extinguished now. She knew with a certainty that felt like a ball of lead in her heart that Wes wasn't going to change his mind. About any of this.

"What about the rest of the horses?"

"I've got a buyer lined up for Whiskey Chaser. A young steer wrestler from Helena. He'll be coming by with his trailer later this week."

She swallowed. "And the others?"

"Going to a nice family outfit down by Ronan. I know the people. They'll treat the horses well."

"This is going to break Wren and Portia's hearts." They'd been six when Princess Bride and Madame Curie

121

were born, within days of each other. Wes had told them, "If you take care of these foals, when they're old enough to ride, you can help your mom train them—and then they'll be yours." The girls had been devoted to their horses ever since.

"It'll be easier for them this way."

"You mean it's easier for you." He never had liked saying good-bye. When it was time to head to a rodeo, he'd always waited to drive off until the girls were in school and she was out working with the horses. Even his homecomings were low key. Usually he'd slip in during the wee hours of the night, inserting himself back in her bed, and their children's lives, with the minimum of fuss or fanfare.

"Look, I'd better go. I'll—"

"Wait!" She had things to say and this might be her only chance. "I spoke to Stan earlier today. He told me you'd been talking to him about—" She might as well say the word. Put it out there. "About our divorce."

"Yeah...?"

"You might have told me there wasn't going to be any discussion. That your mind was made up."

"I thought I had."

This cold, cold man. Had he really ever loved her? It was so hard to believe now. "Fine. If that's what you want, that's what you'll get. But this stunt you pulled with the horses—don't you dare do the same thing with our land. Our house."

"I aim to give you a fair settlement, Mat. But the land and house—they're in my name."

"Don't I know it." She'd been such a naïve fool, to think she didn't have to worry about legal technicalities once she was married. "But I have rights, too. And I want some say on the timing of the sale."

She'd find a lawyer, just as Stan had suggested. She'd see if there was anything she could do to block Wes's plans. Only a few days ago, Wren and Portia had found out their family was breaking up. Now their horses had been sold out from under them. They couldn't lose the family house, as well.

With only eight horses, and none of them in the barn, chores took less than thirty minutes. Mattie was all done when Jake pulled up in his truck. She'd expected him to notice the missing horses right away and come running, but he took measured steps toward her and they met by the patch of raspberries Wes's mother had planted between the main barn and a smaller one that was used for weaning foals.

The sadness on Jake's face took her by surprise.

He knew.

But she had to say it, anyway. "Wes sold the horses. Fourteen of them." She almost started crying again, and had to press her lips together and stare out at the road.

"He called me an hour ago."

Before he'd phoned *her*. The blows kept coming. She couldn't believe how much they still hurt.

"Not sure what you're going to do around here anymore, Jake." She tried to smile, like it was some kind of joke, but couldn't.

"Not an issue anymore, Mattie. He laid me off."

"What?"

Jake shrugged. "I saw it coming. But I have to admit. I don't like it." He touched her shoulder. "I'm going to miss those pies of yours, Mattie."

No more Jake coming round the property two times a day, like clockwork. She couldn't imagine it. But then, if Wes had his way, she wouldn't be here much longer, either.

Damn it. Damn *him*.

"This is temporary. Don't go taking another job Jake."

"Wasn't planning on it. Figure I've done enough talking about Arizona, I might as well drive down there and check it out. Maybe you should get in your truck and take a trip, too, Mattie. Head to Marietta and stay with your family a spell. According to Wes, the rest of these horses will be gone by the end of the week."

"I'll think about it."

"Do it. I hate the idea of you all on your own out here."

But she was alone. And she'd actually been that way for quite a while. It was time she faced that. No more wishing for the past, or crying about her future. She was pulling herself together. Starting now.

She felt as if she'd reached a sort of turning point and that the moment needed to be marked in some special way. "Jake, want to come out to dinner at the Smoke House with me tonight?"

Jake looked surprised. "What for?"

"It was just a thought." She shrugged, a little embarrassed, hoping he hadn't taken her offer the wrong way."

"And not a bad one. But I've got a fellow coming over tonight to look at my old car. Wren put a sales notice up on that Internet Kijiji thing for me and I just may have myself a buyer."

"That's good news." He'd been wanting to sell his car for over a year now. And if he was going to travel to Arizona, that plan made more sense than ever.

"We'll go out for that dinner another time," Jake promised.

"Sure," she said. But she was still going tonight. Even if she was a party of one.

Mattie checked her reflection in the restroom mirror of the Smoke House Bar & Grill. She'd curled her hair, put on a bit of makeup, a dress and heels, and the results were satisfactory, if she did say so herself. She exited the door and headed to the bar, where Ryan Garry, owner of the local Lake County Gazette, was waiting for her.

He'd been sitting at the bar when she first came in, twenty minutes ago. She'd been nervous.

It had been a long time since she'd gone by herself to a bar—actually she never had—and though the Smoke House was far from a pickup place, she still felt conspicuous.

But she knew the bartender. Blake Coffey was in his mid-twenties, cute and charming. When he was younger she'd given him and his sister riding lessons. They chatted a little, and his good-humored banter helped eased her tension. She ordered a cranberry and soda, and kept an eye on the football game playing on TV screens positioned strategically so almost everyone in the room had a view.

Shortly after that, Ryan had come in. Forty, a divorced father of three kids, besides his newspaper, his main passion in life was protecting the ecosystem of the Flathead Watershed. Last time she'd spoken to him, he'd sold her a membership to the Flathead Lakers, a grassroots organization that worked to ensure responsible land and water stewardship.

As soon as he'd spotted her, he headed for the empty stool next to her.

"Hey, Mattie. Were the girls home for Thanksgiving?" Ryan was a tall, reed-thin man, with very curly, sandy-colored hair. His trendy, dark-framed glasses gave him an intellectual appearance, but Mattie knew he loved fishing every bit as much as his beloved books.

"They were. I just drove them back to the airport this morning and I miss them all ready."

He shook his head. "Hard to believe you have kids in college."

Mattie was used to comments like this. She and Wes had started their family young—not necessarily on purpose, but she had no regrets. "How are your kids doing?" The older boys were Murray and Shane. She couldn't recall his daughter's name.

"Ah, you know. Teenagers." He gave a rueful shrug. "The boys were bad enough, but Katie just turned fourteen and wow. All of a sudden I can't do anything right. I used to be her hero." He paused, then added, "They're with their mother for the holiday."

Mattie remembering hearing that he had a complicated joint custody arrangement with his ex, Amanda, who lived about forty-five minutes away in Big Fork. She wondered if Ryan's current predicament would one day become hers. Was she going to have to share her daughters with Wes in future? Right now, it seemed impossible to predict.

Ryan held out a hand to signal Blake. "Rye and ginger,

here." Then he glanced at Mattie. "Can I buy you a drink?"

Mattie hesitated. She couldn't remember the last time she'd had anything with alcohol. Maybe champagne last New Year's Eve? But—she'd had a really bad day, topping off a dreadful month. And she could always call a cab to drive her home.

"Sure. I'll have the same."

So now, coming out of the washroom, Mattie slipped up onto the barstool and took her first sip of the drink. It tasted pretty good. "When's the next meeting of the Flathead Lakers?"

That got Ryan started. And after fifteen minutes' discussion of the latest conservation initiatives, he ordered them both a second drink.

And suddenly the conversation stopped being so serious. Mattie found it easy to laugh at Ryan's jokes. And to make a few of her own.

Then a local band, a guy on a fiddle, a female with a banjo, and another guy on bass, took their places on a small stage, and started playing bluegrass. Soon couples were getting up on the dance floor, and when Ryan held out his hand, Mattie smiled and thought, *why not?*

It was good fun, at first.

But after three heel-kicking numbers the bass line slowed and the fiddle turned soft and sweet. All of a sudden Ryan was holding her a little too closely. Mattie realized she must have been sending out the wrong signals. She pushed back on his chest. "How about we sit this one out?"

Ryan didn't look pleased.

I t was just past dinner, when the phone rang. Eadie had left for the day and Nat took the call in his office, door open to the foyer. He sank into the leather chair that had once been molded to his father's frame and now to his. Not that there was much difference between his father and him. They'd both topped six feet, had strong frames, broad shoulders, and a metabolism and work ethic that kept the accumulation of pounds to a bare minimum.

Nat put his feet up on the walnut desk and stared at the oil painting over the fireplace. His mother had commissioned a local artist to paint the scene that he saw every morning when he went out to start his day—Mission Mountains at Sunrise.

"Hello?"

"Hey, Nat. Wes Bishop here."

Nat felt a knot form in his gut, but he kept his tone relaxed. "What's up?"

"I'm checking back to see if you're interested in Bishop Stables. You asked for a week, I've given you a month."

He'd weighed the pros and cons and had come up with this: the purchase didn't make sense, given his goals to downsize. But if he didn't buy the land, Mattie would almost certainly lose her home.

"I'm interested." He named a price that was borderline acceptable.

Wes swore. "You're low-balling me." He named a higher figure.

Nat held firm. "You won't get a better offer."

"I wouldn't be so sure about that." Wes hesitated, then added, "I have another interested party. I'll check in with him and get back to you."

"Fair enough." As he disconnected the call, Nat worried that he may have been foolish to gamble. His instincts told him Wes was bluffing. But what if he wasn't? What if he really did have a second prospective buyer interested in Bishop Stables?

Nat decided he had to talk to Mattie about this. Did she even know how close Wes was to closing a deal on the property? He dialed her home number, and when there was no answer, he felt a pinprick of worry.

He knew she'd driven the girls to the airport that morning. Even if she'd done some shopping in Missoula, she would have been home hours ago. It was late for chores, but maybe she was still out in the barn?

Her cell phone rang through to messages.

He thought for a minute, and then called Jake.

"She isn't home? That's odd," Jake said, when Nat asked if he knew where Mattie was. "She mentioned something about going for dinner at the Smoke House. But I had some business to attend to. I wouldn't think she'd go alone." He thought a moment, then added. "I hope she hasn't had a fall or some kind of accident at the ranch."

"I'll swing by her place and check," Nat offered.

"Thanks. Keep me posted."

"Will do."

As he talked, Nat was already walking to the mudroom, where he found his coat, boots, and car keys. He fed Buffy, and turned on the radio to keep her company, then went out to his truck.

Only the light above the door was on at Mattie's house. And her SUV was missing. He slipped his vehicle into park with the headlights aimed into her driveway. He could see what looked like fresh tire tracks in the snow.

Maybe she'd gone to the Smoke House, after all.

If so, she was probably fine. But he needed to talk to her about Wes's phone call. So he decided to keep driving into town.

Twenty minutes later he was at the Smoke House, pushing open the door of the Montana styled log building and finding himself being greeted by a cute young woman in dark jeans and a button-up black shirt with a discreet Smoke House logo.

"Here for dinner? Or the bar?" she asked, looking behind him, to see if there was anyone with him.

Nat's gaze scanned over the diners on the left hand side of the building. No one sitting alone there. Then he checked out the bar. And the dance floor.

And there she was, dancing with Ryan Garry, looking about as pretty as a woman could be. But not very happy. She was pushing Ryan away, and Ryan, in turn, was scowling back at her.

Nat didn't think about what he was going to do, he just did it. Brushing past the hostess, he strode to the dance floor where he put a hand on Mattie's shoulder, insinuating himself between her and Ryan. "Hey Mattie. My turn now?"

No denying the relief on her face as she smiled at him and said, "Why not?"

Ryan backed off, with a modicum of grace and Nat placed his other hand at Mattie's waist. The song was slow and romantic, and the temptation was to pull her petite, curvy body up close to his. She was always a lovely woman, but he had to admit, even more so with her hair styled and a little color on her lush, kissable mouth.

Carefully he held her at arm's length, none of his actions betraying his inner yearnings.

"You and Ryan on a date or something?"

"Hardly. I needed to get out of the house. And ran into him here."

Her words came out a little slurred. He noticed then that she was leaning on him, to keep her balance. In all the years he'd known her, he'd rarely seen her take a drink. And never more than one. "Have you been drinking?"

"Just two."

"You do know they serve doubles on Monday evenings?"

Her eyes widened. "So I've really had four?" She looked shocked. Then giggled. "No wonder I feel so... strange. I forgot to have dinner, also. That was silly, huh?"

"For you, I'd say this classifies as a full-on bender." And if anyone deserved to let loose a little, it was her. When the song ended, he walked her back to the bar. Ryan Gerry had left, and Mattie looked a little concerned about that.

"I hope he isn't upset. I'm afraid he might think I was leading him on." She frowned. "But as far as he's concerned, I'm a married woman, right?"

"Legally, that's true." Nat signaled to the bartender, one of the Coffey kids, he couldn't remember his name. "Could we get a plate of nachos here? And some water?" He was fine with Mattie letting off some steam. But he was pretty sure she didn't want to get totally plastered.

"You think people around town know Wes and I are... separated?" She leaned forward on her stool to whisper that last word into his ear, and almost slid to the floor.

He put an arm over her shoulders to steady her. "Yeah. Judging by how fast Gerry moved in on you, I'd say they know."

"Oh." She sounded deflated. But she perked up when

the plate of food was set in front of her. She ate a few nachos, took a sip of water "He sold our horses today. Fourteen of them, gone, like that." She tried to snap her fingers, not quite pulling it off.

He'd noticed the big trailer driving down the road around three o'clock. No wonder Mattie was drinking. She loved her horses, and loosing fourteen in one day. "I'm sorry."

She popped another chip in her mouth, then wiped her mouth delicately with one of the small paper napkins stacked on the bar. "He didn't even warn me first. This truck just shows up out of the blue..."

Tears welled in her eyes, and she dabbed them with the same napkin.

"That reminds me. The driver was supposed to send me a message..." She fumbled for her purse, and he leaned over to snag it off the back rest, then held it steady while she fished inside.

Finally she found her phone, and turned it on to check her messages. "Some stupid reality TV star bought the horses for his ranch. I wanted to know whether the people working for him know what they're doing."

"Looks like I have a message..." She fumbled with the touch screen, then handed it to him. "Could you read it, please?"

"Sure." He studied the screen. "The one from Guy Medley?"

"Yes. He was the truck driver."

"Okay, he says, *Checks out OK. Don't worry.*"

"Well, thank the lord for that, at least." Mattie carefully extracted a chip loaded with melted cheese and guacamole. "These are tasty. Thanks, Nat. I'm starting to feel more like myself." She smiled, rather sadly. "Though it was nice to sort of forget all my problems there for a while."

"Does that mean you've had enough of Polson's exciting night scene for now?"

She smiled faintly. "Yeah. I suddenly feel absolutely beat. Do you think you could give me a lift home?"

"That was my plan," Nat pulled out some bills to settle the tab, then helped Mattie off her stool. "If you pass me your keys, I'll have a couple of my hands drive into town in the morning to fetch your vehicle."

"Thanks, Nat. What did I ever do to deserve a good neighbor like you?" She was leaning on him as he walked her toward the door and he didn't mind a bit.

"Yeah, I'm quite the guy."

She giggled, which sounded cute, though he preferred her normal throaty laugh.

Outside the cold night air sobered her a bit more, and she sucked in a breath. "Darn it's frigid."

"Yeah, that storm's coming in."

Already it was snowing lightly. The delicate flakes looked pretty now, but soon they'd be dealing with a full-on blizzard. Mattie's high heels were useless on the slick surface of the parking lot and he wrapped his arm around her waist to hold her up as they made their way to his truck. He buckled her in, then got behind the wheel and headed for home. They hadn't been on the road for five minutes before she slumped against the door, head tipped against the window, and fell asleep. When her yard light came into view, he slowed.

He didn't feel right about leaving her at home, alone, in this condition.

"Mattie, how about we pick up Tuff and the two of you sleep over in my guest room tonight?"

He had to repeat his offer a few times before he got an answer from her.

"Tuff..." a few mumbles he couldn't decipher, then, "... barn."

"Okay. Hang on a sec while I get her." He left the truck running and jogged through the fresh layer of snow to the main barn. The radio was playing, set to the local country music station. He walked up and down the central aisle, noting all the empty stalls. The place was deserted. Finally he located Tuff, sleeping soundly in a cordoned-off area in the feed room, a plump tabby cat curled up next to her.

Damn, they were cute. He lifted the little border collie gently and Tuff immediately perked up. He let the pup outside to pee and chased her through the snow a few minutes, playing the little thing out before picking her up again and carrying her to the truck.

Mattie was back asleep. Or maybe she'd never even woken up.

At his place, Nat helped Mattie to the guest room, while Tuff and her sister celebrated their reunion with a little tussle.

"Nat?" Mattie was sitting on the bed, her posture slumped, her eyes closed.

He'd already pulled off her heels and removed her jacket. He had no plans to touch that dress. She'd have to sleep in it and deal with the damage tomorrow.

"Yes, darlin'?" He pulled down the covers for her, quite certain that she'd remember none of this in the morning.

"Stay with me?" she mumbled, as she fell back to the pillow.

Had he heard that correctly? Nat couldn't be sure. But did he want to curl into that bed beside her? Hell, yes.

Instead, he pulled the quilt up to her chin, hesitated, then kissed her forehead. "Sleep well, Mat."

He sure wouldn't.

Chapter Eleven

Mattie hadn't had much experience with hangovers. A fact she was profoundly grateful for the next morning when she woke up staring at the wood plank ceiling in Nat's guest bedroom. She felt like she had the flu, but at least she remembered where she was, and how she got here.

She shifted up and studied the room. It was decorated in upscale western style, with a log-framed poster bed and an original oil painting above the polished oak bureau. Color scheme was gold and blue. Nice. She swung her feet out to the floor, wincing at the throbbing in her head. Her stomach felt pretty crappy too.

In the en suite bathroom, folded on the counter, was one of Nat's oversized flannel shirts and a thick pair of woolen socks. She put the shirt over her wrinkled dress, doing the buttons up to her neck. For a finishing touch she slipped on the socks. Quite the ensemble.

She avoided her reflection as she made her way sheepishly out of the room.

Down the hall and to the right, she found the kitchen. Nat was helping himself to a cup of coffee. He looked up.

Smiled.

She felt self-conscious about her bare legs—somehow her stockings had gotten several ghastly runs last night, she didn't recall how it happened, but she'd had to toss them in the trash this morning.

"Morning Mattie."

Suddenly she remembered how it had felt to have his arms around her when they were dancing. He'd held her so properly, but his touch had still created a heat in her body quite unlike her reaction to having Ryan Gerry pull her close.

She shuddered, remembering. Boy, she hadn't handled that very well.

"Sleep okay?" Nat asked.

"Better than I deserved." She slipped onto a stool at the butcher block island, about three times the size of her own at Bishop Stables.

Everything at the Double D was bigger. And more beautiful. Nat's house could have been the lodge for an upscale mountain resort, and yet he rarely entertained, so she'd only been inside a handful of times in the past nineteen years.

Two pain pills were on the counter, along with a glass of water. When Nat nodded at them, she said, "Thanks," and swallowed them down. Glancing at the microwave, she winced at the time. It was almost nine o'clock. She'd slept through his morning chores and her own. Not that there was much in the way of chores for her anymore. There was plenty of hay in the shelters for the eight horses that were left. When she got home, she'd check and make sure the water troughs weren't frozen. But since Jake had just repaired all the pumps in October, the chances of that happening were slight.

"Where's Tuff?" Her voice came out hoarse. She took another drink of water.

"In the mudroom with Buffy. Probably flaked out. They exhausted themselves playing in the new snow this morning."

"Mind if I go say hello?"

"Be my guest." He pointed the way.

She vaguely remembered coming into the house through the side entrance that led in from the garage last night. Just beyond the kitchen was a rather forlorn-looking dining room—she'd bet it hadn't been used since Julia left—and then the hallway opened up to a large gracious foyer. Straight ahead was the main entrance, and to the left a corridor that led to a bathroom and the mudroom. Here she found Tuff and her sister curled up together. So adorable, she wanted to scoop them up, but puppies were like babies. When they were sleeping, only a fool disturbed them.

Quietly she backed out of the hall and from this vantage point noticed that the door to Nat's study, on the other side of the entry, was open.

Feeling a little snoopy, she couldn't resist a peek.

The room was masculine, but cozy, decorated in navy blue and chocolate browns. Dominating the space was a massive, walnut desk. On top of the desk were blueprints, curling up at the edges.

"Everything okay?" Nat had come to check on her. His gaze went from where she was standing, to where she was looking.

"Have you got a new construction project in the works?" she asked.

Nat closed the door to his office. "Just some minor renovations to the house."

While Nat had been married, Julia had done a complete update of the place. Fortunately, while she had no interest in living in a ranch house, she'd had excellent taste in decorating one. "Really? It looks perfect just the way it is."

"Oh, you know, just a few changes here and there," he said vaguely. "Hungry?"

"Honestly? No."

But she followed him back to the kitchen and watched as he sliced some cantaloupe, then arranged it on a plate with two slices of toast. He slid the plate across the gleaming wooden surface to her.

"I'm bit foggy on some of the details from last night." She picked up the buttered rye toast and took a nibble.

"How did you happen to be at the Smoke House? Was it a coincidence?"

"No. I was looking for you. When you didn't answer your phone, I called Jake and he said you'd mentioned going to the Smoke House."

He must have wanted to speak to her urgently, if he hadn't been willing to wait for the morning. "Is there a problem?"

Nat's forthright gaze slipped a little to the left. "Wes called here last night after supper. He sounded pretty serious about finding a buyer for your ranch."

Mattie gasped, then choked on the piece of toast she'd just swallowed. She gulped down more water. "That bastard. He phoned me around five o'clock yesterday to tell me he'd sold the horses—fat lot of good that was, since I'd already seen Guy Medley drive off with them thirty minutes earlier. I told Wes he'd better not pull the same stunt with the ranch."

A request he'd obviously point-blank ignored.

Nat refilled his coffee cup, then took a seat to her right. Leaning forward, he turned his head in her direction. "And what did he say to that?"

She hesitated. "He told me to hire a lawyer."

"You're right. He *is* a bastard."

"He wants a clean, fast break, that much is clear. But he's such a coward. Just once I'd like to have him look me in the eyes and explain why he has to not only end our marriage, but sell all our horses and our home, too."

"But he won't," Nat predicted. "That would require him to admit that he's the bad guy here."

"Well, maybe I shouldn't give him a choice. He's been calling the shots for too long. It's my turn." Mattie straightened her shoulders. Finished off the water. "Could you give me a lift home, Nat?"

"I could. But what's your plan? You're cooking something up. I can see it in your eyes."

"If he won't come to me, then I'm going to find him."

"In a few days, you mean?"

"Now."

"Have you looked out a window today?"

She had, briefly, but now she turned to the large picture window behind her. The view was almost entirely white. The predicted blizzard was in full onslaught.

"I've driven in storms before. I've got good tires. I'll be fine."

"Do you even know where to find him?"

"A month ago Wes told me he was staying with some old friends of his, Peter and Marg Wilkinson. They have an acreage up near Billings. I'll start there."

Nat processed this. Then looked deeply into her eyes. "You're really determined to do this?"

"I am."

"You know... I wouldn't mind having a few words with Wes myself."

This was interesting. She narrowed her eyes as she studied him. "About buying Bishop Stables?"

Nat nodded. "Finish your breakfast Mattie. We need to get on the road."

"You sure?"

"Yup. Even if I didn't have my own reasons for this trip, I sure as hell wouldn't let you drive to Billings alone."

Maybe she should have been insulted by his alpha male attitude. But she liked the idea. Nat would be a good person to have along if anything went wrong.

And even if it didn't.

At home Mattie took a quick shower, then threw some jeans, sweaters, underwear and her toiletry bag into a duffel. Nat had made arrangements for Eadie to take care of Tuff and for one of his men to check on her horses and the barn cats. Mattie didn't know what would happen when the buyers Wes had lined up to purchase Whiskey Chaser and the rest of the families' horses came by. There'd be no one here to sign any paperwork, so they could hardly just drive off with them, even if they had already forked over their money.

But that was Wes's problem.

She felt so much better now that she had a plan of

action. She was sick of waiting and praying for Wes to get in touch, being on edge to see what he would do or say next.

Nat insisted that he would drive, and that they'd be taking his truck. She didn't argue, knowing there would be no point.

He was waiting for her out there, now, checking the address she'd given him for the Wilkinson's on his GPS.

On her way out the door, Mattie paused for a final check over her shoulder. She didn't often leave her home unattended, but she knew she could count on Nat's men to watch over everything.

Snow pelted the exposed skin on her face as she dashed from her door to the passenger side of Nat's truck. Gratefully she jumped up to the heated seat and stared out the windshield to an almost complete white-out.

"Sure you don't want to wait this storm out?" Nat's hands were on the steering wheel as he turned to look at her.

"I've driven in worse." And she knew he had too. You couldn't live your entire life in Montana without driving in less than optimum conditions a lot.

But she did feel guilty for taking Nat away from his comfortable home. "I can handle this. Really. You don't need to drive me."

She didn't expect him to capitulate, and he didn't. He just eased the truck out of park and pushed through the snow drifts toward the main road. What was normally a seven hour drive was going to take a lot longer today.

But she didn't mind. Nat had his iPod hooked up so they could listen to tunes. And despite the raging storm outdoors, it was warm and cozy in his truck.

Surreptitiously Mattie studied the man beside her. Nat had a gorgeous profile, with his straight nose, firm jaw and chin and perfectly proportioned lips. Despite the dreadful conditions he seemed perfectly at ease behind the wheel.

She had to laugh at the incongruity of the situation. "Three months ago—if someone had told me you and I would be driving to Billings in a blizzard, I never would have believed it."

"Yeah. Life can turn on a dime. I've experienced it, myself."

Was he talking about his ex-wife? "Do you and Julia keep in touch?"

"She sends me an e-mail every now and then. It's usually about three pages long, telling me everywhere she's been and all the people she's met. She never did marry again. But she keeps looking."

"She's a beautiful woman." Mattie wasn't insecure about her own appearance, but being around Julia had always made her feel like plain, beige wallpaper.

"I once thought so."

"Not anymore?"

"Disillusion warps a guy's perspective. Not that I blame her for what went wrong between us. I was a fool to marry her. It was like I'd made a list of qualities I wanted in a wife, then went out and looked for someone who had none of them."

The rhythmic swish, swish, swish of the windshield wipers, blended with the sweet voice of Alison Kraus singing about not letting go, now that I've found you. Mattie leaned her head back and thought about what Nat had said.

"What were those qualities you wanted?

"Someone who could be happy with the simple things. That's a key one. Love animals. Nature. Not afraid of hard work, or getting her nails broken."

"I see those kinds of people every day."

"Me, too," Nat agreed. "One in particular is so beautiful, she puts Julia to shame."

Mattie felt a zap of pleasure, tinged with surprise... and sexual awareness. Was he talking about her? He smiled, but said nothing further. And she didn't dare open her mouth, either.

Neither one of them was compelled to fill every minute with chatter. Yet, about ten minutes later, it felt completely natural to Mattie to continue their conversation.

"I was so young when I met Wes. I never gave a thought to what qualities would make a good husband. My dad told me I should insist Wes give up the rodeo and focus full time on the ranch. I ignored him, but it was pretty good advice. Of course, I never dreamed that nineteen years later Wes would still be bulldogging for his living..."

Now she couldn't help wondering if the reason Wes had stuck with the rodeo for so long was because he hadn't been happy at home.

With her. The ranch. The girls.

Was it one of those things more than the other? Or all three that he'd tired of?

Mattie felt anger heating up in her midsection again. Wes could quit ranching. He could divorce her. But he couldn't opt out of being a father. It would kill her to see him hurt the girls that way.

But of course, they'd already been hurt.

And it might get worse...

At Missoula they stopped for coffee and sandwiches. The little local coffee shop had Wi-Fi, and seeing all the customers with their laptops and smartphones, made Mattie think of something.

Wes must have been paid a lot of money for those horses he'd sold.

Had he deposited the funds into their bank account?

"Nat, did you pack a laptop with you?"

"Need to check your e-mail?"

"Actually, I want to access my online banking. I'm wondering what Wes did with the money he got for our horses."

Nat's eyes narrowed. "Hang on. I've got an iPad in the truck."

Five minutes later, Mattie was logged in and able to see all of her and Wes's account balances, checking account, as well as savings. The balances were just what she'd expected.

"The money isn't here." She logged out, then handed Nat back his iPad.

"That isn't right. Half of that money belongs to you."

Suddenly not hungry, Mattie tossed the crust of her

tuna sandwich, then picked up her to-go coffee mug. Nat was ready, as well, and soon they were back on the road, listening to Blues Traveler Legend sing about mountains and not doing much talking. Mattie sensed Nat was just as angry as she was.

They needed gas and a bathroom break by Butte. All the while, the snow never gave up, not even for a minute, and Nat refused Mattie's offer to share in the driving.

"I'm not tired. Besides, I make a cranky backseat driver."

"Yeah, you and every other male over eighteen in the state of Montana," she muttered.

"What was that?"

She just smiled. Actually, she didn't mind being a passenger. She'd already had a few naps and the extra rest had helped clear away the fog from the previous night.

"I'm embarrassed about last night. Thanks for rescuing me. I can't believe I had so much to drink. I must have looked ridiculous."

"No. That's not the word I'd use."

She waited to see if he'd supply an alternate descriptor. But he didn't. She used a mitten to wipe away a patch of fog accumulating on her passenger side window. It didn't help. She still couldn't make out a thing, even though it was three in the afternoon. She figured they'd be in Billings by seven. Despite the poor conditions, Nat was making decent time.

"I don't know what came over me."

"So you let your hair down for a couple of hours. Don't beat yourself up about it. A few drinks. A little dancing. A lot of folks would call that a normal night on the town."

"Thank you."

"For what?"

"Making me feel better about myself. My life has been in such a deep rut I didn't even realize that stepping out of it now and then might actually be a good thing."

"That's the attitude."

"Of course, we're really out of the rut now, aren't we? I couldn't read that last sign. How many more miles to Bozeman?"

"Just hit city limits," Nat replied, easing off the gas and

letting the truck slow to the reduced speed limit. "We're good with gas. Want to stop for something to eat?"

"I stocked up on some trail mix and candies at that last gas station. Unless you want a break from driving?"

Frown lines creased Nat's forehead. Was he tired? If so, he didn't let on. "Let's push through."

Mattie shared her snacks with him, and forty minutes later they were approaching Livingston. She thought longingly of Sage's Chocolate Shop in nearby Marietta. But if she suggested a stop, she and Sage would start chatting and they'd lose precious daylight hours.

"We're less than an hour from The Circle C." She peered past Nat, out his window. The clouds had lifted a little and snow was falling in lazy flakes now instead of driving ice pellets. She could just make out the distant peak of Copper Mountain, one of Marietta's key landmarks.

In the other direction lay the road that cut through Paradise Valley. She imagined Callan and her father holed up in the house, impatiently waiting for the storm to break so they could go about their usual routine. It never ceased to amaze her that their youngest sister had chosen to stay at the Circle C with their father. How could she take being around all that negative energy on a full-time basis?

Mattie sometimes wondered if she would have married Wes so quickly if she'd had a happier home life.

"Want to stop in and visit? Stay the night, then carry on to Billings in the morning?" Nat suggested.

"No." She'd never sleep. Not when she was this close. Her palms were beginning to sweat as she imagined finally facing down Wes. He had a hell of a lot of explaining to do.

As the weather improved, they were able to make better time, and they pulled onto the access road that led to Peter and Marg's acreage at quarter to seven. Nat stopped his truck on a rise, from which vantage point they could see the Wilkinson's sprawling, ranch-style home, a huge detached garage, and what seemed to be a small guest cottage.

Two vehicles, a truck and a mid-sized SUV were parked outside of the Wilkinson's home. Neither one of them belonged to Wes.

"I wonder what they keep in the garage," Nat said.

"An RV. And a boat."

"Do they have any livestock?"

"Nope. They both work at Peter's family's lumberyard. Peter's a manager and Marg does the accounting. A long time ago Peter had a few horses, but when he quit the rodeo—probably ten years ago now—those were sold."

"Well. Should we go knock on the front door?"

"I'm not sure. At one time Wes said he was staying at their guest cottage. But I don't see his truck." She felt nervous, almost scared. But that wasn't her reason for hesitating. She didn't want the Wilkinson's warning Wes and giving him yet one more chance to avoid her.

"Let's just pull in on this side road and sit for bit." Nat had spied a small turn-off that once must have been used as access to a field. There were lots of trees on either side, that would block their truck from view of the lane and house while they pondered their next move.

Once the truck was tucked out of sight, Nat switched off the headlights.

"Wes might not be staying here anymore." Mattie tried to think through the possibilities. Having arrived in the early evening of a Monday, she'd fully expected to see Wes's truck here.

"Or maybe he sold his truck and bought one of those two vehicles we saw?"

"That could be." After all, he'd changed out his phone.

"Whatever the answer is, we have to go talk to these people," Nat said. "We don't have any other leads."

She was about to agree with his plan, when lights flashed on the road in front of them, a few seconds later, Wes's truck bumped past them on the gravel road.

"That was him, right?" Nat checked with her for confirmation.

"Looked like his truck," Mattie agreed. But there'd been two people in the cab, not just one.

"Drive up behind him, Nat." Even as she said the

143

words, Nat was putting his truck back into gear. Slowly he turned onto the lane and followed the other vehicle as it coasted past the main house, then stopped by the smaller one.

Mattie felt her throat tighten and her stomach clench as her husband got out from the driver's seat. Their headlights shone straight into his face when he tried to look at them. He brought his arm up to try and shield the light.

And then, from the other side of the cab, a woman descended, a bag of groceries in one hand, her purse in the other. She turned to stare at their truck, eyes squinting into the lights, and giving them a full look at her. She was tall, pretty, with long, wavy dark hair.

And kind of familiar looking.

Five seconds later Mattie realized why. This was Dex Cooper's widow.

CHAPTER TWELVE

"Talk to me, Mattie." Nat had been afraid another woman might be in the picture. He'd debated trying to prepare Mattie for the possibility. But he hadn't had the heart.

She was staring out the windshield, as still as if she'd been turned to ice. Her breathing so quiet, she might not be doing any.

He put a hand on her shoulder. And squeezed. "Are you okay?"

With a whoosh of air, she exhaled. And turned to him. "That woman? She's Dex Cooper's wife. He was a bull rider, killed on the circuit in Texas last spring. I met him and his wife a few times. He and Wes were friends..."

Her mind turned over the fact that her husband now seemed to be pretty good friends with Dex's widow. In fact, it looked like they were shacked up here together, if the one vehicle and those groceries were anything to go by.

A tap at the driver's side window interrupted her thoughts.

Nat unrolled the window and Wes stooped so he could see inside.

"Nat Diamond?—" He leaned a little further so he could see the passenger side. "Jesus—Mattie? What the hell is going on here?"

"Your wife wanted a few words, so I offered to drive her out here." Nat's voice was calm, but not friendly. Not even close to friendly. "Step back, Wes, so I can open my door."

Mattie got out of the truck, too. Her legs shook a little as she walked around to the front. Dex's wife—she wished she could remember her name—was watching her, but didn't move any closer.

"Are you crazy, driving in this weather?" Wes had removed his hat. Now he was combing through his dark hair with his free hand, as if there was an itch somewhere that he couldn't calm. He looked good. He was wearing a new sheepskin jacket that fit him well. And his hair looked like it had finally been cut by someone who knew what they were doing.

She knew he wouldn't be noticing any improvements in *her* appearance.

"If I'm crazy, it's because of you," Mattie said. "All I want is a little honesty, Wes. After nineteen years you'd think I deserved that much, at least." Her gaze drifted to the other woman and a name suddenly popped into her head. Suzanne.

"Hey, Suzanne." Mattie changed course, moved away from the men and headed for the woman. Suzanne was wearing fashion boots and skinny jeans, and a double breasted black jacket with a coordinating scarf looped around her neck. "Have to admit—I didn't expect to see you here."

"Hi Mattie." As soon as she spoke, Mattie recognized her voice. Suzanne glanced from Mattie, to Wes, then to her bag of groceries. "I should get these in the fridge."

She all but turned and ran inside, at which point Nat said, "So Wes. Going to invite us in?"

Wes glowered and Mattie half expected him to tell them to hit the road.

If he had, she didn't know what she would have done. Maybe started beating his chest with her fists?

But then Wes capitulated and led the way to the front

door. Inside was a cozy kitchen and sitting area. Two doors on the far wall were open just enough for Mattie to see a bedroom and a bathroom. "Isn't this sweet," she said.

Suzanne pushed the entire bag of groceries into the half-sized fridge, then ran to the bedroom, without a word to anyone.

The sound of the slamming door reverberated for several seconds.

All three of them were left standing in the kitchen. Wes's arms were folded over his chest, while Nat glared down at him, taking advantage of his extra four inches of height.

"So how long, Wes?" Mattie could hear the anger vibrating in each of her calmly spoken words. Never in her life had she felt this furious. She wanted to hurl her fists at Wes's chest, then shriek at Suzanne and kick her out of the house.

"What?" Wes went to the fridge and pulled out three beers. He set two on the table, some sort of invitation, Mattie supposed, though he didn't say anything. He twisted off the cap of the third and took a long drink.

"How long have you and Suzanne been... together?"

"Does it really matter?"

"We're still married. We haven't even been legally separated. So, yes. It matters."

"Okay, so if I say, like, forty-two days that's going to make you feel better than if I say fifty-nine?"

"Stop it." Nat brought a hand up to his face, in a gesture that betrayed how tired he was feeling. "Mattie's had a long day. Do you suppose you could cut the bullshit Wes and be straight with her?"

"What the hell are you doing here, anyway?" Wes's voice was contemptuous. "You always were a little quick to step in and be the hero when I was out of town."

"You're not just out of town now, though, are you?" No mistaking the anger in Nat's tone. "You've moved out on Mattie. You're having an affair with another woman. And you're selling communal property without a word of consultation. So don't blame me for being Mattie's friend."

"Friend. Is that all?"

Both men looked on the verge of throwing punches, so Mattie had no choice but to move between them. "Nat, would you wait for me in the truck, please. This won't take long."

"You sure?"

She nodded.

"I hear any trouble. I'm coming back in."

"Okay." She waited until he'd left and closed the door before she turned to face Wes. She didn't say anything, just studied his eyes, tried to see in them and past them, to his very heart and soul. It was something she'd been longing to do for a very long time. Hearing his voice on the phone wasn't enough. It didn't feel real. This did, though.

Almost nine hours of driving and over four hundred miles and she still had no idea *why* this man who had promised to love her "until death did them part" wanted a divorce. But she could see that he *did*. There was absolutely no love, no caring in Wes toward her anymore.

"Tell me when it started. Was it before Dex died?"

"Of course not. Dex was my friend." He was standing with his back against the wall, arms still shielding his chest, the bottle of beer held tight, like it was a charm with protective powers. If he wanted to talk this way—standing up—Mattie didn't mind. She'd spent most of the day sitting in the cab. It was good to stretch her legs...

Even if she did feel a little weak... she masked the trembling in her legs by grabbing onto the back of a chair.

"Are you telling me your friendship with Dex meant something. And your marriage to me, didn't?"

"You're twisting my words. I never meant to cheat on you Mattie. This just—happened. You knew Dex named me executor of his estate."

She'd forgotten, but yes, he had mentioned the fact.

"Which meant Suzanne and I had to spend some time together. I felt sorry for her. She was pregnant when Dex died. And she lost her baby the next week."

Mattie looked at the closed bedroom door. She knew she ought to feel sorry for the woman in the other room, but she couldn't. Instead, she was picturing the distraught widow, phoning up *Mattie's* husband and crying on his

148

shoulder.

And yes, Mattie could see how it had happened, how Suzanne's vulnerability and need had bolstered Wes's yearning to feel strong and manly. He'd stepped in to help—maybe with good intentions at the start—only to get more and more entangled.

"You think she needs you more than we do. But that isn't true."

"Actually, it is. Mattie—you've never needed me. You've always been the strong one in our family. And the girls are gone, living their own lives."

"They still love you. And miss you."

"And I love them too. If I haven't been in touch lately, it's only because I'm not sure how to explain this to them."

Mattie stared down at her fingers, turning white as she squeezed the chair so hard she thought the pine might snap. "What happened to the money you got from selling our horses? Why didn't you deposit it into our bank?"

"What—you think I'm trying to cheat you? I deposited the funds into an investment account. It was too much money to sit around without earning interest. Don't worry, when the time comes to divide our assets, you'll get your share."

Oh, he sounded so cool and calm about all this. Speaking about the dissolution of their marriage as if it were as simple as a tallying and dividing of assets and liabilities. "You should have talked to me before you arranged that sale."

"It's not like I had a choice. We have to sell. Everything. That's the only way we can get enough money so we can both have a fresh start. I'm too old and tired to work the rodeo anymore. You know it was showing in my scores the past few years. But I don't want to run the ranch, either. It's too much work, twenty-four hours a day, seven days a week, never getting a break, always worried about something or other."

"But that's been our life."

"And I'm tired of it. I like working at the lumberyard. I put in my eight-hours, work hard and earn good money, then come home and I can relax. I get my weekends off.

Once the ranch is sold, I'll have enough money to buy a nice house. Travel, like regular people get to do."

The life he was describing was not what she wanted. Why had she never seen this side of him before? "What if we sold the land, but kept the house? It isn't just another asset to me, or to Portia and Wren. It's our *home*."

"But it's also on the property I want to sell. And why would you want to live so far from town if you weren't ranching anymore? Believe me, I've thought about this a lot, and selling is the only option."

"I want to talk to my lawyer, first."

"Fine." Wes sighed. "But I promise you he's going to tell you the exact same thing." He took another long drink of his beer, then set the empty bottle on the kitchen table. He glanced at the closed bedroom door, then back at her. "Anything else?"

The words stung. His desire to get rid of her was so obvious, and nothing more than that made the end of her marriage feel real. She'd come here hoping for answers, but they were a lot harsher than she'd anticipated.

He was in love with someone else.

He had absolutely no feelings left for her, anymore.

So now it all boiled down to accounting. What was his and what was hers. Divide it up and move along to the next phase of your life.

And what would that look like?

She had no clue.

"If you haven't already, please give the girls a call. Let them know that you love them. They need to hear that right now."

Wes didn't answer, but he nodded. She waited to see if he would ask any questions of her. Was she okay? What were her plans?

But he remained quiet. No doubt anxious for her to leave.

She went to open the door. Paused, and glanced back at him.

"Goodbye, Mattie."

That was it.

She didn't respond. Once she'd hoped to grow old with

this man. Together they would watch their daughters grow up, maybe get married and have children of their own. Now those dreams were officially dead.

Waiting in the truck was one of the hardest things Nat had ever done. More than anything he longed to drag Wes outside and give him a good pounding. The guy was a damned jerk. A total idiot. Did he really think that lightweight Suzanne was any sort of replacement for Mattie? Even if he did—was it necessary to end his marriage in the most hurtful way possible?

Across the yard, lights glowed from several windows in the big ranch house. Had the people inside noticed Wes had guests? Or were they making a point of ignoring the happenings in their guest cottage?

Nat shifted in his seat, considered getting out to stretch. All these hours of driving had been hell on his body. He'd already popped his limit of pain pills for the day. No doubt he'd be limping later tonight.

He tensed as Mattie came out of the cabin with a shell-shocked expression on her face. Nat wanted to wrap his arms around her. But since he couldn't do that—he'd come up with an alternate plan.

"I don't want to talk about what just happened," were Mattie's first words when she'd climbed back into the truck.

"Okay." He'd expected as much. What she needed was time to decompress. And he'd already taken steps to help the process. "I've made reservations for two rooms at the Northern Hotel in downtown Billings."

She looked at him, surprised.

"It's too late and too far to drive home tonight."

"That's true. I'm sorry. I didn't think this through."

"Fortunately they have lots of room at the hotel. I think you'll like it. It's right downtown, a renovated historic building, named after the Pacific Northern Railway."

"That does sound nice," she murmured.

He lost no time pulling out of that place and heading back to the highway. GPS told him the hotel was fifteen minutes away. He used that time to chat about the history of Billings, how it had begun as a rail hub with the first train arriving in August of 1882. Montana history had always interested him. At home he had a library of about fifty books—and most of them he'd read cover to cover.

At the hotel, he handed over the keys to his truck, then went to the front desk. When Mattie pulled her wallet out of her purse, he told her no.

"We'll settle up later." He said that so she wouldn't argue. But he had no intention of letting her pay for anything tonight. After what she'd just been through, she deserved a treat. And he was determined to give it to her.

Once they had their key cards in hand he suggested she go up for a shower then meet him in the restaurant, called TEN, in the lobby. "Food is supposed to be great, and we deserve a decent meal."

She nodded, still looking a little numb.

"You okay to meet in thirty minutes? I asked the desk clerk to make us a reservation for eight-thirty." He didn't intend to give Mattie enough time to fall apart. She could do that later, if she wanted. First she needed some TLC, Nat Diamond style.

M attie wished she'd packed something pretty to wear, but the best she could do was to put on clean underwear and a fresh sweater after her shower.

The multiple shower heads in the step-in marble stall had been fabulous. Nat must have booked her the most expensive room in the place. She had a sitting area and huge king-sized bed. The bathroom was like a gorgeous spa, with lots of complimentary bottles of lotion and soaps, as well as a plush white robe and matching slippers.

She almost wished they'd decided to order in, but given the circumstances—she was still legally married and Nat was just her neighbor—going to the restaurant was probably wise.

As she rushed to get ready in thirty minutes, she made

a conscious effort not to think about the scene with Wes. Wounds had been inflicted that were going to hurt like hell when the shock wore off.

And she wanted to be at home when that happened. On familiar ground. And not with the man who'd already done so much to help her and didn't deserve to witness her falling apart. Again.

The restaurant was beautiful, all modern with clean lines, beautiful red velvet chairs pulled up to round tables sets with crisp, white linens. Nat stood when he saw her, even pulled out a chair for her.

"Feel better? You sure look good."

"Thanks. That shower was awesome." She noticed the bottle of sparkling mineral water already on the table. "That's perfect for me, but if you want something stronger, please go ahead. It's been a hell of a day."

"That it has, but since we'll be driving home tomorrow, it's probably a good idea for me to keep a clear head."

He touched his water glass to hers, then gave her a smile. As their eyes met, she felt a zing of excitement and pleasure, which was truly the last thing she ought to be feeling right now. Quickly she lowered her gaze.

"Mattie, there's something I need to say. Just to be clear. This hotel, and dinner... well, I don't want you to get the wrong idea."

"You mean you're not hitting on me?" she asked wryly.

His answering smile was quick and relieved. "I don't deny there was a time when I might have done exactly that."

Another pulsing of pleasure. She couldn't deny what it was this time. Desire, plain and simple. Followed by a dashing of hopes. What did he mean when he said *there was a time?* When had that time been? And what had changed?

She shouldn't be having these thoughts. She knew it.

But she'd just found out her husband had left her so he could console a pretty, young widow. And what woman on earth wouldn't want Nat Diamond? The understated lighting made him look even more attractive than usual. With his incredible bone structure, plus his attitude of confidence and ease, he pretty much owned the room.

But what made him even more attractive were the qualities that couldn't be seen. His kindness and generosity. His love of the land and animals—and of history and Montana. They shared the same passions in life, and to Mattie, that was the biggest turn-on of all.

Yet, here he was, trying to make sure she didn't misread his intentions.

With perfect timing the server came and handed them menus. Nat ordered slow braised bison short ribs.

"Sounds good. I'll have the same." She passed back the menu, then glanced around the room. Although it was a Monday evening, at least half the tables were occupied. She took a deep breath and could feel her body relaxing on a cellular level.

"This is nice. I haven't been in a restaurant this fancy in a really long time."

"Good. Relax and enjoy it." Nat gave her a lazy smile. "You class up the joint, if I may say so."

She raised her eyebrows. "Even in my jeans and old sweater?"

"Even so."

She thanked him with a smile. She appreciated hearing that *some* men still found her attractive... though she hadn't meant to think about the encounter with Wes, a mental image of Suzanne popped into her head. Dex Cooper's widow was cute, and probably only just thirty, if that. Had she *tried* to steal Mattie's husband away from her?

Or had it *just happened*—Wes's words?

She'd never know, for sure. But seeing her husband with this other woman hadn't cut her as deeply as she'd thought it would.

When she probed her emotions to understand why this was so, she realized that the love she'd felt for Wes had been hurt so badly these past few months that it was close to dying. The way he'd treated her tonight had been the last straw.

She was done. Ready to accept that her marriage was over. And the future—whatever it might hold—was suddenly looking a lot less bleak.

"I know we agreed not to talk about it..." she leaned closer to Nat. "But I'm surprised I'm feeling okay right now. Seeing Wes with Suzanne. Two months ago it would have killed me."

"Two months ago it almost did." Nat reminded her. "Thankfully a shipment of tea and tissues arrived in time to revive you."

She grimaced, feeling rueful. "Were you afraid I'd go to pieces on you tonight?"

"Afraid is the wrong word. I can take it, Mattie. But I hate seeing you suffer. Mainly because you're a good person, and you were a good wife. I know you can't judge a marriage from the outside. But I saw enough to know that if anyone wasn't giving a hundred and ten percent in your relationship, it sure as hell wasn't you."

"Thank you for saying that." Despite the fact that it was Wes who had left, Wes who'd refused counseling, and Wes who'd cheated, she still found herself probing her feelings and the past, trying to find the ways that she'd let him down, or not been there for him.

Happy husbands didn't go looking for trouble.

But then, maybe asking a wife to be responsible for her husband's happiness was asking too much. A lot of the factors that had strained her relationship with Wes had been out of her control.

"I'm done with falling apart, Nat. The last few months have been brutal. And I don't want to feel that way, anymore. Subconsciously I must have known Wes was having an affair. Because seeing them together didn't devastate me. Once it would have. But he's been such a jerk these past six months..."

"I'm glad to hear that. And I can relate. When Julia finally packed her stuff and left the Double D, I was mostly just relieved."

"Exactly." Mattie relaxed back into her chair as the server brought their meals. The bison melted in her mouth and the roasted vegetables were packed with flavor. She ate every bite, even though there was more food here than she needed.

"Save room for dessert. I was hoping you'd share the chocolate soufflé with me. I ordered it when I first sat down."

"Seriously?" She laughed. "I may explode, but I will definitely join you for that."

"So I made a good choice?" His smile was indulgent, and it felt nice, knowing that he'd been trying to pick something she would like.

She couldn't remember the last time Wes had seemed to care about making her happy.

But no. She shouldn't entertain such bitter thoughts. Especially not tonight, when Nat had gone to so much trouble to plan a nice evening for her.

"I've only had chocolate soufflé once," she confessed. "We were in Marietta for the rodeo and my sister Sage was experimenting in the kitchen."

"She's the one who owns the chocolate shop?"

Mattie nodded. "Before then. Even when she was a barrel-racer, Sage loved baking anything that had cocoa in it."

"Sounds like a good sister to have."

"I love all my sisters, but I do have a sweet spot for Sage."

He groaned at the double entendre, which she appreciated because it proved he was really paying attention to their conversation.

The soufflé was served then, along with a pot of Earl Gray tea. The first mouthful was so divine, neither one of them spoke until both of their servings were gone. Mattie warmed up their teacups, emptying what was left in the pot.

"Was that as good as your sister's?"

Mattie had to admit that it was. "But don't tell Sage."

"I doubt if I'll have the opportunity in the near future. Mind you, Sage is the only one of your sisters I've met. Red hair, right? Kind of quiet."

When Mattie nodded, he continued, "What about the others? Portia was talking about Dani, your sister in Seattle. She seems to be rather in awe of her. A professor of psychology?"

"Yes. She's the brain of the family. The most sophisticated and definitely best dressed. She's never come to visit me at Bishop Stables—usually we meet up at The Circle C during the fall rodeo. A few times I've taken the girls to Seattle for sight-seeing and shopping. She's a great hostess."

But now that the topic had been raised, Mattie wondered why it was that never once, in nineteen years, had Dani ever come to Bishop Stables. She made a mental note to ask next time they were chatting. In fact, calls to both Dani and Callan were overdue. The situation with Wes was not going to be resolved and she wanted everyone in her family to hear the news first from her.

Except her dad. She'd let Callan tell him. She was pretty sure her dad would find a way to blame her. She just didn't need to go through that.

"And your youngest sister—Callan—how does she like working at The Circle C with your father?"

"I honest don't know how she copes. He is so ill tempered—one of those old-timers who is pretty much impossible to please. I used to avoid him as a kid—he was always taking me to task for one mistake or another. Full marks to Callan for putting up with him. She only does it because she loves the ranch so much..."

Mattie could relate. She loved Bishop Stables the same way. "Tell me, Nat." She leaned forward, conspiratorially. "Are you considering buying the ranch from Wes? I know he's asked you about it."

Nat leaned back in his chair. For the first time that evening he seemed uncomfortable.

"I'm sorry. It's none of my business."

"Actually, it is, Mattie. Your name may not be on the land title, but that place has been your home for almost twenty years. And the truth is, I'm torn. I don't like the idea of strangers moving in right next to me. On the other hand, I was thinking of scaling down my operation. Not expanding."

She was shocked to hear him say that. "Scaling down? Why?" Like her, Nat was doing the work he'd been born to do. Living in the one place in the world where he most belonged.

"I'm not getting any younger. And I don't have kids coming up behind me, the way I did with my father."

"Not getting any younger. Don't be ridiculous, Nat. You're not even middle-aged."

"By most people's standards, I most definitely am. I'm forty-nine, Mattie. Next year I'll be fifty."

The number took her by surprise. She'd always considered Nat a contemporary. But then, at this stage in life a ten year age-gap wasn't that much. "You don't *look* middle-aged."

"Thank you." The corners of his eyes crinkled as he smiled though, belying her compliment. "I sure feel it sometimes though."

She knew what he meant. She'd heard Wes complain often enough about how much it hurt to get out of bed in the morning. Of course Wes's body had taken plenty of hard knocks in the rodeo ring. But years of working with cattle took a similar toll on the body.

"Did you and Julia ever talk about having kids?"

"We did more than talk."

Mattie laughed.

"But—wasn't meant to be. Sometimes I think that was a good thing. Would have been hard on kids after we'd broken up, especially since Julia moved around so much." He finished his tea, and set the cup back on the table. "Other times I wonder if kids maybe could have saved our relationship. Who knows. I suppose it's possible."

Is that what he wished, Mattie wondered. Perhaps a lingering love for Julia was the real reason Nat had never remarried.

CHAPTER THIRTEEN

Nat was a perfect gentlemen when he said good night—something Mattie found herself slightly regretting, as she closed the door to her luxurious suite. If she'd been a different sort of person, she might have invited him in for a drink. Maybe they could have watched a movie together.

It would be better than being alone.

She'd never had a hotel room to herself before, let alone an entire suite. If she were in a happier frame of mind, she would have taken photographs of the gorgeous tub and luxurious bedding and texted them to her daughters.

But what words would she use to accompany the pictures?

"Hi girls, just found out your dad has a new woman in his life. Nat Diamond and I are staying... here!"

Oh, no, that did not seem like a good idea at all.

Mattie ran water into the tub, pouring in half of one little shower gel bottle to make some bubbles. She ran the water in the sink until it was cold, then filled up one of the water glasses provided. No sense drinking bottled water, when the real stuff here was as good as it got.

Next she turned on the TV. Not because she wanted to watch a show, but so she didn't feel lonely. Like some televised voices and laugh tracks were going to change that. Then she stripped out of her clothes and sank her weary body into the hot, perfumed water.

Heavenly.

She never took the time for leisurely soaks in the bathtub at home.

So why was she crying?

She could feel moisture running down her cheeks and knew it wasn't humidity from the bath. Just a few hours ago she'd been bragging to Nat about how good she was feeling. She'd said seeing Wes with that young beauty hadn't been that hard.

But it wasn't true.

It *had* hurt. A lot.

She just hadn't let the betrayal sink into the deepest part of her heart. But now she had time to recall all the little things she'd noticed in that cabin.

The rumpled blanket on the sofa, reminding her of how she and Wes used to cuddle up together to watch movies. The two dirty coffee mugs and cereal bowls sitting by the sink, testament to a breakfast eaten together. Oddly enough, though, it had been the sets of boots by the door that had stung the most. His and hers.

His. But not hers, anymore. *Suzanne's.*

Mattie cried.

And cried. And cried.

Despite the mattress that felt like a cloud, and linens softer than summer breezes, Mattie hardly slept. She tried to watch movies, but her eyes stung, and she just couldn't concentrate.

She switched on some music next, but almost every song seemed to come with a painful memory or haunting emotion attached.

When morning finally arrived and Nat tapped at her

door—the prearranged signal—she was already dressed and ready to go.

Nat only needed one glance. "Tough night?"

She nodded, bending to get her duffel, hiding her face so he couldn't get a closer look. She knew she looked rough. She almost didn't care.

"You should have called."

"I came close," she admitted, giving up on the duffel bag, because new tears were forming in her eyes and her vision had blurred.

"Oh, Mattie." He dropped his own bag and pulled her close for a hug.

They'd shared polite semi-hugs and cheek-kisses before, but this was the first time he'd ever folded his body around hers, offering comfort, warmth, and strength. He was such a large man, and his hug made her feel like she'd been spirited away to a safe spot where no one, and nothing, could ever hurt her again.

She pressed her cheek against the soft sheepskin of his jacket, which smelled of freshly chopped pine and timothy hay. She felt his hand on the top of her head. Gently he stroked her hair, still holding her like something precious. Closing her eyes, she let the good feeling seep into her pores.

And finally took a deep breath, then looked up with a smile. "Damn, but you give good hugs, Nat."

He carried both bags down to the truck, then they went to get coffee and breakfast bagels to eat on the road. The sky was clear today, an icy blue, with a freezing wind chill to match. Mattie was thankful Nat had thoughtfully warmed the engine, so her seat wasn't a block of ice when she sat on it.

"Sure you're okay to drive?" She'd noticed Nat limping a little this morning. The long trip must have been harder on him than it had been on her.

"Yup. Sit back and enjoy the ride."

In the bright light of a new day, Mattie felt much better. But after just an hour on the road, her eyes felt heavy. Her lack of sleep was catching up to her and even the caffeine in her coffee wasn't enough to perk her up. She struggled to keep awake, to make small talk with Nat. It wasn't fair of her to sleep when he was doing all the driving.

"I wonder how much snow we got at home?"

"I talked to Seth last night. He said about two inches. Don't worry, though, I asked him to have our men plow your lane and yard after they finish at the Double D. Should be all clear by the time we get home."

"Thanks Nat. I'll be glad to pay you—"

"Come on now, Mattie. You know better than that."

She let her head relax against the side window. Her eyes drifted closed and she let them stay that way for a few seconds, before prying them open again. To the north, a flock of geese in V-formation were flying toward the low winter sun. "Those poor geese. I guess they must have had enough of this weather."

"They aren't the only ones. If the past few weeks are any indication, we're in for a long, cold winter." Nat turned to glance at her, catching her just as she was stirring herself awake, again. "Go ahead and sleep. I know you had a rough night."

"But—"

"No buts. I have satellite radio to keep me company." He pressed a button on the audio display, selecting a station that played classic rock.

The songs were perfect. Upbeat, but not so raucous that she couldn't sleep.

In the end, Mattie didn't think heavy metal could have kept her awake. She dozed most of the way home, feeling warm and safe in the truck as they covered the long miles between Billings and home. Thanks to their early start, they arrived back at Bishop Stables an hour before dinner time.

Mattie's mood took a upward turn when she spied the familiar outline of their blue metal roof through the grove of dark green pine trees. But then she remembered her home might not belong to her much longer—and depression swamped her.

Nat rolled his truck up next to the side door. He put the gearshift into park, then gave her a rueful smile. "I wish we'd had a better outcome to our trip."

"At least I know the truth now." She hoped the answering smile she gave him was brave. He must be so tired of propping her up. The urge the invite him in for dinner was strong. But he'd be wanting to get back to his place.

Tuff wiggled in her lap, sensing they were home, and anxious to be free. She was glad Nat had thoughtfully stopped by the Double D first, to pick up the excited little puppy. Tuff would make her homecoming a lot easier.

She dug out her house keys, then opened the truck door. A blast of cold north wind sucked the air from her lungs. Quickly she turned her back to it, protecting Tuff like she was a baby, pressing the warm puppy up to her chest. Nat came around the hood side of the truck with her duffel bag in tow.

As he'd promised, her driveway was plowed. The walkway to the house had been shoveled too, all the way to the covered stoop over the door leading to the mudroom. She unlocked it, then stepped inside, letting Tuff free, then making room for Nat to join her.

"I can't thank you enough for all you've done."

"You need anything," he said, his voice suddenly gruff. "Tea, tissues...a friend to talk to. You call. Don't think it's imposing. It won't ever be that."

"Okay."

"Good."

She looked into his honest and caring face. From her tiptoes she reached up to kiss his cheek, balancing herself with one hand on his arm. Instinctively Nat's arms moved around her, holding her steady. For a moment it seemed he would kiss her back. But he ended the contact and stepped to the door. After a final nod, he was gone.

Mattie played with Tuff for about half an hour before finally tackling the red blinking light on her phone. There were two messages, both related to the sale of her horses.

The cowboy coming to get Whiskey Chaser said he'd be

by tomorrow, assuming the weather had warmed up by then. The other call was from Jon Claypool, the guy Wes had said had a nice family outfit near Ronan. He was also delaying the pickup of his new horses until tomorrow. "Warm front's supposed to come in tonight," Jon drawled. "Won't be so hard on the horses if we send someone to get them then."

She knew the horses had to go.

But this final confirmation hit her hard.

She dressed in her warmest work clothes, wrapped Tuff in an old blanket, then headed out to the barn. Hermione was happy to have her playmate back and immediately lunged at Tuff, who retaliated by assuming the border collie pounce stance, front legs down with her butt up in the air, and barking excitedly.

Mattie turned the radio on low, then went out to call her horses. They were all happy enough to come indoors, especially when she offered them an extra ration of oats. Horses burned a lot of extra calories in weather like this.

She spent hours that evening, grooming each horse in turn, talking to them tenderly as she worked, saying her own private goodbyes to each of them.

She saved Princess Bride, Madam Curie, and Copper to the end. These weren't just horses. They were family members. With all her heart she wished there was some way out of selling them tomorrow. If only she had access to the money Wes had earned from the earlier sale. Maybe the Ellingtons would let her buy them back.

It was scary to realize that while she had legal entitlement to a fair share of what she and Wes had accumulated during their marriage, she didn't even have enough money to buy three horses. Though what she would do with them if Wes found a buyer for the ranch was another problem to ponder.

By the time she'd finished up in the barn, it was almost nine o'clock. Mattie showered, then made herself some toast slathered in peanut butter for dinner. She sent text messages to her daughters, asking how they were doing, then while she waited for their replies, she called her sister Dani.

They chatted for a while about Dani—her life and her job. She had a few things to say about Portia, how she seemed to be putting too much emphasis on the social scene and not enough on studies.

"She's always been a social butterfly," Mattie said. "As long as she isn't neglecting her classes too much...?"

"She's achieving average grades. But she's capable of much better."

Mattie had heard these comments from most of Portia's teachers over the years. But she'd learned that you couldn't push Portia too hard, or she'd simply give up and stop trying altogether. In high school Mattie had encouraged Portia to raise her grades so she could have options for college, but Wes had told her to lighten up, that the ability to get along with people was pretty important in life, and not everyone was meant to be a scholar.

So Mattie had backed off. But she'd worried. And it had turned out to be unnecessary because Portia seemed to have the knack of knowing just how hard to work to get what she wanted—without expending an iota of extra effort.

"Have you see Portia this week?"

"Not since the Thanksgiving break. In fact yesterday was the first time she skipped out on my psych class. I suppose she was making up for lost time with her friends."

"Maybe." Mattie sighed. She supposed she just needed to blurt out the news. "Or maybe she's still upset from the news I told her when she was home. Wes and I have split up."

There was a long silence. Then Dani, who usually spoke in a logical, no-nonsense tone, said very gently. "I'm sorry, Mattie. When Wes didn't come for the rodeo this fall, I was worried there might be problems."

"I thought it was just a rough patch. But it's a lot more." Mattie stared into the fireplace wishing she'd thought to start a log burning earlier. It felt so cold in here. Outside, the wind was blowing hard, causing the house the creak and moan. Hopefully blowing better weather in for tomorrow.

"Did it have something to do with his buddy getting

killed last spring?"

"Yes. More than I thought. I figured the accident would make him re-evaluate his career. At least I hoped it would. But what I didn't count on was the fact that Dex Cooper had named Wes executor of his will—which seemed to require that Wes spend a lot of time with Dex's wife, Suzanne."

"Oh, hell. Don't tell me Wes and Suzanne...?"

"Yup. My neighbor, Nat, just helped me track them down. They're living together in a guest cabin on a friends' property up by Billings."

"She sure moved on fast."

"According to Wes, she was pregnant when Dex died. She lost the baby soon after."

"Oh my God. This just gets worse and worse, doesn't it?"

"Hang on. You haven't heard it all, yet. Wes is looking for a buyer for the house and the land. And he's already sold all our horses. The last of them are getting picked up tomorrow."

"Oh, honey, I'm so sorry. I never did take to horses like the rest of you, but I know you love them almost as much as your kids."

Mattie was surprised by how compassionate and sympathetic Dani was being. She was about to thank her for her support, when Dani's logical side suddenly kicked in.

"I hope you've got yourself a good lawyer?"

"I-I'm working on that. First thing tomorrow." She'd phone Nat. Surely he could recommend someone.

"Good. You've got to protect your rights. Once you've done that, you should think about coming here for visit. Or head to Marietta and stay with Sage for a bit. She's spending so much time with that hunky cowboy of hers, that you'd have lots of privacy."

"I'll think about it, Dani." She hesitated, wondering if Sage had ever told her about their mother having an affair—and how their dad had known about it all along. But, even if Dani did know, that situation was totally different from the one she and Wes were in that there was no point in bringing it up.

Even so, she thought it was telling that Dani didn't once suggest that she and Wes try to work things out. "Nineteen years ago," she said softly, "I never would have guessed we'd end up this way."

"I wish I could claim to be equally surprised."

"You never did warm up to Wes, did you?"

"Wes is one of those cowboys whose eyes light up when he's in the company of a beautiful woman. I wanted my sister to be with a man whose eyes lit up only for her."

Portia read the text message from her Mom and responded quickly with, "I'm good. You?" She was in a funky coffee shop, miles from campus, with Kirsten, Jared, and Noah. It turned out that neither Noah nor Jared was enrolled in the university. They were struggling artists who worked at Twisted Perceptions, a cooperative coffee and art shop where a collective of workers alternated between working in the kitchen, behind the counter, and cleaning tables. The rest of the time they were free to create their art in the open gallery on the second floor.

All the walls, almost every square inch of them, were covered in works from the various artists. Right now Portia was studying one of Noah's. It was a mixed media effort. She couldn't think of anything intelligent to say about it. So she just sort of went, "Wow," every now and then.

Noah seemed happy with that.

She'd been hanging out here for two days now. Tomorrow she'd definitely have to start going to her classes again. But she liked being at Twisted Perceptions, where there was always action and music, new people coming in, and all the free coffee she could drink, thanks to Noah.

In the evenings, a few tables were pushed together to make room for live musicians, who played for free, just for the practice and exposure. Then she and Noah would dance, sneaking out back every now and then for the beer that they were both officially too young to drink.

They made out some, too. Portia had made it clear that

she was only willing to go so far—and Noah seemed, if not happy, at least resigned.

She wasn't sure how much longer that would last, which was a worry, because she didn't think she could come here on her own. It was such a cool place, it made Portia wish she had some sort of artistic talent. Though, she *did* think she could paint as well as most of the artists who hung out here.

"I'm getting the evil eye again," Noah said, getting up from his chair. "I've got to go load up the dishwasher and stuff."

"Me, too." Jared, who'd had his arm around Kirsten, while they whispered and laughed in the corner, pushed back his chair, the legs scraping obnoxiously on the wooden floor. "I'll be back in a bit. You'll still be here?"

"We will," Kirsten promised. She kept her eyes on the guys until they'd disappeared behind the curtain that closed off the kitchen from the rest of the café, then turned to Portia and gave her a big smile. "Aren't they yummy? *Soooo* cute."

Portia nodded. Jared reminded her of the guy who played Arrow on TV. He had short brown hair, nice features, and a muscle-builder's body. Both guys went to the gym almost every day. Plus they were obsessed about these green smoothies that tasted to Portia like blended grass.

"My Mom would kill me if she knew I cut classes two days in a row." Kirsten's eyes were bright as she leaned forward conspiratorially.

"Is that a good thing?"

"It feels good to me. I don't know what your life was like before college, but for me every hour was filled with school, or activities, or tutoring. I had to account for where I was every minute of the day. To go from that, to this—perfect freedom—is just amazing."

"It is." She and her sister hadn't had crazy schedules, but their mother had been the kind who always wanted to know where they were. *Her* mother wouldn't be angry if she could see her now. She'd be disappointed.

Portia glanced around the room, seeking some sort of

distraction. The reason she was here was to forget about her family problems. And being reminded of her mom didn't help. "I'm going upstairs to see how that girl is coming along with her picture of that turtle." One of the artists was working on a life-sized water color of a sea turtle she'd seen on a vacation to Maui. It was Portia's favorite and she could hardly wait for it to be completed.

"I'll let you know if the guys get a break," Kirsten said, staying in her seat.

Portia took the stairs slowly, her exhaustion catching up to her. She hadn't slept well at home and even worse since she'd arrived back in Seattle. It seemed that no matter how late she stayed out at night, she still couldn't fall asleep once she went to bed. Last night she'd made the mistake of phoning her sister around two in the morning.

"Wren? I can't sleep."

"What are you doing calling me at this hour? I have to get up for class in four hours."

"Oh, God. Are you still going to classes? How can you concentrate?"

"My classes are the only thing keeping me sane right now." Her sister had paused, then asked, "Are you skipping class?"

"Of course not," Portia had lied. It just figured, didn't it, that her brainy sister would react to the breakup of their parents by studying even harder than she had before. Wren was going to end up with stellar grades, while she'd probably get kicked out of college before Christmas.

"Have you heard from Dad?" she asked.

"No."

Portia could tell that Wren was hurt by this, as well. "What do you think is going on? Has he forgotten about all of us?"

"No," Wren was quick to answer. "I think he's going through some weird stuff. He's probably afraid we'll be on Mom's side and give him a hard time. Which is probably true. I totally feel like giving him hell. But—"

"He's still our dad," Portia had whispered, holding her phone with both hands, curled up under her covers, and remembering all the times he'd tucked her in when she'd been a child. Their father had been away a lot.

But he'd also been home a lot too.

She'd sighed, then. "I hope he calls me soon."

"Me, too. Go to sleep now Portia."

The line had gone dead, but Portia had lain awake for hours, staring out her window and wishing she could see the moon and the stars the way she could from her bed at home.

Wednesday morning Mattie had just finished her breakfast when she heard a rig pull into the yard. Actually Tuff heard the rumbling first. She let out one sharp bark, then ran from the front door to the side one, clearly wanting to be let out.

"Oh no, you don't. You're staying in here where you can't be run over." Mattie passed her a chew toy and pointed to the dog pillow by the back window. It was Tuff's favorite place to rest, because all she had to do was lift her head and she could see everything happening in the back yard.

After this morning's chores, Tuff had been reluctant to leave the barn and come back to the house. She was only four months old and already she was showing signs of being a good ranch dog. But Mattie could hardly be pleased about that when she wasn't sure she would even be living on a ranch one year from now.

Mattie paused by the window herself, watching the progress of a silver and white half-ton pulling a two-horse trailer, the kind with living quarters attached. The driver went about as close to the barn as he could get, then climbed out of the cab and took a big stretch.

She recognized him. Tip Duvall was an up-and-coming star in the steer wrestling world. A little shorter than Wes, he had the ideal build for a cowboy—compact, wiry and solid muscle. Three years ago, Wes had pointed out the young rookie to her, saying he was going to be one of the best in the business in five years. Tip was well on the way to proving Wes correct. In fact, in every rodeo they'd been at together this year, Tip had scored much higher than Wes.

With a heavy heart, Mattie went to the mudroom to layer up. The temperature today was just below freezing—a lot warmer than when she and Nat had made their impromptu road trip to Billings. She hadn't heard from him in the two days since. Several times she'd wanted to call, to hear his warm, reassuring voice. But she resisted. The boundaries of their long-time friendship were shifting and she was nervous about pushing them too far.

Besides, she had to learn to stand on her own two feet.

Outside, she stuck her gloved hands deep into the pockets of her parka. Sun glinted off the frothy mounds of fresh snow, making her wish she'd remembered her sunglasses.

Tip watched her approach, his stance displaying the bow in his legs common to most men who spent a lot of time on horses. It had been a few years since Wes had introduced her, but he acted like he remembered her well.

"'Morning, Mattie. It's good to see you again." He gave her a smile with his handshake.

"Hey, Tip. You've had a good year." He'd come very close to qualifying for the Wrangler National Finals scheduled for mid-December. It was an accomplishment Wes had never achieved. Only the most talented and dedicated cowboys—those willing to be on the road almost all year long—had a shot at it.

"Thanks. Next year I hope to make the Finals with Whiskey Chaser.

"He's a good horse," Mattie agreed. So, down to business already. She still couldn't believe Wes was giving up his beautiful golden quarter horse. Much as she hated this transaction, she felt obliged to be hospitable. "Are you hungry? I have coffee ready in the house. And muffins in the freezer I could thaw in the microwave."

"I'm fine. Thank you, though. Is your barn warm? We could do our paperwork there and not need to take off our boots."

"Sure." She led the way, sliding the door open for him, then feeling a rush of pride as he let out a whistle.

"Now this is what I call a horse barn." He glanced

inside one of the empty stalls, then admired the parade of blue and red ribbons running down the aisles. "Is this the arena back here?"

She nodded. "Go ahead and take a look."

He slid the door open and stepped into the dirt-packed arena where the Bishops had trained and worked their Tennessee Walkers for many decades. "Very impressive."

"This barn was built thirty years ago and it's still in excellent shape. I brought Whiskey Chaser in to get him all nicely groomed for you. Would you like to ride him a bit before we finalize things?"

"Not necessary. I gave him a nice workout back at the Belt Rodeo in June. We made a good team."

Mattie felt shocked to hear this. The Belt Rodeo had been mid-June, about a month after Dex Cooper's death. Had Wes already been thinking of selling back then? Planning to leave her as well?

"Do you have an office in here?" Tip asked.

"Sure." As she headed for it, Tip was already pulling the papers out of the breast pocket of his jacket. In no time they had everything taken care of and it was time to take Tip to his new horse.

Princess Bride and Madame Curie nickered at her as she passed their stalls. They'd rather be outside, frolicking in the bright sunshine, but in here they'd be clean and rested for their upcoming journey. If the Ronan outfit showed up this afternoon as scheduled, tomorrow, all that would be left in the barn was the cats.

Tears had filled her eyes by the time she reached Chaser's stall. She felt like she had a tennis ball in her throat and a dark pit of sadness where her heart ought to be.

Fortunately Tip was too busy reacquainting himself with the quarter horse to notice her sudden quiet. She stayed in the aisle, turning her back as she swiped away the tears. She'd said her goodbyes to the horses yesterday when she'd groomed them, then again this morning as she gave them what would probably be their last feeding at Bishop Stables. Today she would keep her distance and try not to break down in front of people who were virtually strangers.

"Yup. Still looking good. Thank you, Mattie. I can tell when a horse has been taken care of by someone who loves him."

His words brought tears to her eyes again, despite her resolve. "Want help loading him in the trailer?"

"We'll be fine." Sure enough, once Tip had attached the lead rope, Chaser followed him contently out of the barn.

"Go ahead," Mattie kept her face averted "I have some things to finish up with in here."

"Okay, then. Thanks again. You take care now."

"Drive safe. And good luck to you both."

"We'll go far. You'll see." Tip winked, before leading the horse out the main door and disappearing from her view. She slid the door back into place, closing her eyes and resting against the solid pine for a moment. It was somewhat reassuring to know that she'd be able to follow Tip and Chaser's career next year—it would be a way of maintaining contact with the courageous and hardworking quarter horse.

She puttered in the tack room, waiting until she'd heard Tip's rig rumble on down the road before emerging and heading toward the house. She hadn't taken three steps, however, when she noticed a new vehicle driving in from the main road. Another rig, a bigger one this time. She shielded her eyes and watched as it drew closer, until finally she recognized Guy Medley's white and silver unit.

He drove in slowly, raising one hand in greeting, before maneuvering the trailer for an easy exit. His head was bowed slightly when he walked toward her, as if he was fascinated by the tips of his boots. Finally when they were only a few yards apart, he halted and lifted his round face. He looked at her rather sadly with his little brown-button eyes.

"Mrs. Bishop. I don't suppose you're be happy to see me again."

She didn't need to ask. Obviously he was here to pick up the rest of their horses for the family outfit near Ronan. "Thanks for letting me know the first batch went to a decent place."

"No problem. I wouldn't have felt good about it myself,

otherwise. I don't often get to handle horses of this caliber. Frankly they'll be under-utilized on that swanky ranch. But they'll have a good life and be treated well. As will this batch. I know the Claypools myself and they're good people."

Mattie had heard of them, too, and despite the fact that they had a small outfit, their reputation was fine.

So that was reassuring.

"Want some coffee?" Mattie offered. "I'm afraid I'm all out of pie, though I could find you something else."

This time he shook his head. "If I get moving now, I'll be in Ronan in time for lunch. Might as well pull the Band-Aid off fast."

He felt bad. Poor man. None of this was his fault. He was just doing his job. "They're all in the barn. I gave them a good grooming yesterday. I—" her voice hitched and she stopped talking. In her mind she could picture them, Copper, Princess Bride, Madame Curie, lining up and trustingly getting into that trailer. Never guessing they would never come home again...

How could she do this to them?

If only she had some other option.

CHAPTER FOURTEEN

Nat was just driving out of Polson, about to get on the Memorial Bridge that crossed the Flathead where it ceased to be a lake and narrowed into a river, when he noticed the truck with the Wyoming license plate. The cowboy at the driver's seat was pulling a horse trailer with living quarters attached. Not an uncommon sight on these roads. Still, it made Nat's lips thin into a hard, angry line.

'Cause he had a good idea where that cowboy had been and which horse was in the back of that trailer. Nat turned off the radio, no longer in the mood to listen to up-beat rock tunes. Fifteen minutes later he was off the highway heading south toward home—and the Bishop place. When he saw the huge tractor-trailer rig parked next to Mattie's barn, he swore. Losing them all in one day. This was going to kill her.

He didn't even consider driving by. He pulled in and parked his truck next to Mattie's, by the house, then hurried over to the big rig. The horses had already been loaded and Mattie was talking to a rotund man with a round face and small, dark eyes. He thought she looked glad to see him, but she didn't say anything. She was gripping onto the corral fence, though, like she needed the support. And she looked like she'd been crying.

Nat walked up to the man with his hand outstretched. "Hi there. I own the place up the road. Nat Diamond."

"I've heard of the Double D," the trucker driver acknowledged, shaking his hand willingly. "I'm Guy Medley. I was out here last week picking up some horses for transport out to the Whitefish area. Now I'm back for the rest, though I can't say I'm very happy about it. This little lady is having a hard time seeing her horses go."

Mattie had turned away from them, was pretending to fuss with a section of fence closer to the barn. Nat knew she wasn't meaning to be rude. She was just trying to hold herself together.

"Where are you taking these horses?" Nat wanted to know.

"John Claypool's place, they just have a small outfit, mostly looking for nice horses for their kids to ride."

"What will they do with the yearlings?"

"No idea. Train them I suppose. It's too bad about that nice bay, though, looks pretty old. Would have been nice for her to finish out her days in a familiar place."

He had to be talking about Copper, who'd been Mattie's horse since she married Wes and moved out here. "That's for damn sure," he agreed.

Once Guy had taken off with the horses, Nat took Mattie by the arm and led her inside. He could feel her trembling and didn't know if he felt more sad for her, or plain furious at Wes. Tuff greeting them enthusiastically, but not even the puppy's cute antics drew a smile from Mattie.

He couldn't leave her alone this way.

"How about you change out of your work clothes and we go into town for some lunch?" So he'd just been in Polson. Wouldn't hurt to drive back.

Rather than hang her jacket and tuck away her boots the way he'd seen her do before, Mattie dropped everything to the floor, mechanically washing her hands before she headed to the kitchen. He removed his own boots and followed her.

"Mattie? Lunch?" he repeated, since she seemed to be in something of a daze. She'd gone to stand by the window. It made him kind of crazy to see how beautiful she was, even in her sorrow. He didn't want to be feeling any sort of attraction to her. It wasn't right. Not in these circumstances.

"I—just can't, Nat. I don't want to be around people right now."

"Does that include me?"

She gave him a feeble smile and a gentle head shake.

"Then come with me to the Double D. I'll bet Eadie has made something good we can eat for lunch. We'll bring Tuff and she can play with her sister again. It'll be a win-win."

Mattie ended up agreeing, mostly Nat suspected, because she lacked the energy to argue. She did seem a little less fragile once he had her seated at the kitchen table at his place. The blueprints for the renovations were still on the counter where he'd been studying them that morning. He had a few last minute changes to run by Timothy. Nat rolled them up and took them back to the study. Then he put on the kettle for tea.

A minute later Eadie came through, carrying a laundry hamper of freshly folded sheets and towels.

"Hello Mattie—I thought I heard two sets of footsteps. I was in the laundry room." She turned to Nat. "I'll put away these towels, then make up your bed and I'll be finished for the day. I made a chicken enchilada casserole for your dinner. It's in the fridge, along with a dry salad."

"Perfect. We can have the casserole for lunch."

"Then what will you eat for dinner?" Mattie wanted to know.

"Oh, there will be lots of leftovers," Eadie assured them, before heading down the hall toward the master bedroom.

An hour later, Eadie had left, and Mattie and Nat had finished lunch. The casserole had been delicious, but Mattie only picked at her portion. She was going through tea, however, like nobody's business. He picked up the empty pot. "Should I make some more?"

She let out a long, unhappy sigh. "I should be getting

home. You must have work to do."

"Not really," he insisted. "Why don't we be decadent and watch an afternoon movie." Not the action, adventure type that he preferred but something feel-good that would cheer her up a little. Without waiting for her answer, he turned the TV on then gave her the control so she could scroll through the offerings.

"Oh, this is cute," she said after a few minutes. "It's about two women who switch houses for the holidays. Have you seen it?"

He glanced at the screen as he carried the fresh pot of tea in from the kitchen. "Nope, haven't seen it. Let's give it a try."

It soon became clear that she *had* seen it before, but she seemed to enjoy it just as much despite the fact. "Oh, I love this part," she said, touching his arm as the American girl trudged in her high heels in search of the English cottage. "Isn't she a hoot?"

At some point Nat realized he was watching Mattie more than the movie. He hadn't seen her smile this much for a long time. She had a haunting beauty when she was sad. But happy, she glowed, effervescent and irresistible.

When the woman from England ran through the beautiful, sophisticated, LA house, delighting with each new discovery—from outdoor pool, to gourmet kitchen—Mattie looked as wide-eyed and happy as the actress.

They'd been sitting side by side, a good two feet between them. But somehow they were closer now. Every time she laughed, Mattie would reach for him, touch his arm for a second or two, nothing inappropriate, but man, how he was aware of those touches. And then, when the couple celebrating Christmas in England shared their first kiss, pulled back, then kissed again, a new tension entered the room.

Mattie looked at him with raised eyebrows. "You probably hate these mushy scenes."

"Do you?"

"I love them." She wasn't looking at the screen, though, she was looking at him.

Never had he wanted to kiss a woman as much as he

wanted to kiss her. He'd found her perfect from the first moment he'd met her. But seeing her withstand the onslaught of the past few months had only made her more precious to him. Her strength, *and* her vulnerability, the combination was irresistible.

"Nat? We don't have to watch this if you don't like it."

"Why do you think I don't like it?"

"Because you're not watching the TV..." her gaze dipped to her hands, then rose back to meet his. "It seems more like you're watching...*me.*"

"Guilty," he admitted. "It's just nice to see you smiling for a change."

Her smile broadened, real and warm. "You've really seen me at my worst, haven't you?"

"Even your worst is beautiful."

They were both quiet for a moment, the soundtrack to the movie quite superfluous at this point.

Her eyes grew luminous. "Nat... you're so good to me." She reached a hand to the side of his face. And then she was leaning in toward him, lips sweetly parting.

She had probably meant for them to share a chaste kiss. But magic sparked from the first light touching of their lips. He cupped the back of her head, kissed her more deeply, inhaling her, tasting her, drowning in her... then pulled back to check her beautiful warm eyes.

They were glowing. He could tell she wanted more. He could feel the surrender in her body, as well as the heat and the need.

Just like his. Every fiber of his being wanted him to kiss her senseless then carry her to his bedroom. He wanted to explore every inch of her body. Claim her and please her. He groaned, imaging how intense and amazing it would be.

"Mattie, how I want you." He stopped himself from adding, *how I've always wanted you...*

"I feel the same way."

He touched his lips to her smooth, high forehead, while he searched inside himself for the strength to hold back. "In another time... we could have been so good together."

"Why do you say another time..."

He chose his words carefully. "For one thing... you're still married."

"After everything that Wes has done—you really feel my being married is an obstacle?"

"Legalities aside, there's the rebound factor. A lot has happened in a really short time. You need to deal with the end of your marriage—really come to terms with it—before you jump into another relationship." She looked so crushed. He felt as if he had rejected her, when the very opposite was true.

"What you say is wise." She sighed. "I'm sorry if I made you uncomfortable. I know I started that kiss of ours..."

"Maybe you started it. But I'll bet I wanted it to happen more than you did." He didn't try to hide his emotions when he looked at her now, and was rewarded when a wash of pink spread up from her neck, until even the tips of her ears were red.

"This is kind of a mess, isn't it? But please don't tell me we shouldn't see each other anymore—not even as friends. I couldn't stand that."

"I couldn't either," he admitted, wrapping his arms around her to give her a warm hug. He'd been walking an emotional tightrope with Mattie from the beginning. Only now the rope was so much higher.

Mattie was confused by her sudden sexual awareness of Nat Diamond. She'd known him for almost twenty years, during which time she'd certainly been aware of his drop-dead gorgeousness. Why was it only now that her heart raced when he was near, and his every touch made her long for more?

Trouble was, Nat—so off-limits when she'd been a happily married woman—was no longer the forbidden fruit. The fact that he'd been the one to put the brakes on a potential sexual encounter between them made her feel slightly guilty, but also frustrated.

If he *really* found her attractive, surely he wouldn't be so noble.

A week after spending the afternoon at his place, however, she saw the situation more sensibly. She *was* still legally married. And a rebound affair wasn't really her style—or Nat's, obviously. One good thing about that kiss though. It gave her something to think about that had nothing to do with Wes or the sold horses, or the fact that a realtor had been by to measure each room in the house for the sales listing.

With no chores to do in the morning and evening, no horses to exercise or groom during the day, Mattie filled her days by cleaning the house with a thoroughness that she'd never had the luxury to indulge before, including washing walls and polishing light fixtures.

And then it was time to think about Christmas. Since her marriage, she'd always celebrated here at Bishop Stables. But with no livestock tying them down, there was no reason they had to stay put. Mattie decided to give Callan a call.

"So I'm the last to know," Callan said bluntly, even before hello.

"Honey, I'm sorry if it seems that way. It's just that— getting divorced isn't the sort of news that's fun to spread. I hoped Sage would fill in you—and Dad."

"She did," Callan conceded. "And I've been meaning to call to see how you're holding up. So. How are you holding up?"

"Good days and bad days. I was hoping we could talk more about this in person—how do you feel about the girls and me descending on you for Christmas?"

"Seriously? That would be awesome! I've always wanted to celebrate the holiday with my nieces. You, too, of course."

Mattie wasn't offended at being an afterthought. Her parents had spaced their children about four years apart, which worked out to a twelve-year gap between her and her baby sister. Callan was only six when Mattie married and left home, so it was no wonder they weren't very close.

"That's good to hear. Since Wes sold all our horses, we're free to travel this year."

"He sold *all* of them?"

"Yes."

"Oh my God. I couldn't stand it if—" never the most tactful person, Callan did have the sense to end her sentence there. "I'm so sorry, Mattie."

"Yes, it's rough. And it'll be even worse when Wes sells the land and the house."

"Surely that won't happen for a while?"

"I didn't think so—but everything's been happening at breakneck speed. I figure I should be prepared just in case. Right now Wes is working at a lumberyard in Billings. He likes the job and wants to buy a house in the area. To do that he needs to sell this place." It was so weird to talk about her husband as someone totally apart from her.

But she was starting to get used to it.

"Well, of course you and the girls should come here for Christmas. And stay as long as you like."

"Possibly the girls will be spending part of their holiday with their dad," Mattie cautioned. Which was another argument in favor of celebrating at the Circle C this year. Marietta was much closer to Billings than Polson.

"Right," Callan said. "I guess that's only fair. Even though their dad's a jerk."

"I'm inclined to agree. But don't say anything like that in front of the twins."

Portia wanted to study, but she didn't know where to start. Why hadn't she buckled down sooner? She had exams every two days for the next ten days and was so far behind it wasn't funny. Thanks to all the classes she'd skipped, her notes were patchy at best. And she hadn't kept up with the readings. She'd scraped by on most of her assignments—mostly by copying bits from some of her and Kirsten's friends who were more studious.

Usually she'd have been studying with that same group now, but their parents had sprung for tutors who were working with them in a private group. Portia didn't dare ask her Mom for money to do the same.

Portia groaned and let her head sink onto the stack of

books on her desk. She'd been in this stupid library cubicle for forty minutes and hadn't accomplished a darn thing.

If only Wren were here. In high school, her twin sister had been her savior at times like this.

"Looks like you could use one of these."

She lifted her head. A take-out coffee cup was now on her desk, next to the books. Beside her was a tall guy with dark hair. One corner of his mouth lifted in a smile. Gradually the other corner went up, too, in a sweetly crooked smile.

The pretend cowboy from Helena.

"I am in big trouble," she confessed.

He slouched in the cubicle seat next to hers, tossed a binder on the desk. "I figured. We could hear your moaning from all the way over there."

Portia glanced where he was indicating and saw Annie Larimer and several other kids sitting at a round table. They all had coffees, too. The cowboy from Helena must have bought a round for everyone.

She took a sip. Vanilla flavored latte. "Delish. Thank you. I'm not sure the caffeine is going to be enough though." She pulled her psych text off the pile of reading material. "I don't even know where to start."

"Must be hard when you haven't been to half of the classes."

"Why bother, when I can get lectures from you?" she asked sweetly.

"So I take it you're not interested in seeing my study notes?" He started to get up.

"Hang on," she said quickly. "Did you say *study notes?*" She looked at him suspiciously. "How much are you charging?" Maybe the coffee was just to warm her up, before he hit her for some big-time cash.

"I'm hurt. That you would suspect my motives, when I'm just trying to be a nice guy and get you out of a jam."

She studied his expression. Was he serious about helping her? If so, it wouldn't be the first time. "Is this about my Dad? Do you want his autograph or something?"

He seemed amused by that. "No strings, Portia. I even made a copy so you don't have to return them." He pulled a set of notes from his binder, neatly typed and stapled. "You learn all this, you'll have no problem passing. That's a guarantee."

She grabbed the notes eagerly. "Thank you—" he still hadn't told her his name, but before she could ask, he was gone, rejoining his friends at the other table. Ten minutes later, they were packing up their books and leaving.

Portia stayed where she was. The notes were fabulous. Several hours later, she still hadn't taken a break when she heard an incoming text message on her phone. She could tell by the generic text tone that it wasn't from anyone she had programmed into her contact list.

Had the guy from Helena somehow tracked down her number?

She couldn't resist a look.

But the message was from her dad.

Finally.

"Hi Portia. How are you? Wondering if I can see you this Christmas?"

Mattie knew Sage would do tons of baking for the Carrigan's Christmas, but she decided to bake shortbread cookies using her mother's traditional recipe. She made six dozen snowflakes, throwing any that weren't perfect into a plastic bag. She'd crush them up for use as a crumb piecrust at a later date.

Carefully she iced the snowflakes, then dusted them with silver sparkles.

Once they were dry, she bundled two dozen onto a plate, covered it with plastic and a pretty silver bow.

Then drove to the Double D.

She hadn't seen Nat since the afternoon they'd kissed. He'd phoned a few times, "how are you doing" calls— probably making sure she wasn't contemplating slitting her wrists or anything. But actually, she was doing better these days, getting to a place where she could contemplate the uncertainty of her future without too much panic or despair.

It was only five when she reached the gate to the Double D. She drove slowly over the cattle guard, then down the long approach that branched off about a quarter-mile later. To the left were the outbuildings, to the right, the house. Despite the early hour, the shortest day of the year had just passed and the sky was already dark. Red and green lights twinkled on the long roof-line, as well as on two thirty-foot pine trees that flanked the front yard.

It was a festive sight, and helped put a smile on her face as she knocked on the large pine door. Nat answered within a few seconds. He was wearing faded jeans and a flannel shirt over a white T-shirt and the welcome in his eyes was unmistakable. "Mattie. Come in."

"I love all your Christmas lights. They look so festive."

"That's as far as I got, unfortunately."

"More than I did this year. Decorating seemed like a waste of time since the girls and I are spending the holidays at the Circle C. And speaking of the holidays—" she handed him the plate of cookies.

"Thanks. These look too pretty to eat."

"Don't let a little sparkle stop you." She'd been worried they would be awkward in each other's company, but she felt completely at ease and Nat seemed the same. "It's nice to see you, Nat. I hope you don't mind me stopping in unannounced, but I'm leaving early tomorrow for Marietta."

"I'm glad you did. Come in for a drink."

She intended to refuse, but he already had the door closed behind her, and was one handedly helping her off with her coat.

"How does an eggnog sound?" he offered. "I was just going to have a glass myself."

"Sure." She followed him to the kitchen, and noted that he'd been totally right about not having done any decorating beyond the outdoor lights. There wasn't so much as a poinsettia inside to indicate that this was the holidays.

A fire crackled in the hearth, however, and Christmas carols played quietly in the background. Nat poured their drinks, then carried them to the family room. Together they sat on either side of the sofa where they'd watched the movie together two weeks ago.

She noticed his gaze slide from her eyes, to her lips. Was he remembering their kiss?

Too bad there was no mistletoe over her head.

She took a sip of the eggnog which was fresh, creamy, and sweet, and felt granules of nutmeg stick to her upper lip. Before she could discreetly lick them off, Nat reached over and did the job with his index finger.

"So what are *your* plans for Christmas?"

"Not much. A bunch of us bachelors are going to the Smoke House for dinner on the twenty-fifth. They do a nice job—lots of decorations, and a traditional turkey meal with all the fixings."

That sounded fine. But very different from the Christmases *she* was used to. House full of family, stockings hung for Santa, noise, confusion, laughter and games... did Nat ever hunger for a holiday like that? "And you don't have to worry about washing a bunch of dishes at the end of the evening."

"Another plus." He leaned back, stretching out his legs. "I know it probably sounds lame to you. But I'm used to having a low-key Christmas. I was an only child growing up. And since Julia and I never had kids..."

"Just because you didn't have children with Julia, doesn't mean they can't ever happen. You *could* marry again." She wasn't thinking of herself when she said that. Of course she wasn't. Anyway, she'd had her children. And while getting pregnant was a possibility for her, it was definitely not a road she intended to travel again.

"At forty-nine? No."

He sounded very decided. "What are you saying 'no' to—children? Or marriage?" Maybe it was a bold question. But after all they'd been through together the past few months, she didn't feel it was inappropriate.

"Both."

Again there seemed no room for doubt in his answer. Which she just didn't get. No one was ever too old to get married again. Heavens, she'd heard of people in their eighties doing it. "Was being married to Julia so terrible that you've sworn off women?"

Nat smiled. "Who said I've sworn off women?"

Her mouth went dry. Did he mean to sound provocative? She sipped at her eggnog and regarded him cautiously, while he just laughed.

"Relax, Mattie, you're safe with me."

That was the trouble, she thought. Maybe she didn't want to be.

Fortunately the weather was sunny and temperate the next day and Mattie had an easy drive to Marietta. She arrived just before six, and was able to admire the Christmas lights her dad always strung on the big Douglas Fir at the top of the yard—a task that must be getting progressively more challenging with each passing growing season.

Mattie opened the crate so Tuff could jump out and explore the new territory. Bob, her father's current border collie—he'd owned one since Mattie could remember— came to check out the newcomer. While the dogs did their requisite sniffing, Mattie clipped Tuff onto a leash to prevent her running off. She was too inexperienced to run unsupervised around an unfamiliar cattle ranch.

The front door opened and Callan came out on the front porch in her work shirt, jeans, and stocking feet. As usual, her long brown hair was in a ponytail and she wore not a dab of makeup. Not that her thick-lashed blue eyes needed any.

"Mattie! You're here!" Just a little over five feet tall, slender, with delicate features that belied her toughness and grit, Callan was constantly being underestimated by people—a mistake that they soon came to regret.

What took a little longer to discover about Callan, however, was her big heart—which was easily won over by the new puppy.

"I forgot you said you'd be bringing your new dog. Oh, she's so cute! Come here, Tuff. That's a good girl."

As Tuff happily claimed a hug and scratches from the

friendly stranger, Mattie grabbed her suitcase, then the bag of Christmas gifts. Her dad appeared then, just under six feet tall and closing in on two-hundred pounds. He had a time-worn face, tired eyes, gray hair that needed a trim. He lumbered down the stairs and took the case and bag out of her arms.

"Mattie," he said. Not "hello" or "it's good to see you" or "how was your drive?" Just—"Mattie."

"Hi Dad, how are you?"

"Getting old," he grumbled. "Might as well get in here. We're about to have dinner. Good thing we made extra."

Mattie felt her heart lighten as she stepped inside. Coming home, the first few minutes, always hit her the same way. Beyond the aroma of Callan's signature chili and the fresh scent of newly cut pine, was the underlying smell that was home. The foyer wasn't grand, but it was large enough for an eight-foot Christmas tree—decked out in colored lights and an array of western-themed ornaments. Mattie stopped for a moment to admire it.

"That one was Sage and Savannah's project." Callan sounded like she wasn't sure if she approved. "We have all the family decorations on the big tree in the living room."

They walked through to the back of the house where the kitchen, dining and living areas sort of blended together. Dominating the space, and taking advantage of the open rafters in this part of the house, was a twelve-foot white pine, covered in golden lights and handmade ornaments.

Not having been home for Christmas since she was eighteen, Mattie had forgotten about all the decorations she and her sisters had made as little girls. Their mother had bought them craft kits every November so they would have something new to add to the tree. Four daughters, times eighteen Christmases, equaled a lot of hand-made ornaments, and Mattie felt her eyes fill with tears as she recalled the happy times they'd spent at the kitchen table, cutting, pasting, gluing, and painting.

"This is the most amazing tree ever." And then her gaze was drawn to the fireplace, where Callan had hung the stockings their mother had made for them, as well as two new additions for Sage's beau Dawson, and his daughter Savannah.

"I don't have any for Portia and Wren. I was hoping you'd bring them with you."

"I did." They had both been cross-stitched by her mother, the year the twins were born.

"Good," Callan said. "Are you okay to sit and eat now?"

The meal was basic—chili, cornbread, and salad—but delicious. Mattie asked how the ranch was doing, and Callan filled her in on the latest machinery breakdowns. Their dad didn't believe in buying new when it was possible to fix something they already owned. The only problem was, after so many years of repairs, most of the equipment on the ranch was on its last legs.

Mattie waited for her dad to mention something about Wes, or to ask how she was doing, but he didn't broach the subject of her impending divorce. When the meal was over, Hawksley made no apologies about retiring to his office to "watch his shows." This autumn Callan had informed them that he spent more time snoozing than watching, but then, as Hawksley himself was quick to point out, he wasn't getting any younger.

"Does he look like he's aged to you?" Callan asked as they were washing up.

"Maybe a little." The truth was, on her past few visits she *had* been surprised by how old her father looked. But she didn't worry. Her dad was as tough as boot leather. His father had lived until his nineties, and Mattie was sure Hawksley would do the same.

"When do the girls arrive?" Callan asked. "I've made up Sage's old room for them."

"They're coming tomorrow afternoon. Portia and Dani are on the same flight from Seattle and Wren arrives about thirty minutes later, so I'll be able to pick all three up in one trip."

"Great. I have a few things I need to get done in the barn. Hopefully I'll finish in time to get dinner started before you get back."

"Don't worry about cooking. I'll do the prep work before I head to the airport. And I can help in the barn, too.

You already handle too much around here, without having to treat us like guests."

"I like being busy."

Her tone was defiant, but Mattie could see dark circles under her sister's eyes. And she didn't like it. "Have you thought of hiring a housekeeper? Then you wouldn't have to worry about cooking and the laundry."

"We have a cleaner come in twice a month. Dad thinks that's enough."

"Dad would. He doesn't do the cooking or laundry, does he?"

Reluctantly Callan conceded that this was so.

Mattie hung her dish towel to dry. "Have you ever considered doing something different with your life? You know you don't have to stay here, right?" Callan was twenty-six. Mattie was afraid she would one day regret that she'd spent so many of her best years toiling away on the family ranch, instead of starting a new life—and possibly a family—of her own.

"I can't imagine doing anything else."

"But living alone with Hawksley. It can't be easy."

"He doesn't say much, but I know he cares. You can't let his gruffness get under your skin."

Mattie left that unchallenged. She knew she ought to be more generous toward her father. But she couldn't seem to get over resenting him for their mother's death. Even though it had happened so long ago now. And even if Mom hadn't been entirely faithful...

Did Callan know about the affair with Bill Sheenan? She'd have to check with Sage. She sure didn't want to be the one to tell her.

Almost never did Mattie and Callan get to spend time together, but that evening they made gingerbread cookies and chatted for hours. What they shared above all was a love of horses, and a talent for working with them. Callan's eyes filled with tears when Mattie told her about saying goodbye to Copper and the twins' horses, too.

And then, later, they both laughed as Callan shared tales about training a new three-year-old filly with a strange affinity for an old sheep that had come to live on the ranch ten years ago, abandoned by a family who'd moved on, and adopted by Callan.

Their father came into the kitchen around nine-thirty, sampled a cookie, pronounced it, "good," then declared he was going to bed.

"Good night, Pops," Callan said, and Mattie added, "Sleep well." She waited for him to make eye contact. Once he did, she would round the counter and give him a hug.

But he didn't even glance their way, just brushed the gingerbread crumbs off his fingers then shuffled off.

Mattie watched his exit feeling sad, disappointed... resigned. It was always this way with her father. Why had she expected any different this time? Lots of fathers might have expressed sadness or disappointment when one of their children was going through a divorce. They might offer counsel, or at least sympathy.

But Hawksley had always left every aspect of child-rearing to their mother. And that hadn't changed after her death. At least Mattie had been twenty-one by then. But what about poor Callan?

"He's something else." Mattie's gaze lingered over the empty space her father had left behind. "You were so young when Mom died. Only eight. However did you survive?"

"I had Sage and Dani. I was fine."

Sage had been twelve and Dani sixteen. Mattie had no doubt that the three sisters had banded together and looked after one another during those hard years after Mom's death. But it still must have been a lot more painful than Callan's matter-of-fact words let on.

Mattie felt there must be softness at the core of her baby sister. She just wished Callan would let her close enough to see it.

As they cut out the last batch of wreath shapes from the dough, Mattie asked, "So what have you been doing for fun? Is there a guy in the picture these days?"

"There are always guys. Most Friday nights I head to Grey's Saloon for a few drinks and some dancing."

"But no guy in particular? What about Dillon Sheenan?"

"Dillon is just a buddy. He does a lot of traveling

around, but when he's in town, sure we get together for a few beers."

"That's it?"

"He's a friend. I could never see him as anything else."

"Must be some other contenders around town...?"

Callan shrugged her slight shoulders. "I'm only twenty-five. Too young to get serious about a guy."

She'd had a husband and four-year-old twin daughters at Callan's age. But everyone was different. Mattie slid the last cookie tray into the oven, then started washing up the dishes. She'd no sooner turned on the water, than her phone let out a chime.

"That's Wren." She hurried to the phone she'd left on the far corner of the counter. Then frowned as she read the message.

"What's wrong?" Callan asked.

"Wes has been in touch with the girls. He wants them to spend a few days over the holidays with him in Billings." Mattie had been expecting this and knew she should feel happy for her daughters. They'd missed their father. Needed to be reassured that he still loved them.

But she'd been so looking forward to having them home for two weeks. Now that time was being cut short. Worse, this made the whole divorce thing feel so real. Wes had a new life. A life that excluded her.

And she still hadn't figured out what her new life would look like, excluding him.

CHAPTER FIFTEEN

That night Mattie dreamed of Nat. She saw him at her bedroom door, wearing jeans but no shirt, the way she'd seen him many times on the ranch, working hard in the blazing summer sun. He was smiling at her in his usual warm and tender way. But there was a heat in his eyes. Desire.

She'd sensed it in him before. Tamped down and concealed, but still present.

He wanted her.

And she wanted him, too. Was so aroused, her entire body tingled. Ached.

Come to me. In the way of dreams, he was instantly with her, naked, under the covers.

Kiss me, Nat. Touch me...

She hovered on the brink of orgasm as she tried to will him to do the things that she needed. Slowly though, the dream became lucid.

Why am I dreaming of Nat this way?

It wasn't right. She wasn't yet legally separated.

Her muscles slackened as the dream lost its hold on her. She opened her eyes to a room that was still dark. Her old room, from when she'd been a child. Pink and white striped wallpaper. An upholstered cushion in the window seat of the dormer window. She'd read so many books curled up there. Dreamed so many dreams.

Many of them, in her adolescence, as steamy as the one she'd just had.

Back then it had been Wes Bishop she'd longed for. She'd thought he was her true love, the man she was meant to spend her life with. So how was it she had managed to forget him so quickly? What did it say about her that two and half months after her husband left her, she was already lusting after another man?

Lusting?

No. Her feelings for Nat went much deeper than that.

Which was probably why she found them so frightening.

In the hall, she heard bedroom doors open, footsteps. The house gurgled as the plumbing was put to use. Faintly a radio announcer's voice traveled from the kitchen, telling her to expect a sunny, but cool, winter day. By the time she'd dressed and made her bed, she could smell the coffee.

A new day on the Circle C Ranch had begun. Before it ended, her daughters would be here. And Dani. She would look forward to the days they would spend together.

And try not to worry about the ones when they'd be apart.

Portia had never been to her grandfather's ranch in the winter. The fields looked alien covered in snow, the aspen naked, the outbuildings somehow grimy and run-down. She was in the backseat of her Mom's SUV, with Wren, Tuff between them, nuzzling them in turns, demanding scratches and petting.

In the front her Mom and Dani hadn't stopped talking since they'd left the airport. Actually Dani was doing most of the talking—about her work, about some paper that had been recently published and a planned trip to South Africa where she was going to present her findings.

Portia glanced at her sister. On the surface she looked like the same old Wren in her generic blue jeans, baggy sweater, and two-year-old gray wool coat, just slightly out of style this season. Of course Wren wouldn't care about that. She'd never bothered about fashion and college didn't seem to be changing that about her.

But Wren had evolved in other, more subtle ways. She had a calm, collected, sureness about her. As if she'd somehow figured out what it meant to be a grownup, and was cool with it. Portia had always admired her smart twin sister. But this new confidence made her almost daunting.

"We're here!"

Her mother's announcement as she drove through the wrought iron gate was unnecessary. Since their first hellos, her Mom had been almost forcefully merry, as if it was a good thing that she and Dad had split and they were spending their first Christmas away from home. Mom parked the SUV in a lineup of trucks, two of which Portia recognized as belonging to her grandfather and her Aunt Callan. The other, she'd never seen before.

"That isn't Sage's truck," Dani said. "Must be her new honey's."

"Callan invited Dawson and Savannah for dinner," Portia's mom agreed. She turned off the ignition, then got out of the SUV to help Portia and Wren with their luggage. Once everything had been unloaded she put a hand on each of their shoulders, drawing them into a little circle.

"I hope you don't mind spending Christmas here," she said in a low tone so only the three of them could hear. "With the horses gone... and your father..." she sighed. "Well, I was afraid Christmas at home would have been too sad."

"This will be fun," Wren said. "Right Portia?"

There was Wren, being all adult-like and understanding, making Portia feel as if she had to pretend to like the situation, too. So she nodded. "It'll be cool to spend Christmas here for a change."

Mom smiled, then gave them each a huge hug that went on and on—for the first time Portia had the sense that their mother needed the comfort more than they did.

"It's really good to see you, Mom."

Portia could see the relief in her mother's eyes when Wren said that. *She's alone now. She needs us.* The realization was unsettling, a promotion to adulthood that Portia wasn't sure she could handle.

"Take your bags to Sage's old room, then wash up for dinner. I made a couple of pans of lasagna this morning. I hope you're hungry." Portia was relieved to hear her mom talking like her old self once more.

They hadn't made it any farther than the porch, when the front door flung open and Callan and Sage rushed out to hug them. Callan was petite like their mother, with dark hair and beautiful blue eyes. Sage was tall and lean, with golden red hair that Portia had always coveted, and eyes that were changeably green and then brown.

"Come in, come in," Callan said, "It's freezing out here."

In the foyer Grandpa and Sage's smoking hot new cowboy boyfriend, Dawson O'Dell, were waiting to take their suitcases out of their hands. Mom disappeared with her sisters into the kitchen. And suddenly Portia and Wren were left facing a cute five-year-old girl in pigtails and a Christmas dress, the kind Portia remembered loving when she was little, with ruffles and a crinoline and a satin sash at the waist.

"Don't you look pretty, Savannah."

The little girl didn't acknowledge the compliment. She glanced from Portia to Wren. "Are you really twins? Why aren't you wearing the same clothes?"

Wren choked out a laugh. "We aren't that kind of twins. We like being different."

Savannah took a moment to process that. "Okay. Did you see our tree? Sage and I did it. She's going to be my new, second mommy. I get to have two because my first mom doesn't like to stay in the same town very long. She thinks it's boring, but I like it."

"Nice tree," Wren said, fingering one of the many miniature cowboy boots that had been hung from the branches, along with little horses, cowboy hats, and other western-themed ornaments.

"It's really funky," Portia agreed. "And I'm glad you like living in Marietta. It's a nice town."

"I go to school now." Savannah took each of their hands, started leading them to the kitchen. "I have to go every day, unless I'm sick. Did you have to do that when you were little?"

"Sure we did." Portia smiled over the little girl's head at her sister, who seemed equally amused and charmed. No wonder people liked having kids so much. They sure were cute. And this little Savannah was something else.

At the dinner table Portia sat next to her mother, carefully out of her Aunt Dani's eyesight. They'd had a "chat" on the taxi ride to the airport.

"You've missed a lot of classes since Thanksgiving. And been late handing in assignments. I know you have a lot going on at home, so I'm not going to say anything to your mother. But you should talk to her over Christmas, Portia. Okay?"

The speech sounded like it had been rehearsed. But the concern in her aunt's eyes had looked genuine.

Portia had nodded, of course.

"Good. We won't discuss this again. I want you to enjoy your break, Portia. Maybe when it's over, you'll be able to focus better on your studies."

Did her aunt really believe that all it would take to make life normal again was a couple of weeks on grandfather's ranch—with a few days thrown in to visit her dad in Billings? *Not likely*.

At least finals were over, that was one relief. If she managed to pass, the credit would belong to her cowboy friend. His study notes had been amazing. But though he'd shared them with her, he hadn't ever lingered at her desk or shown any interest in talking.

One day when she'd been paying attention in class, she'd heard a professor call him Austin, so at least she knew one of his names. She had no idea if it was his first or his last though.

"A toast," Callan called out from the head of the table. Grandpa sat on the other end, looking cross as usual. When she was younger, he'd frightened her. Her dad used to tease them when they were on the road to Marietta. "Now, don't be afraid of your grandfather this time, girls. He looks scary, but as far as we know, he still hasn't killed anyone. Well, not recently, anyway."

"Wes!" Her mom would make a show of being shocked.

But it was pretty obvious she was struggling not to smile.

Sometimes Portia wondered if her grandfather *had* killed someone. He sure looked like the sort of guy who could do it. His eyes were so cold, when he focused on her—which wasn't very often, thank God—she would actually shiver.

"To having the family together at Christmas," Callan continued, and everyone raised their glasses—some containing wine, most others sparkling apple juice.

As she sipped the refreshing fruit drink, Portia couldn't help wishing for something stronger. Something to help her relax and soften this feeling of impending disaster. It was nice to be at the Circle C—but she couldn't help worrying about the upcoming visit with her dad. They were meeting at a hotel in Billings on the afternoon of the twenty-sixth and staying with him there for two nights.

Would he be different?

Would his new girlfriend be there?

Portia's stomach twisted every time she thought about it.

By the day after Christmas Portia was so nervous she could hardly eat. The holiday had passed in a blur. Opening stockings—normally her favorite moment—hadn't been the same without her dad. He'd always put at least one totally goofy thing in their stockings. And then he'd make them Eggs Benedict for breakfast. It was the one meal her dad was really good at cooking that didn't involve the barbecue.

The egg and ham casserole her Aunt Callan served just didn't compare.

Later, Portia hardly tasted the turkey dinner, either.

When they were all in the kitchen cleaning up at the end of the day, she couldn't focus on anything that was said. Normally she loved being around her Mom when she was with her sisters. The way they chattered, it was like her Mom turned into someone much younger and more interesting.

But tonight, all she wanted was to go to bed. Not that she expected to sleep. She just needed some time to process what was going on with her family.

Shortly after they turned in, though, her Mom came into the room she was sharing with Wren. All three of them squished together on one of the twin beds. "I know this Christmas has been difficult. So much has changed. I promise it will get easier. Over time."

Her mother looked so sad as she said this, that Portia knew the answer, even as she asked, "Is there any chance you and Daddy will get back together?"

"Your dad is with someone else. The horses have been sold. Pretty soon the ranch will be, too. So no, I don't think things will change. This is our new reality."

"But—once the ranch is sold, where will you live? What will you do?" Wren asked.

Their mother's bottom lip quivered. "I-I'm not sure. Callan's invited me to move back here, and Sage offered me a spare room at her place, too. I could even take over the lease, once she moves in with Dawson and Savannah after their wedding this fall. But—I have to say, I'm not excited about moving back to Marietta. It was my home for eighteen years. It doesn't feel that way anymore."

"No," Portia whispered. She couldn't picture her mom living anywhere but in their house. The house she and Wren had grown up in.

"It's okay, Mom," Wren put her arm around their mother's shoulders. "You'll figure something out. It's going to be okay."

Portia wished she could have had the strength to say those things. More importantly, to believe them.

The next morning, as they piled into the SUV to make the drive to Billings, Portia felt as if her world would never be whole again. She let Wren have the front passenger seat, knowing she would make better company for Mom as she drove them to the city, to the Country Inn where they were to meet Dad.

"You sure you're okay in the back?" Wren asked. She was used to having to negotiate for the opportunity to ride shotgun.

"Yeah. I'm going to sleep." She'd taken a pillow and the comforter from her bed with her. Both had quilted coverings that had been stitched by her grandmother. Portia liked the feel of the flannel backings. She pressed the fabric to her check and closed her eyes, but she was only pretending to sleep.

Instead she prayed for a flat tire. A road closure. An unexpected storm.

Something that would have her mom turning back to the relative safety of the Circle C.

Much as she'd missed her dad the past few months, Portia wasn't ready to see him again.

She was afraid he'd be different.

And he was.

She knew it the moment he stepped out of his truck. The twinkle in his eyes was missing. Instead of coming toward her and Wren, still in their mother's SUV in the parking lot of the Country Inn where they'd been waiting for twenty minutes, he walked around to the passenger side of the cab and opened the door for a pretty brunette with a small, soft mouth and a tiny dot of a nose.

"Bye Mom. I love you." Wren was the first to get out of the SUV.

Though the window Portia watched as her sister gave their Dad a hug, then shook hands with the woman.

"It's okay, honey. He's still your father."

Portia leaned forward, kissed her mother's cheek. Her mom touched her head softly, then nodded. "Go."

And then Portia was outside, with the cool air snaking inside her open jacket and blowing her hair across her face. It only took three steps for her father to reach her. He pulled her in for a deep hug and she was amazed that he smelled the same, like coffee, Head and Shoulders shampoo... and his own dad smell. His hug was as strong as ever and his voice rumbled in her ear.

"Portia. It's good to see you, honey."

Driving away, leaving her daughters with their father, was the hardest thing Mattie had ever done. She managed to wave and smile before turning out of the parking lot. She made it a full block before the tears made it difficult to see. Pulling into the nearest parking space—which happened to be at a fast food outlet—she finally let it all go, sobbing like a baby for almost a full minute.

"Enough." She couldn't keep doing this. Hadn't she shed enough tears over this man?

With a tissue, she mopped up her tears, then joined the drive-through lineup. She felt eviscerated without her daughters and their absence mocked the roominess of the SUV. At the window it took three attempts before her voice finally cooperated enough to order a medium-sized coffee with cream.

Fifteen minutes later, Billings was in her rear-view mirror. She longed to pull over again, this time to text her daughters.

How needy was that? No. She had to let them be. They already had too little time with their father.

Still, she fought the urge to reach for her phone. Maybe she could call Nat. It would be wonderful to hear his voice. To know that she still had a friend in this world who wasn't one of her sisters.

She resisted that urge, as well. Whatever their relationship was—and it wasn't simply neighbors, or friends, she was sure of that—she didn't want Nat to become an emotional crutch. He'd already been there for her during some of her darkest hours. Which she appreciated. But she didn't want to continue being that woman around him.

By the time she'd returned to the Circle C, dinner was ready to be served. Hawksley had left, making his annual pilgrimage to visit his cousin Arron and family in St. Paul's. He and Arron—a second cousin, actually, as Mattie recalled—had spent summers together on the ranch when they were boys, and their bond remained strong throughout the years. Mattie remembered her mother suggesting that the entire family go with him to St. Paul's one year. Or that Hawksley invite his cousin and his wife, Renee, and son, Court, out to the ranch for a visit.

"No," was all Hawksley had said.

And the solitary visits had continued.

In the bathroom, Mattie washed her face and then reapplied her eye makeup. She found her sisters in the kitchen, waiting for her.

"Let's fill our plates and eat by the fire in the family room," Sage suggested.

"Where are Dawson and Savannah?"

"They stayed home today. Savannah wanted to play with her new toys and Dawson—well, he loves you all, but he has to start a new shift tomorrow and felt he could use a day to just veg."

"We love him, too," Callan said. "But it is kind of fun to just be the four of us. Doesn't happen often."

That was true. And Mattie felt she ought to be happy at this chance to spend the evening with her sisters. But as she helped herself to a serving of turkey casserole and green salad, she felt little appetite. Crawling into bed and crying was all that really appealed.

"I bet it was tough," Sage said. "Dropping the girls off with Wes?"

Mattie nodded, watching as Sage poured white wine into three glasses.

"Want some?" Sage asked.

Mattie was tempted to make another exception tonight and say yes. Remembering what had happened the last time, though, she resisted. "Water's good for me."

"I admire your willpower," Dani grabbed one of the goblets, as well as her plate, and headed to the family room. The warmth of the fire drew Mattie to the hearth, where she settled on one of the plush pillows that were kept on the stone ledge. She couldn't help wondering what the twins were doing now. Having dinner in some restaurant with their dad and Suzanne? What did the girls think of Suzanne? She was younger, more fashionable than Mattie. Would those things impress them?

"Pay attention, Mattie." Callan kicked her leg, and Mattie noticed she was wearing the red, wool socks with jingle bells at the ankle that Mattie had put in her Christmas stocking. "Sage is trying to tell us something important."

"Actually, Mattie already knows. I told her this fall when I went to visit."

"That was right after Wes moved out," Dani calculated.

Sage nodded. She was looking at Mattie now, clearly intending to tell the other two about Mom's affair with Bill Sheenan. Mattie sighed. She supposed it was only fair that they all know.

"Don't judge Mom too harshly," she said.

"Why would we do that?" Callan sounded exasperated. "Tell us, Sage. What is this big secret of yours?"

Sage used pretty much the exact words she'd used when she'd told Mattie about walking in on Mom and Bill Sheenan. It didn't sound any prettier the second time around.

"Eeew—oral sex?" Callan wrinkled her nose. "How gross."

"I was pretty shocked," Sage agreed.

"And you were only what—twelve at the time?" Dani seemed determined to put everything they talked about tonight into chronological order. "That must have been traumatic for you."

Sage nodded.

Mattie wondered if Dani was remembering what a chatty, happy child Sage had been when she was younger. And how abruptly she'd turned quiet and secretive. At the time Mattie had blamed adolescence. But now she knew that this event, even more than surging hormones, had created the change in their little sister.

"Why did you keep it to yourself?" Dani wanted to

know. "It would have been much healthier for you, psychologically, if you'd talked about what you'd seen."

"With who?"

"Well... Mom?"

Sage shook her head. "I was so afraid Mom was going to leave us and go to live with the Sheenans."

Bill Sheenan had been a widower of ten years by then, so it had certainly been a possible outcome.

"Maybe we all would have been happier living with the Sheenans than here." As soon as the words were out, Mattie was shocked she'd spoken them.

"Come on, Mat. Dad wasn't that bad. Sure he was kind of gruff. But he never hurt us. Never."

Was that all it took to be a good father in Callan's opinion? Never beating your children? What about love? Providing guidance and support? Even just the occasional kind word would have been appreciated. But no sense starting that argument with Callan. She was convinced their father had a soft center. How else could she continue to live and work with him every day?

"I can't say I blame Mom for having an affair," Dani said softly. "But even though dad was a tough bird, I'm still kind of surprised. Maybe I've been keeping her on too high a pedestal."

"She was a great mother," Mattie said. "She deserves to be on that pedestal." She felt utterly tired suddenly. It had been a long day. And this conversation was almost more than she could handle. More than anything she wished their mother was still alive. That she was here, sitting with them. Mattie felt sure that she would be able to explain, to her adult daughters, why she'd been unfaithful to their father.

"Anyway, I just thought all of us should know the truth," Sage said. "Because eventually, when Dad dies, we're going to have access to her diaries. And I'm pretty sure she wrote quite a bit about Bill Sheenan in them."

"Why? Have you read them?" Callan wanted to know.

"As if. You know Dad keeps them under lock and key in his bedroom. This fall cousin Eliza asked if she could see Mom's diaries for the Bramble history book she's writing. I asked Dad if he'd give her access and he said a very firm no."

"That doesn't prove he knew about the affair," Dani countered. "Maybe he was just being cantankerous."

"Who? Dad?" Mattie asked, in a mock surprised tone.

They all laughed then, even Callan.

Sage got up to refill everyone's wine glasses, and Dani and Callan went to the kitchen for seconds on the casserole. Mattie rinsed her food down the sink, hoping no one had noticed how little she'd eaten. But she'd no sooner placed her plate in the dishwasher, than she felt Sage's hand on her shoulder.

"I'm sorry, Mattie. You must miss the girls."

Mattie nodded. "I'm kind of tired. The drive and everything." She avoided looking at her sister, afraid that if she saw sympathy, she'd start to bawl. "Sorry to jam out on you guys, but I'm going to bed."

"Sure. We understand."

The fact that no one gave her a hard time about going to bed so early told Mattie that she must be looking as rough on the outside, as she felt in her heart. She hadn't been lying about feeling exhausted, but once she was in bed, sleep seemed far away.

Again she thought of Nat.

Why was he always on her mind these days? Was she falling in love with him? Or just taking advantage of his kindness and dependability to help her through this tough time in her life? He'd always been the kind of neighbor—and friend—she could call if she had a problem. Like the time a black bear had found her way into one of the barns. Wes had been at a rodeo and Jake was gone for the day. She and the girls had been alone. And so she'd called Nat.

He could have sent one of his hired men. But he had come, himself, and he'd managed to lure that bear out of the barn, then scare it off the property and back into the hills. Over the years there were so many times he'd come to her aid, that she could never remember them all. Wes had always been slightly annoyed when Nat stepped in like that.

Once he'd even said to Mattie that he thought Nat was in love with her. She'd scoffed at the idea, then reassured her husband that he was the only man she needed.

Back then, that had been true. Only recently had she started dreaming about Nat in a sexual way. *That* was new.

But what did it mean? And was Nat feeling the same way about her?

The visit with Dad turned out to be equal parts good and weird. Fortunately Suzanne was the quiet type. She didn't try to bond with them, or act like she was a member of the family. She was pretty quiet actually. If anything, Portia thought she seemed a little sad.

Dad didn't seem all that happy, either, though he put on an act. He'd bought her and Wren T-shirts with stupid sayings that made them both laugh. And he also gave them a check, to help with the extras at college.

Though Portia was dying to know what her father's plans were, it was Wren who put the questions to him, talking calmly and rationally, like one adult to another.

"So, Dad, are you planning to live in Billings now?"

"Yeah. I like working at the lumberyard. It's a good, steady job. Suzanne and I are going to buy a house once— once the money stuff is settled with your mom."

"And are you going to keep rodeoing?"

"No. Getting too old for that.

Their Dad looked at Suzanne as he spoke. Her face was suddenly pale, her lips pinched. Mom had told them that Suzanne had been married to Dad's bull-riding friend, the one who'd been killed last spring in the rodeo arena. Portia could tell that was what Suzanne was thinking about. And as much as she was inclined to dislike the woman, Portia couldn't help feeling just a little bit sorry for her.

"Were you there when your husband had his accident?" she asked.

She could tell her Dad was annoyed, and Wren surprised, that she was being so blunt. But Suzanne answered as if she was relieved to talk about it.

"Yes. I had a bad feeling that morning, when I heard he'd drawn Black Cyclone. He'd had trouble on that bull before."

"Most all of us had," her father agreed. "That was one mean animal."

"I begged Dex to give it a pass. But he was stubborn. I wasn't in the stands. I was too nervous. I watched on one of the screen monitors and when I saw him go down, I covered my eyes. When I heard the crowd go silent, I knew Dex had been badly hurt."

That was the most Suzanne had spoken since they'd met her. Dad put a hand around her shoulders and she leaned into him, accepting his comfort. But Portia could tell by the dull sheen of her eyes, that she was still thinking back to the day her husband had died.

"I'm sorry," Portia said. She knew what it felt like to watch someone you love get on the back of a wild bull. Even when she was younger, before she'd fully appreciated how dangerous her Dad's job was, she'd been nervous watching him compete. Her stomach twisted now, just remembering.

"This is a grim topic," Dad said. "You girls should be telling me about college. All the stuff you're learning and the friends you're making."

Portia hesitated. Theoretically she should have lots to talk to her father about. But they hadn't spoken for so long, she didn't know where to start. Even Wren seemed nonplussed by the request.

Then she had an idea. "There's a guy in a lot of my classes who says he met you, Dad, and even shook your hand. At a rodeo this summer, I think it was in Great Falls."

"Does this guy have a name?" her father sounded amused.

"Austin something-or-other," Portia mumbled.

Her dad straightened. "Would that be Austin Bradshaw?"

"That. Sounds. Right." Portia was on her phone, checking to see if an Austin Bradshaw was on Facebook. Sure enough, the guy had a profile. And his photo showed him on the back of a bucking bull. Oh my God. He'd called himself a cowboy, and she'd scoffed. But he was the genuine thing.

"The kid shows a lot of talent. And courage. I think it

was his first time lasting eight seconds in a PRCA sanctioned event. He was so excited." Wes smiled, shook his head, then looked at Portia again. "So, you two are just friends, right?"

Portia groaned. "Dad."

But inside, she felt a warm glow. Maybe because, for a second there, her dad had finally sounded like himself again.

Or maybe it was because of Austin...

CHAPTER SIXTEEN

No sooner had Mattie returned home after Christmas, than a storm set in, leaving her house-bound for three days. Fortunately she'd stocked up on groceries at the tail end of her drive home from Marietta. So she had plenty of food, tea... and tissues. Not that she needed the tissues so much these days. She figured she was pretty much cried-out now.

The question remained, what to do with her life now? Since Wes had left there had been no new deposits to their joint checking account. Her expenses were few, but she would soon run out of cash.

She needed to make a living, somehow. But all she was qualified to do was train and take care of horses. It was maddening to have an empty stable at her disposal, plenty of hay and feed—but no horses.

She missed the girls so much. Would she ever get used to this empty house? Every day she gave thanks for Tuff, who gave her a reason to get up in the morning, to go outside for walks... and someone to cuddle in the evening when she was watching TV or reading.

When the snow finally let up, one of Nat's hired men

came by with the plow to clear out her lane and yard for her. She went out to thank him, squinting against the bright sun hanging just above the hills to the south. "Would you like some coffee? I have some fresh muffins, too, if you're hungry."

"I'm fine, Ma'am." He looked to be in his early twenties, dark blonde hair, his face covered with a light stubble, that had red glints in the sunshine.

"Well, thank you very much." She looked around at the work he'd done, snow mounded well out of the way, making it possible for her to access the main road with her SUV and walk around the yard with ease.

"No problem, Ma'am. Nat says hi." And then he was off, driving his tractor along the freshly cleared lane, turning right on the main road, headed back to the Double D.

Over the next few days Mattie kept expecting to hear from Nat. That he would call, or drop in—but he didn't. Several times she happened to be outside playing with Tuff when he rode past the farm in his big truck. He always slowed, smiled and waved, but never stopped.

She felt confused by this. And distressed.

Obviously she'd assumed there was more to their friendship than Nat intended.

But that didn't stop her from thinking of him. Dreaming of him...

Mid-January Mattie finally had a meeting with a divorce attorney. She used the one Nat had recommended, Jemma Humphries, a family lawyer in Missoula.

She felt awkward dressed in a skirt and blouse, sitting in the office boardroom, coolly discussing the end of her marriage with a virtual stranger. Jemma Humphries was about Mattie's height, pretty, plump, and very well groomed. She had lovely gel nails and Mattie couldn't help but notice how well her hands set off her thick wedding band with the large diamond perched above.

The meeting was torture. But at least she left with the information she needed to start building her new life.

Montana was a no-fault divorce state, as well as an equitable distribution state. Jemma figured that since the farm had been in Wes's name when they were married, that she would share in any appreciation in value that had occurred during the twenty years of their marriage.

That was a relief.

She wouldn't leave the marriage with nothing.

Back at home, Mattie fought the urge to call Nat and discuss what had happened with the lawyer. Instead, she called Sage, who listened sympathetically, then urged her to stop waiting to see when Wes was going to sell the farm, and just get on with her life.

"You said the barn is just sitting there?"

"Yes."

"Then why not start boarding horses again? Make sure the commitment runs month-to-month so if Wes does find a buyer, you won't be stuck."

It was such a great idea—Mattie wondered why she hadn't thought of it first. Getting the word out didn't take long. A few phone calls, a notice at her church and at Murphy's Feed Store, and she soon had eight horses delivered to her care.

Early February a ninth horse was delivered by parents of one of Portia's friends. Ray and Becky Turnball had a beautiful Tennessee Walker they'd bought from Bishop Stables ten years ago.

"We're selling our acreage and moving to a condo on the lake in Big Arm," Becky explained, while her husband Ray unloaded the beautiful sorrel mare. "Ray's tired of the upkeep, and I don't need a big garden anymore now that the children are all grown up."

Becky and Ray had had four children. Their youngest, who was the same age as Portia and Wren, was now working in Missoula. The rest had settled around Polson. One had married a man whose family owned a cherry orchard on the east side of the lake, and the other two were in law enforcement, working for the Sheriff's office.

As she and Becky chatted, Mattie realized how much her previous social life had revolved around the twins' activities and friends. Attending school sporting events, sharing car pools and volunteering at the school had ended for her now that the girls were in college.

It was time she developed her own interests. Her own activities.

So when Becky mentioned a new book club that she'd started that fall, Mattie was quick to show interest, and soon she had an invitation to the next meeting. Once Clementine had been made comfortable in her new paddock, Mattie invited Becky and Ray in for coffee.

The visit was good for her, and as she watched them drive off an hour later, Mattie promised herself she was going to accept every invitation that came her way for the next while. She'd become too isolated living out in the country on her own with only a dog for company.

When Ryan Garry called two weeks later wondering if she'd have dinner with him, however, she hesitated.

"To be honest Ryan, last time we saw one another, I'd had too much to drink. Something I don't usually do. I'm kind of embarrassed about it now." What she didn't add, was that she'd found his own behavior a little intense that evening, as well. Though maybe it wasn't fair to judge him, when her own actions may have been leading him on.

"You're not the only one, Mattie. I would have called you sooner, but I was embarrassed as well. I probably came on a little too strong that night. How about this time we meet for just dinner—and hold the dancing and drinking? Frankly, I would really enjoy a meal with some adult conversation. The kids have been driving me crazy, lately."

Mattie laughed. "At least you have kids to talk to. I've just got horses and a dog."

"Is that a yes?"

It was.

Mattie was careful how she dressed for her dinner out with Ryan. Her main interest in him was as a friend—though she supposed it was possible that could change.

But not likely.

She couldn't help remembering how she had felt dancing with Ryan at the Smoke House last December. No sparks, whatsoever. And then Nat had stepped in. Instant heat.

Maybe she should have turned down Ryan's invitation. But it had been so long since she'd had an evening out. And he'd made it clear that the night was just going to be about good food and conversation. Where was the harm in that?

Mattie wore a long sweater with a narrow belt, black skinny jeans and boots. Not an inch of inappropriate skin was showing. Just to be sure she sent the right message, she kept her makeup minimal, with only a light gloss on her lips and some mascara.

Ryan had insisted on driving out to the ranch to pick her up, and he arrived right on time, at seven. Working for the Lake County Gazette meant Ryan had lots of interesting stories and conversation on the twenty-minute drive to the Finley Point Grill was not a problem.

Mattie commented on an article she'd read that week about a minor earth tremor in the Flathead Valley that had been erroneously reported as a magnitude nine-point-nine earthquake.

"Totally ridiculous," Ryan commented. "Not sure how that error happened."

"I didn't realize Polson was on a fault line."

"We are. The same fault line runs from here, down to Yellowstone and onward to Salt Lake City. Most of our shakes are tremors almost no one notices, but back in 1969 we had an earthquake that measured around four or five on the Richter scale."

At the restaurant, they continued their conversation, moving easily from one topic to the next. Ryan was intelligent, with a good sense of humor. Glancing up from her menu, she thought he was not only pleasant to look at, but also well groomed. His thick sandy hair had been recently trimmed and his shirt was well pressed.

Funny that a man could have so much going for him, and yet she felt zero romantic interest.

Was it because her separation from Wes was too recent?

But that didn't explain the way she felt around Nat...

By the time dessert had been served, Mattie had come

to the conclusion that Ryan would be perfect—for Dani. Surely her academic sister would find his type totally appealing. She, on the other hand, could never feel anything but friendship for him.

As the evening progressed, Ryan suggested an idea for a second date. "It's been ages since I've seen a movie in a real theater. Maybe next week we should take in something at the Showboat?"

"Maybe. But I've been a lot busier since I started boarding horses, again." Mattie segued into a cute story about how Tuff had reacted when she'd taken her out to the stables a few weeks ago. She was getting older, and her herding instincts were kicking in. Trouble was, the horses didn't take her seriously—she was still too little.

On the ride home, it took a lot of effort to keep the conversation light, and Mattie's head started to hurt. This dinner had been a bad idea. Yes, she needed to start socializing more, but she'd already known that Ryan wasn't the right guy for her. By agreeing to have dinner with him, she'd given him false encouragement.

Staring out the side window into the dark, she felt a similar despair about her boarding business. She loved having horses to look after again. But the minute Wes sold the farm—and he would find a buyer eventually—her new business would be dissolved.

She'd started the year determined to build a new life for herself.

But it wasn't proving an easy thing to do.

When Ryan pulled into her yard, she tried to make a quick exit. "Thanks for dinner, Ryan. I had a nice time."

To her surprise, he followed her out of the truck and walked her to the front door. She could see the expectation in his eyes as he smiled at her and took her hand. "Can't remember when I've enjoyed an evening more, Mattie."

She took a step toward the door. "I'd invite you in, but I've got a headache coming on. I'm not used to late nights, I guess."

"Now that doesn't sound good." Ryan opened the door once she'd unlocked it, following her so deftly she would have had to push him to prevent him from coming inside.

"Why don't you lie down while I find you some water and pain pills. Where do you keep them?"

"I'm fine, Ryan. Really. You should get going."

"I'm not the kind of man to leave a woman on her own when she isn't feeling well, Mattie. Here, let me help you with that."

Before she knew it, he'd removed her jacket and helped her off with her boots. Tuff came to check him out, and Ryan gave the puppy a few friendly scratches, soon winning her over. "Lie down, Mattie. I'll get you a cool cloth and some pills."

Mattie sighed. She supposed she'd have to let Ryan do his fussing so he could go home with a clean conscience. "I keep pain medicine in the cupboard over the sink. With the water glasses."

"That's handy."

"First thing Wes would want when he got home from a rodeo. He used to go through a lot of it—especially as he got older." She settled on the sofa, placing a hand on Tuff when the puppy rested on the floor next to her.

She listened as Ryan ran some water, then heard him shake a couple of pills from the bottle. Her headache was no ruse. Her head was really pounding now and she was thankful to take the medication when he brought it to her. "Thanks Ryan. I hope you don't mind letting yourself out."

"You sure you're okay on your own? I don't mind spending the night on your couch, especially if it makes you feel safer. Can't be fun living alone, miles from the next neighbor."

"I'm used to it, Ryan. Thanks anyway." His solicitousness was started to make her crazy. Yet, she didn't want to risk making him angry. She'd known Ryan Garry for years. But did she *really* know him?

How would he handle outright rejection, once she gave it?

Frankly, she would feel a lot safer delivering the message over the phone, than in person. Especially after he'd just reminded her how alone they were.

"Mind if I use your washroom?" he asked.

"Go ahead." She waved him toward the powder room

and as soon as he'd closed the door, got out her cell phone and sent a quick text to Nat.

"Need to borrow a cup of sugar? Ryan Garry here. Doesn't seem to want to leave." It wasn't exactly a desperate plea for help. But if she knew Nat, it would be enough.

Nat was on his way home from poker night with the guys, when his phone made the sound he'd assigned to Mattie's contact info—a magical chime, which he thought suited her and the way she made him feel. He took his foot off the gas. No cars within sight in either direction, so took a quick glance at the screen.

Ryan Garry? *Hell.* Was she serious? Hadn't she learned anything from the last time?

Nat put his boot back on the gas, a lot harder this time. He was only minutes away from Bishop Stables. A cup of sugar? Hell, this time he was going to flatten that man.

He blew into her lane like a Montana blizzard, jerking his truck to a stop and leaving the keys in the ignition as he stormed out and headed for her door. After one sharp rap, he let himself in. "Mattie? Saw your lights on—is everything okay?"

His heart was thumping as he strode down the hall, into the main living area. Mattie was lying on the couch next to the fireplace, where Garry was working to get a good blaze going. The scene looked real cozy, and he felt a flare of anger of a completely different sort than before.

Was she toying with him?

But then she sat up and he saw the relief in her eyes. Her skin was pale, he could tell she'd been scared.

"Nat, you're the best neighbor in the world. Thanks for checking in on me. I'm not feeling great, I'm afraid. Ryan was just lighting that fire for me and then he was going to leave."

Ryan Garry looked pissed. His long, bony legs creaked as he stood up from the hearth. "Kind of late for a neighborly visit."

"I keep an eye out," Nat said curtly. "Mattie's lights aren't usually on so late." This was stretching the truth some. But Mattie clearly wanted this man gone. And he was going to make sure it happened.

"Unlike you, I'm an *invited* guest," Ryan said, squaring his shoulders to Nat, and curling his hands into fists.

"Oh, Nat has a standing invitation at Bishop Stables," Mattie said quickly. "And it isn't true that I invited you in, Ryan. I do have a headache. All I really want is to be left alone."

Ryan looked from her, to Nat, then back again. "Did you *ask* Diamond to come here?"

"Sort of," Mattie admitted.

"Jesus." He shook his head. "Why did you even agree to have dinner with me? Clearly you two have something going on here."

Mattie said nothing to that and neither did Nat. He just stepped to the side, giving the man ample room to leave. A few seconds later, the front door slammed shut behind him.

"Now that's an angry man." He picked up the poker, moved one log over, then added another. Soon the fire was blazing hot.

Mattie laid her head back against the sofa cushions and groaned. "I really messed that up. We were out for dinner, and when he dropped me home I just wanted him to leave. But he kept ignoring all my polite social cues."

"Polite social cues? Hell, Mattie, why didn't you just tell him to go?"

"I was nervous about making him angry."

Nat stared at her. Mattie wasn't usually one to pull her punches.

"I'm terrible at dating, okay? Last time I was in a situation like this I was seventeen years old. I didn't have to tell the guys to go home. I had a father to do that."

Nat chuckled, then sank into the arm chair next to the sofa. It felt crazy good to be around Mattie again. Maybe she did have a headache. But she still looked about as delicious as a slice of apple pie with whipped cream on top.

"What were you doing out with him the first place? As I

recall the last time you were socializing with him at the Smoke House he was getting a little too friendly."

"Yes. Well. We'd both been drinking that time. He called me up and suggested dinner and I figured why not give him a second chance."

He looked at her incredulously.

"Don't judge me. I'm not like you, Nat. I don't like being on my own." She hesitated. Glanced at the fire. "It's lonely."

Nat swallowed hard. Did she really think he liked being alone? If she did, he'd better not disabuse her of the idea. "So you took a chance. I guess I can understand that. But it didn't turn out so well, huh?"

"Not really. I mean, Ryan's *fine*.I think. Just not my type."

It was wrong of him, Nat knew, but he felt so happy to hear her say that. "Seems like you better trust your instincts next time.

The look she gave him then made his heart squeeze in an exquisite mix of pleasure and pain.

"You want to know what my instincts tell me, Nat?" She got up from the sofa, polished off the glass of water on the table, then went to stand by his chair. Her invitation was unmistakable.

"Mattie. I've been staying away from you for a reason."

She was close enough he could smell her delicate perfume—like linens drying in the sun on a summer day. As he watched, she undid the thin belt holding her sweater together. She let the belt fall to the floor, then shrugged the sweater from her shoulders. Underneath was a simple white T-shirt that hugged her breasts and clung to her petite waist.

Hugged.

Clung.

Those were two things he wanted to do to her. Very much.

"Don't you ever get lonely, Nat?"

"You were married for nineteen years. Of course you feel lonely. But it gets easier with time."

"You didn't answer my question. Do you ever get

lonely," she repeated.

"Only for you," he admitted.

She held out her hands. And he took them.

Then he pulled her into his lap, where she curled in like a sexy, little kitten. He couldn't believe how light she was. He brushed back her hair so he could see her face. Read her eyes. Kiss her mouth.

As soon as he tasted her, he wanted more. Everything.

"Mattie. You should send me packing. This is too soon for you. And I'm—I'm not the right guy."

"You said I should trust my instincts."

She was so lovely. Bewitching. When she leaned in for another kiss, God help him, he couldn't resist.

"Headache?" he managed to ask, a long time later.

"Gone."

Real life wasn't anything like her dreams. Nat was not a tractable plaything, he was a big, solid man with a presence that commanded her full attention. He kissed her for a long time, made her want him so much, she realized the desire in her dreams had been nothing. He spread the quilt from the sofa on the floor, then peeled away her jeans and her T-shirt. His own clothes went next and suddenly she was shy. Not just of her own nakedness, but his too.

"Close your eyes," he instructed, as if he could sense her unease. It was good advice. With her eyes shut she could concentrate on how he made her feel. Tenderly, slowly, he teased her body with his touch and his kisses.

"You're beautiful," he murmured.

The shyness wore off, replaced by a very deep need to make love to this man. "Take off your clothes, Nat. Come next to me."

He did as she asked, joining her on the quilt. The glow from the burning logs made his skin golden, hiding the scars she could feel with her hands

He kissed her possessively, his head above hers, and she reached out to touch the side of his face. Such a gorgeous man. But what mattered most to her right now was the way he looked at her—as if he adored her.

I love you. The words popped into her head, but she didn't speak them. Instead she put her hands on his back, pulling him close so she could kiss him again. She had to give a few quiet instructions. They both asked questions and gave breathless answers. It was their first time, but it wasn't awkward.

More like slow and intense.

The first time, she came so easily, with just a brush of his fingers. And then he was digging out a condom and letting her put it on him. She felt a little awkward. But amazed, too, by the intimacy and how totally natural it felt with him.

Finally they were doing it, having the sex she'd been longing for. And again, everything felt so right, she knew her instincts had been absolutely true.

After, Mattie collapsed onto his chest and he held her there for a long time, until the dying fire and their cooling skin made her shiver.

"You're cold?"

"A little," she admitted.

With a groan, and using the arm of the chair for support, he pulled himself up. "My leg must have fallen asleep."

He wrapped her in the quilt, then, favoring his right leg, limped to where his clothing lay and quickly dressed.

Mattie snuggled into the warm fabric, but it wasn't the same without him. "What are you doing?" It would feel weird to invite him to spend the night in the bed she'd shared with Wes. But it was part of moving on, and she wanted him to stay.

His expression, however, didn't look promising.

"What's wrong?"

"I have to go."

She sat up, bringing the quilt with her. "Why?"

"I told you. It's not the right time and I'm not the right guy. You have to keep yourself open to new possibilities in your life. Trust me, they'll come along. You're too wonderful to be on your own for long."

After the intimacy they'd shared, his words felt as brutal as physical blows. Was this the same man who'd just made love to her?

"Why are you giving me the brush-off?" She recalled his earlier words, about there being a reason he had been avoiding her lately. But what reason? They had always gotten along well. Had lots of similar interests. And the sexual attraction part was obviously working, too.

"Mat, you're just going to have to trust me on this." He was dressed now, looking down at her with a certain amount of regret and concern. "Do you want me to help you into bed?"

She resisted the urge to say, *only if you come with me.*

"I'm not a *child*. If you want to go, then leave."

Despite everything he'd said, she couldn't believe it when he did exactly that.

Two weeks went by. The girls opted to stay at college during spring break so they could study. Or so they claimed. Portia sounded a lot happier. She kept mentioning a boy named Austin. She claimed they did a lot of studying together. When Mattie asked about her friend, Kirsten, Portia was off-hand. "Oh, we didn't have as much in common as I thought."

With March came longer days, melting snow, and the return of familiar songbirds like goldfinches and meadowlarks. Mattie looked forward to being able to take her horses out for longer rides. Like her, they were suffering from cabin fever after the long, dark winter.

In April, Mattie had to don her uncomfortable skirt and blouse again and drive to Missoula where she met with her lawyer and signed the official divorce papers. She hadn't heard from Wes in all this time, but she assumed it was what he still wanted, and as they'd now been officially separated for more than one hundred and eighty days, she figured she might as well get it over with.

On the drive home, her feelings of sadness and remorse were none the weaker for the warm sunshine spilling in her windshield. She wondered if Wes was still happy with Suzanne and his new job at the Lumberyard. Several times in the past few months his realtor had shown Bishop Stables to prospective buyers.

No offers yet, though she knew that could all change in the blink of an eye.

Still, she did her best to live day-to-day, enjoying the horses and Tuff, spending time with the Book Club ladies and making plans to holiday on Flathead Lake this July with her sisters.

A few other men from the community had called to ask her out since that disastrous night when she'd gone out with Ryan Garry and ended up having sex with Nat Diamond. After that dating faux pas she'd decided she'd better get used to being single for a while, before she experimented with men again.

But that didn't mean she wasn't hurt.

And the oddest thing was, it wasn't the divorce from Wes that stung the most, but the fact that Nat had never called, not once, since their night together.

A week after Mattie signed papers in Missoula and requested her lawyer to send the papers on to Wes, she heard a truck pull up in her lane. Tuff gave a sharp bark, her usual way of announcing that they had visitors.

Mattie was making her bed at the time, pulling fresh, line-dried linens onto the king-sized mattress, thinking for the hundredth time how silly it was that a small woman like her still slept in such a big bed.

She decided to finish fitting the corners over the mattress before going to the door to check out her visitor. But before she had a chance, she heard the door open.

Hadn't she locked it when she came in from feeding the horses that morning? She was sure that she had.

Then she heard footsteps on the hardwood floor, like an echo from the past.

She almost doubted her hearing.

Only one man walked with that particular rhythm.

She abandoned the bed and went out to the hall. There he was, at the other end of it. Hat in hand, but still wearing his boots. No matter how much she nagged, he never took them off at the door.

"Wes?"

CHAPTER SEVENTEEN

"I signed your papers." Wes threw a manila envelope onto the kitchen counter. Mattie glanced from the package, to him.

The man who had once been her husband looked weary and sad. Sun, years, and worry were showing on his face today. He brushed a hand over a two-day growth. "It's early, Mattie, but I could use a beer. Are there any in the fridge?"

She nodded and he helped himself. Watching him move around in the kitchen, made her heart ache. He knew it so well. As well as they knew each other. One year ago their lives had been like familiar slippers, comfortable and formed to fit like a second skin.

In the space of six months, so much had changed.

He popped the tab off his beer, then took a long drink. "I've accepted an offer. Bishop Stables has been sold, and the new owner will take possession in sixty days."

Mattie let out a gasp, put a hand to the wall. The news shouldn't have been so surprising. But she'd assumed he was here to talk about the divorce.

"Nat Diamond bought it," Wes continued, his

expression souring. "He put an offer in around Christmas, but I held off, hoping to sell for more money."

Somehow Mattie doubted that. "But you didn't get any more offers?"

"A few. They were all lower than Nat's."

Mattie wasn't surprised. Nat wasn't the type of man to take advantage of his neighbor's troubles to try and get a bargain.

"So I finally said yes. Can't say it was easy. That man has always made himself too familiar around here. Don't exactly love the idea of all this now belonging to him." Wes shrugged. "But I had to think of the girls. And you. Only made sense to take the highest offer."

Mattie didn't say anything. Wes made it sound like he didn't care about the money, personally, which she knew was not the case. "You don't have any regrets about selling the ranch?"

His gaze was lowered as he shook his head. "Nope. I'm still enjoying my job. Want to buy myself an acreage outside of town. Stay involved in the rodeo, but not as a contestant anymore."

He'd said get *himself* an acreage. "And you and Suzanne... will you be getting married?"

He let out a long breath. "That's history as of last month."

"Oh. I'm—" she honestly didn't know how she felt about it. Part of her felt vindicated, glad that he hadn't found her spot in his life so easy to fill. But she also felt sorry. Clearly Wes had done some real suffering. It made her like him just a little bit more than she had for a long time.

"We were two vulnerable people reaching out during a tough time in our lives. Turns out we're really not that compatible in terms of day-to-day living." He lifted his gaze to meet hers. "How about you? Seeing anyone?"

"No."

His eyes widened, as if she'd given him an unexpected answer. "I thought maybe you and Nat...?"

"I thought so too, for a while. But—no. It doesn't seem to be working out that way." She moved to the windows where she drank in the view she loved so much. Soon the trees would be exploding with green, but she wouldn't be here to see them. Later today, or maybe tomorrow, she'd start making her calls to the owners of her horses, letting them know her business had to close.

Tuff came to stand by her, sitting on her haunches, as if to say, "I'm with you." Mattie kneeled to give her a scratch, at the same time wiping away a tear. Crying seemed so pointless now, given all that she had lost. The sadness felt like an extra thirty pounds that she would have to drag around with her for the rest of her life.

"Where will you go?"

"I don't know."

"I'm sorry, Mattie. Sorry I hurt you."

But not sorry he'd gone. Not sorry he'd sold the home they'd built together. Looking out at the barns, Mattie realized that it was the farm, more than the man, she was going to miss. So maybe he'd been right to leave. Maybe she hadn't loved him as much as she'd thought.

She'd once thought they were so good together. But maybe what they were really good at was being apart.

Wes finished his beer, then put the empty can in the recycling bin. "I signed the papers with Stan today. When the sale goes through, I'll send on your share of the money."

She turned back to face him. "Okay."

"We'll stay in touch...?"

"Of course."

"Good." He gave her a tight smile. Then took a few slow steps in her direction.

She did the same, and soon they were sharing a hug. Such a familiar embrace. But now... different.

"Take care, Mattie."

"You, too, Wes."

And that was it. The final good-bye.

The clock on the microwave said ten-thirty. Mattie wasn't sure how long she'd been staring at it. Maybe ten minutes? Wes had driven off and she found herself frozen here, not sure what to do next. She ought to start phoning her clients.

Instead, she decided to saddle up Clementine and take her out for a trail ride. The snow was finally off the back ranges and she would be able to go on one of her favorite trails, following Chatterbox Creek then up to Ponderosa Hill. Mattie packed water and a couple of apples, then left Tuff in the barn, so she would have some company for the next few hours.

It felt wonderful to be outside, sitting on the back of a beautiful horse like Clementine, who moved through her gaits so smoothly Mattie could have balanced a book, rather than a hat, on her head. Spring flowers dotted the lower meadows, sagebrush buttercups, purple larkspurs, and yellow blood root. Sap was running in the pines—Mattie's favorite scent in the world. She breathed deeply, and pushed all worrisome thoughts out of her mind.

She stayed "in the moment" for three beautiful, soul-cleansing hours. Everywhere she turned she saw beauty in the awakening landscape. A few times Clementine required a strong hand, as she kicked up a little spring-fever excitement, but she was easily managed and Mattie fell a little bit more in love with the horse with each passing hour.

Reality caught up to her, eventually, though, when she was back in the stables. While giving Clementine a much-deserved shower and grooming, she heard another truck roll into the yard.

Immediately her stomach tightened and began aching.

Who was it this time? Was it more bad news?

She set aside the body brush, patting Clementine's hindquarters, "I'll be right back."

Clementine, munching from her feed bag, didn't seem too concerned.

As she stepped out the barn door, she drew in a deep breath. Nat's truck was parked up by the house. She watched as he got out of the cab and began walking toward her. He was wearing a down vest over a navy shirt, jeans, and boots, and his hat all but obscured his eyes from her view. Judging by his uneven gait, it seemed he, too, had been spending a lot of time in the saddle lately.

"Have you heard?" he asked.

She couldn't help but contrast her body's traitorous reaction to him—heart-rate speeding, palms sweaty—to the way she'd felt when Wes had shown up unexpectedly. Nothing could have demonstrated to her more effectively how her feelings toward the two men had shifted in the past six months.

"That you bought our ranch?"

He nodded. "Yeah." Then let out a heavy breath. "I'm sorry it had to be this way."

"A lot of men have been telling me that lately." How lovely that they all felt so *sorry* for her. Didn't that prove how good-hearted they were? No one *wanted* to kick her when she was down.

But they did it anyway.

"Wes told me I have two months to vacate the premises."

"Actually. That's what I came here to talk to you about."

There was a fence between them, but Nat ignored the gate, instead, settling himself on the top rung. She hesitated, then sat on the fence, too, leaving a good five feet between them.

"Don't tell me you want me out of here earlier."

"No. I want you to stay."

Mattie wobbled. Would have fallen off, except somehow Nat reached out in time to stop her with a steady hand to her shoulder, which she shrugged off as soon as she regained her balance.

"You, okay?"

"Of course I am. But what do you mean by saying you want me to stay?"

"I don't have any use for your house or any of these." With a wave of his hand he indicated the main barn, all the outbuildings, the paddocks and outdoor arena. "And I wouldn't feel right tearing it down. Why don't you stay here and keep running your boarding business?"

It was a heaven-sent opportunity, one she'd never expected. But she knew better than to get too excited. "How much rent would you charge?"

He shook his head. "Nothing."

"But—that isn't right. It doesn't make good business sense."

"Mattie, there is nothing businesslike in the way I feel about you. And don't worry that I'll change my mind down the road if you start dating again, or get married. I'm prepared to sign a contract giving you the right to live here and use this land for as long as you're alive."

Mattie's heart galloped at these words, and the sincerity with which they were spoken. Nat was looking at her in the same loving way as that night when they'd made love. He *did* have feelings for her.

He had to.

Then why had he walked away?

Why was he so determined to keep away from her? It couldn't be any lingering loyalty toward Wes. Any friendship they'd shared when they were younger had eroded over the years thanks to Wes's jealousy and resentment.

"I don't understand."

"It's not that complicated. The amount of land I'd reclaim by bulldozing your operation wouldn't be worth the cost of tearing it down. I'd just as soon have a good neighbor like you, someone I know and trust, than rent the place out to some stranger. Honestly, there are no strings attached here, Mattie."

She studied his eyes again, wondering if she'd read too much into their expression earlier.

And the time they'd made love, as well.

Maybe she'd misread Nat right from the beginning. Maybe all he'd been thinking when he heard about her and Wes splitting up, was how to get his hands on their land. He'd kept her close, earning her trust, so he would have an inside track on what she and Wes were planning to do.

The night they'd made love, well, she'd pretty much thrown herself at him, hadn't she? He'd taken what she'd offered, but before he removed his pants, he'd warned her he wasn't interested in a romantic relationship.

Oh sure, he'd made it sound like he was worried about *her*. Nonsense about the timing being off, and him not being the right man. Just words to hide behind when the fact was all he really wanted was her land.

And now that the transaction had worked out exactly as he'd planned, she was getting her payoff.

Oh, how she longed to throw his offer in his face.

And for a long five-minute silence, she battled with her conscience on the right path to take.

But in the end, she had to think of her girls. If she accepted Nat's offer, they would still have their family house to return to during holidays and summer breaks from college. It was enough for them to get used to their parents being divorced, without losing their home as well.

Besides, she loved it here. So much, she wasn't sure if she could ever be as happy anywhere else. She could earn a good living boarding and training horses, doing the work that she'd been born to do.

"That's a generous offer. I'll take it."

Five Months Later

Mattie returned from the drive to the Missoula Airport, feeling a lot better than she had last year at this time. It was getting easier saying goodbye to her daughters when they left for college. They were changing, growing up, but the three of them were still family. She understood now that she would never lose them, that the bonds of love holding them together were elastic enough to withstand distance and the passage of time.

And maybe, if she were truthful with herself, she rather enjoyed the prospect of having the house to herself again. With Wren working rotating shifts at the Polson Aquatic Center, and Portia juggling two part-time waitressing jobs and plenty of weekend visits from her boyfriend Austin

Bradshaw, there'd been a lot of coming and going, arguments over who was using the washing machine next, and whose turn it was to take a shower.

Business had picked up a lot over the summer, too. She now had twenty horses in her stables. A few more and she'd need to hire help again. She wished that person could be Jake, but she'd had a postcard from him last week.

Seemed he'd finally taken that visit to Arizona. And fallen in love with the place.

Mattie parked her truck, looked at her house, then out at the rolling hills to the north. She loved these last days of summer, each one a treat to enjoy before the impending winter. Maybe she'd take one of the horses out on a trail ride.

She went inside only long enough to change her clothes and grab some water and apples. One for her and one for the horse. As she headed toward the pasture where all the horses were turned out at the moment, she heard a truck approaching from the north.

She tensed, the way she always did when she thought Nat was near.

He'd invited the girls to help him move the cattle up to the high ranges this spring, as usual. To be honest, he'd invited all three of them. But Mattie had made an excuse not to join them. Since they no longer had a hired hand, she needed to stay behind to take care of the horses.

In the past Nat would have offered one of his men to do the job.

This year, he didn't.

She didn't think Portia or Wren had sensed the new tension between her and Nat. They were too excited to be going out on a real cattle moving expedition, Portia especially so when Nat had extended the invitation to include Austin.

The summer had offered Mattie a good chance to get to know this young man who seemed to be playing an important role in her daughter's life. She had a good feeling about him. He seemed steady and smart. Only his love of the rodeo had her worried. A few weekends Portia had gone to watch him compete—once at the Livingston Roundup where they'd stayed at The Circle C. A positive report on Austin from Callan had been somewhat reassuring—though Mattie wasn't sure how good her youngest sister's taste in men was.

At the same time, Portia had been able to spend some time with her dad, who'd been working as an out-rider at the rodeo. He seemed good, was all Portia had said. Wren had gone to visit Wes a couple of times during the summer, too. Since she currently didn't have a boyfriend—something she seemed fine with—she had more free time than Portia.

Mattie was glad Wes and the girls were keeping in touch.

As for herself, she'd turned down a few more dates this summer. She still didn't know when she'd be ready to entertain the idea of a new romance. Her girls were pushing her to be brave.

They thought she was having a hard time getting over the divorce. She didn't have the nerve to tell them the truth. Her heart still tumbled every time she thought of Nat.

The truck from the north was closer now. She recognized it now as belonging to the architect Nat had hired to renovate his home. All summer long tradespeople had been driving back and forth. Construction crew, plumber, electrician... and finally, just last week, the County Inspector.

She supposed the work must be done by now and had to admit she was curious. As far as she'd been concerned, he'd started out with a Montana dream home. How could he possibly have improved upon that?

Mattie chose Clementine for her mount that day—the pretty bay mare had remained her favorite. Sometimes she daydreamed about buying back Copper, Princess Bride, and Madam Curie. But her bank account wasn't quite that solid yet.

Once on horseback, Mattie considered heading up to the hills. But on an impulse, she started on the path that followed the road. Within an hour, Nat's homestead was in view. It was two o'clock in the afternoon. No way would he be inside on such a beautiful day.

She turned Clementine to the road, crossing through

the open wrought iron gate, cleverly designed with the Double D brand in the center. From the outside, you couldn't tell much had changed about the house. Though as she drew nearer, she realized something had.

A ramp had been installed at the side door, neatly constructed to blend in with the original building.

Why would Nat want a ramp? Did he have an older relative moving in? If so, she'd never heard a word about it, which seemed strange. She steadied Clementine—who was wanting to move on—and fought an urge to peer in the windows. Before she had settled the matter, one way or the other, Nat's housekeeper came out to the porch.

"Hey there Mattie! You look thirsty. Want to come in for a drink?"

She didn't hesitate. "Thanks Eadie. I'd love to."

She tied the reins to a fence post—making sure it wasn't too close to any of the barrels of flowers that decorated the yard—then followed Eadie inside, leaving her boots on the porch. The kitchen looked the same, as did the family and dining rooms.

"Seems like you've had a lot of construction happening this summer," she said, as Eadie handed her a glass of iced lemonade.

"Sure did. It's a relief to have them finally done, though I still can't seem to get rid of the dust." Eadie ran a finger over her kitchen counter, then showed the tip of her finger to Mattie. "See?"

Mattie murmured in sympathy.

Eadie asked about her daughters next, and once that topic was exhausted, Mattie broached the renovations again. "So what was the big construction project? Everything looks the same here."

The bright light in Eadie's eyes dimmed then, and she sighed before answering. "Nat converted the two main floor bedrooms into a new master suite for himself, with a deck that goes right off the back of the house. It's beautiful, but I don't think he wants to show it off to visitors yet."

"Sounds wonderful," Mattie said, at the same time thinking that something was off here. If the renovation was really such a great thing, why did Eadie look so sad? Her gaze went to the stairs that led to the upper level of the house—presumably where Nat's bedroom used to be.

And then, suddenly, her stomach seemed to drop down to the soles of her feet.

She thought about all the times she'd seen Nat limping, walking stiffly, having trouble with stairs or even that time they'd made love, getting up from the floor and claiming *his leg must have fallen asleep.*

The ramp. The main floor bedroom, bath and deck leading outdoors. She'd bet anything that new bathroom was equipped with a walk in shower and handicap railings.

"What's wrong with Nat, Eadie? You have to tell me. Is he going to be okay?"

She knew it was something. And that it had to be serious. But please, God, don't let him be going to die. She thought of a dozen dreadful illnesses that could lead an active man like Nat, a man who was only in his forties, to have mobility issues. *Please don't let it be ALS...*

"Oh, Mattie. Nat doesn't want anyone to know."

"Is it ALS, Eadie? Is he going to die?"

Eadie put a hand on her shoulder. "No, honey, it's not that bad. He has lots of good years left, possibly decades. The doctors don't know."

Mattie covered her face with her hands. Suddenly she knew. "It's MS, isn't it?"

Eadie hesitated. She glanced behind Mattie, as if making sure they were alone. Then she nodded. "He's known something was wrong for a few years now, but it was only last October that he got a firm diagnosis of multiple sclerosis."

"So—" Mattie had known a few people with the disease, some of them quite well. The speed with which MS progressed, how debilitating it eventually became, varied considerably, patient to patient. Nat hardly showed any symptoms yet. But to have already made all these renovations to his house... "What's his prognosis? Is it bad?"

"They don't know. But Nat. He needed to take action. The only thing he could think to do, besides follow his doctor's advice, was to renovate the house. His worst fear is being institutionalized. To be forced to leave the land."

Mattie could relate to that.

When she got home from the Double D, Mattie couldn't remember anything about the ride back. Her thoughts had been spinning with the repercussions and implications of what she'd learned from Eadie.

It amazed her now that she'd managed to convince herself Nat's kindness toward her had been a ruse—a play to make sure he got his hands on Bishop Stables.

She'd been so hurt by his rejection, she'd been grasping at straws. But the theory she'd chosen had been fragile at best.

Nat simply wasn't that type of man. Besides, what use was the Bishop land to him, really? He had no heirs, nor reason to expand beyond the considerable wealth he already possessed. She recalled him talking a few times about scaling down his operation. Which made a lot more sense than expanding, given his uncertain health.

No, he hadn't been using her.

He'd been helping her.

He'd bought Bishop Stables *for her.* So no one else would buy it, and kick her out of her house and force her to close her business.

Nat was capable of doing such a kindness for a friend. But she knew he felt more than just that for her. She'd seen it in his eyes. Felt it in the way he'd danced with her, kissed her, made love to her.

Mattie spent the evening scouring the Internet for information on MS. She needed to educate herself, because Nat had dug himself into a position, and like any Montana rancher, once he'd settled his mind on something, convincing him to change was almost impossible.

As she tossed and turned in bed, she kept reviewing her arguments, devising and revising her plans. Dawn came as a relief. She'd never been happier to get out of bed and do her chores.

Even Tuff could sense the tension inside her today. The pup kept giving her anxious looks. "It's okay," she tried to reassure her—though she quite honestly didn't know if it was.

If she failed today—it would kill her.

At eight o'clock she put on a fresh pot of coffee, then texted Nat. "Problem here. Can you come over?"

His answer was swift. "I'll send one of my men. He'll be there in fifteen minutes."

"No. It has to be you."

His reply took longer this time. And when it came, it was very brief. "OK."

Mattie poured coffee into two insulated mugs, then went out to the back deck to wait. The flagstone seating area had been their latest improvement to the house. Cushioned furniture was arranged around an outdoor fireplace that had been built into the south wall of the house. From here, she could see the road that Nat would be driving in from.

She settled in to wait.

Fortunately, it didn't take long.

She'd taken only a few sips of the hot coffee when she saw the speck of what had to be Nat's truck in the distance. Her certainty that this was him increased as the speck became larger, eventually recognizable as his gray truck.

Her hands were shaking so much now, that she put her cup down. When he pulled into the lane, she stood and waved a hand, making sure he could see her.

He parked, jumped out of the cab and came loping toward her.

With newly tuned vision, she noticed a very slight imbalance in his gait. But he could still run. That was encouraging.

"What's wrong?" he looked puzzled by the calmness of the scene.

"I have something to tell you. Do you think you could sit for a few minutes?"

Lines of worry creased his forehead. He was still tanned from the summer, and his blue eyes looked even more brilliant that usual for some reason this morning.

She gazed adoringly at him, for once not hiding, or shielding any of the feelings she had for him. Until this moment she hadn't appreciate just how much she was used to holding back when he was around. When she'd been a married woman, she'd schooled her reaction to him, out of respect for her husband and their vows.

But now she was free. And it felt... exhilarating.

Tentatively he perched on the edge of one cushioned seat. She indicated the extra coffee mug. He nodded, but didn't reach for it. Just kept his gaze fixed, clearly expecting some sort of verbal bombshell.

Well, here it came.

"I love you, Nat."

He blinked.

"You once told me it was too soon for us to get together. But Wes and I are divorced. We've been living apart for a year. Frankly, our relationship had been unraveling much longer than that."

Color was rising up Nat's neck. But he didn't say anything. Not for a moment. Changing his mind about the coffee, he took a sip, then set the mug down with a thud. "I won't deny I have feelings for you, too, Mattie. But you can do better than me. There are things you don't know—"

"Like the fact you have MS?"

His eyes widened and his mouth gaped.

"Yesterday I dropped in at the Double D and Eadie offered me a glass of lemonade. I admit I had an ulterior motive. I wanted to see your renovations."

He closed his eyes briefly. Then sighed. "So then you *do* know. Mattie, how can I claim to love you and then ask you to share your life with a man who might end up in a wheelchair?"

"*Might.*"

He hesitated, before insisting, "*Probably.*"

"Maybe. Maybe not. I know several people who cope quite well with MS, Nat. And I've done my research. You can't know what the future holds for you, any more than I knew when I married Wes that we would end up divorced."

"Completely different scenarios," he said, his tone taking an edge of stubbornness.

"In some respects. But consider this. I don't regret marrying Wes. We had a lot of good years. Raised two beautiful daughters." She reached for one of his hands, and he let her take it. His were large and strong, rough with calluses. As she rubbed her thumb into his palm, he rolled his hand over and gripped his fingers around hers.

"Mat—you're messing with my mind. I've already decided. I don't want to be the man who ties you down and makes your life less than what it could be."

"You could never do that. I'm not asking you to promise me forever, Nat. No one can do that. Just tell me that you love me today."

"I do. Have for a long time. Mattie, if I was healthy nothing would make me happier than to ask you to marry me."

He wasn't making this easy. She'd known he wouldn't, but it still hurt. Couldn't he understand that no one—*no one*—could ever mean as much to her as him? She *had* to make him understand that this was too precious to throw away.

"And, if three years from now, I die in a car crash, and you're still basically in the same condition you are now—how will you feel?"

"That's highly unlikely."

"Everything is highly unlikely until it happens. All we can be sure about is today. And I don't want to waste another day apart when we could be together."

He shook his head. "You need to think this through rationally. Talk to your sisters. I'm sure they'll agree with me."

Wrenching her hand from his, she stood up, suddenly exasperated. "Damn it, Nat. There is such a thing as being too noble."

He stared mutely at her, which only made her angry. She felt like hitting something. Instead she threw her arms in the air with frustration. "You're impossible. Let's keep living alone and miserable, then. That seems to be what you want."

She swiveled, started to fast-track it toward the barn. But she didn't get far before Nat caught up to her. Grasping her shoulders, he spun her around, holding her so he could see her face.

"You're not miserable. You love this life. And your daughters."

"Yes. But I'm not a woman who's cut out to be alone. Especially not when the man of my dreams lives just a few miles down the road."

She could see the battle going on behind his pained-looking eyes. And finally, something inside him cracked. "Aw, Mattie. You don't fight fair."

And then he kissed her.

She closed her eyes, absorbed by the sweet magic of the moment. But then reason kicked in and she remembered the last time she'd practically forced him to make love to her, only to have him walk out on her when it was over. Was that what this was—a pity kiss? She pushed her hands against his solid chest. "Stop it, Nat."

"But I thought this was what you wanted?" he said, his breath warm against her skin.

"A kiss?"

"My love. As represented by a kiss." He gazed into her eyes, letting his guard down, too, showing the same emotions she'd seen in him before. "I will never love anyone but you, Mattie. But are you sure you want to take the risk of loving me back?"

"I don't have a choice. We were meant to be. I really believe that."

He pulled her back into his arms, held her like he wanted to make her a part of himself. "Then let's do it. Let's fly the girls down next weekend and get married."

"So fast?" She had to admit the idea was exhilarating.

"You said you didn't want to waste a minute... if we're going to do this, I say let's go all out."

"Yes, yes, yes! Let's have the ceremony at the Double D. Maybe outside, if the good weather holds."

"Absolutely. What about rings?"

Mattie glanced at her left hand. She could no longer see a trace of pale skin where the rings Wes had given her had once sat. "Not important to me. Let's pick up two plain gold bands."

"Then you have to let me buy you a nice wedding present."

She glanced at the barn, then at the man who understood her so well. "Actually, there are three things I want very much."

Nat suddenly looked sheepish. "If you're talking about Copper, Madame Curie, and Princess Pride, well... they're back home at the Double D."

She stared at him, surprised... and yet not. Wasn't this exactly why she loved him so much? Their priorities were perfectly aligned. "When did you buy them?"

"The day after they were sold. I couldn't stand the idea of your horses belonging to someone else." His chest heaved on an exhale. "Just hadn't quite figured out how to tell you what I'd done."

"Oh, Nat." This man was incredible. No wonder she loved him so much. "I can't believe you did that for me."

"I'd do anything for you, Mattie." He spoke the words quietly. No grand avowals for Nat Diamond. Just the simple truth.

Whatever the future held for them—no doubt there'd be downs as well as ups—Mattie knew this: she was a very lucky woman.

THE END

ABOUT THE AUTHOR

Credit: jodiophotography.com

CJ has published over 35 novels and has twice been nominated for a RITA award. She likes to write stories about romance, family and intrigue, usually in small town or rural settings. When it's time to take a break from the computer, she heads to the Rocky Mountains near her home in Calgary where she lives with her partner Michael and their cat, Penny.

Visit CJ at www.CJCarmichael.com.

COMING SOON

Watch for the other books in the
Carrigans of the Circle C series...

Close to Her Heart–Dani Carrigan's story
Courting Trouble–Callan Carrigan's story

For all the latest news and fun from
Montana Born Books, visit our website:

MontanaBornBooks.com!

CPSIA information can be obtained
at www.ICGtesting.com
Printed in the USA
BVOW03s1826091117
499987BV00001B/41/P